Inconvenient Honor

Honor at Heart, Book 3

Caroline Warfield

Merlin's Owl Press

Formerly entitled *Dangerous Weakness*. The new edition is fully edited and enlarged with new material.

Cover design by DAR Albert

For those of my friends and family who have taken time to try my stories, especially those who have liked them enough to come back for more.

Inconvenient Honor

Honor can be damned inconvenient when it upends everything.

If women were as easily managed as the affairs of state—or the recalcitrant Ottoman Empire—Richard Hayden, Marquess of Glenaire, would be a happier man. As it was, the creatures—one woman in particular—made hash of his well-laid plans and bedeviled him on all sides.

Lilias Thornton came home from Saint Petersburg in pursuit of marriage. She wants a husband and a partner, not an overbearing, managing man. She may be "the least likely candidate to be Marchioness of Glenaire," but her problems are her own to fix, even if those problems include both a Russian villain and an interfering Ottoman official.

Given enough facts, Richard can fix anything. But protecting that impossible woman is proving almost as hard as protecting his heart, especially when Lily's problems bring her dangerously close to an Ottoman revolution. As Lily's personal problems entangle with Richard's professional ones, and she pits her will against his, he chases her across the pirate-infested Mediterranean. Will she discover surrender isn't defeat? It might even have its own sweet reward.

Chapter One

Chadbourn Park, February 1819

If women were as easily managed as the affairs of state—or the recalcitrant Ottoman Empire—Richard Hayden, Marquess of Glenaire, would be a happier man. As it was, the creatures made hash of his well-laid plans and bedeviled him on all sides.

"What did we miss now? I can tell you're unhappy." Will Landrum, Earl of Chadbourn, and one of the handful of men who would call Richard 'friend,' was not fooled by the cool façade and bland expression with which the marquess surveyed his ballroom.

"Who invited Lilias Thornton?" Richard demanded under his breath. His eyes followed a slender young woman who paced out the steps of the Quadrille across the parquet floor of the earl's ballroom.

"No 'thank you for turning your country seat into a diplomatic snake pit for an entire week so the haut ton can mingle with exotic visitors from the East while the foreign secretary manages the fate of Greece over Brandy and cards?'" Will demanded.

Richard looked at his friend, one eyebrow raised. "Chadbourn Park fit the need precisely. I thanked your Catherine this morning."

Will grunted. "My Catherine worked miracles when Sahin Pasha showed up with six extra people in his party."

"We can't predict how many retainers the Turks will impose," Richard growled. The Ottomans danced to their own tune; the Foreign Office never knew what to expect. Richard loathed the unpredictable. He went back to surveying the overheated ballroom.

"Who invited Lilias Thornton?" he repeated while he moved along the mirrored wall of the earl's spectacular ballroom to a position next to a massive marble urn that gave him a better view of his quarry. His eyes never left the dancers.

Will snatched two glasses of champagne from a footman stationed discreetly along the softly flocked wall, tray in hand. He handed one to Richard who took it without looking.

"Catherine also had to scurry when your mother demanded that she invite three more marriageable young ladies and their eager mamas," Will complained.

"I would rather that she refused."

"Refuse the Duchess of Sudbury? Surely you jest."

Richard nodded without taking his gaze from the dancers. "I jest. I have less control over my mother than I do Sahin Pasha." He loathed loss of control even more than unpredictability. He had been forced to sidestep the marriage-minded chits for two days.

Right now only one woman interested him, Lilias Thornton. He watched her throw her head back, send auburn curls bouncing, and laugh up at her partner. *She dances with grace, I'll give her that—grace and unbridled joy.* A man could lose his senses over that look. The last thing he needed was to lose his senses.

Will followed his friend's line of sight. "Beautiful woman," he acknowledged. "Catherine called her dress 'beyond perfection.'"

"That dress radiates so damned much continental sophistication she makes the women around her look countrified, my esteemed mother's protégées included."

The woman laughed freely again, and Richard felt himself harden in spite of his determination; the surge of attraction irritated him. I have no time for such nonsense.

"Who invited her?" he demanded. "It's a matter of some urgency."

Will shrugged. "I believe Catherine included some regular attendees at your sister's literary salon. She must be one of those. You said to invite women who could provide intelligent conversation to members of the diplomatic corps."

"So I did. My men tell me she has been in conversation with Konstantin Volkov three times these past two days."

"You're tracking her conversations?"

"Volkov's. He has no official role, yet he follows the Russian delegation and slinks through society in the shadows. I want to know who he works for, why he sought an invitation, and what he intends."

The entire house party had been arranged to provide a discreet opportunity for the foreign secretary—or more precisely, Richard, his second—to persuade Ottoman officials to moderate their suppression of revolutionary rumbling in Greece. England did not want the kind of chaos that would tempt Russia. Expansionist Russia threatened all of Europe. The weak and floundering Ottoman Empire did not.

"Ask him," Will suggested. "Unless diplomacy requires a more devious approach."

"Lilias Thornton accompanied her father to St. Petersburg three years ago. The crown appointed him to the trade delegation at our embassy there," Richard explained. "She returned without him rather abruptly in early January. I wonder why. Volkov arrived shortly after. It puzzles me." He did not like puzzles.

"It isn't unusual for a young woman of marriageable age to seek London before the Season starts," a woman's voice cut in. Catherine Landrum, Will's countess, reached for her husband's glass and took a sip. She tasted it slowly, seemed to pronounce it fit, and handed the glass back. "Lilias made it clear she's seeking a good marriage," the countess told Richard. "Who is Volkov?"

"She's well beyond the age," he answered. He ignored her question about the Russian.

"Surely not!" Catherine laughed. "Twenty-two may be somewhat older than the norm...;" She paused when a young woman of seventeen pranced by and smiled coyly at the marquess over her partner's shoulder.

"Well, perhaps quite a bit older," she acknowledged when they passed.

"She served as her father's hostess in his postings abroad since she turned sixteen. She has shown no interest in the marriage mart until this year," Richard said. "I don't care about the gossip. I want to know about her connection to Konstantin Volkov."

"Ask her," the countess suggested.

"I intend to," Richard said as the last notes of the dance faded. He set out in the woman's direction.

~

Lily Thornton's mouth hurt from smiling. Her feet hurt from dancing. Her neck hurt from the effort to keep track of Konstantin Volkov. So far he made no effort to approach her, but she could feel his eyes on her. The skin on the back of her neck crawled with the knowledge that someone watched.

"...at Vauxhall next month."

She smiled up at the speaker, her most recent partner, even though she had no idea what he had said.

He placed her hand on his arm to escort her from the floor. Was this one's name Roger Heaton or Beaton? Ambitious young men with minor positions in the Foreign Office had flattered her with attention all week. You really ought to pay attention, Lily.

Another one—Walter Stewart, she thought—beamed at her when they approached. This one, she remembered, has at least been to the continent on some brief mission. He will have more conversation. Two others she recognized hovered at his elbows.

You really ought to seriously consider one of these, she chided herself. The need to find a husband weighed her down. The thought of making conversation over breakfast with any of these decent, dim, and woefully narrow-minded young men every morning of her life depressed her even more.

"My dance next, I believe," Stewart said, offering his arm and shooting a smug look at his friends.

"I think not," a cold voice cut in from behind her shoulder. She felt the words vibrate through her. "Your lot has danced Miss

Thornton off her feet tonight. I believe she would like to sit for a set."

When Lily turned to see who had so highhandedly up-ended her evening, a man's cravat and spectacular sapphire stickpin met her gaze. She had to lift her face to look up past his firm chin and stern mouth, to eyes as blue as ice. He glared at the young men behind her who scattered like geese.

Glenaire. No one but the Marble Marquess could have routed the lot of them so quickly. *What on earth does he want with me?*

Before she could formulate a coherent response to his arrogant demands, he said, "Your admirers melted away rather quickly. Shall we sit for a moment?" He took her arm without waiting for a response.

"Do I have a choice?" She tripped trying to keep pace with him.

"I want to speak with you," he said as if it were answer enough.

Does anyone ever tell this man no? She suspected not.

He didn't lead her to the seats where the chaperones looked after their charges. Lily managed only a glance at her Aunt Marianne sitting among them and smiling vacantly about the room. The Marquess gestured instead to two small chairs placed between massive ferns in marble pots that stood shoulder high. The setting allowed a modicum of privacy but prevented any hint of impropriety.

He handed Lily into a seat but stood for a moment looking down at her.

He looks as if he is going to interrogate me...or eat me!

"Do you plan to loom over me or to sit and talk?" she demanded. "My neck will ache from the effort." The pulse in her throat pounded; she couldn't calm it.

She thought perhaps a hint of a smile played at the edge of his mouth just before he sat next to her in one graceful movement.

"Better," she said. "What does the mighty Marquess of Glenaire wish to speak to me about so urgently that he ignores basic manners?"

Eyebrows, slightly darker than his white-blond hair arched up. *Pity*, she thought absently, *hair that fair is wasted on a man.*

"Why are you here?" he asked.

Whatever she expected, it wasn't that. She thought of several facetious answers, but the Marble Marquess would not tolerate trivia.

"Broadening my acquaintances," she said. "A woman who hopes to marry requires a wide circle of friends."

"How do you know Konstantin Volkov?" he demanded.

Lily's heart beat faster. Even the thought of what had passed between Volkov and her naïve self in Saint Petersburg brought a flush of shame. She had been a fool where that man was concerned. Could Glenaire possibly know about Konstantin? People said the Marble Marquess knew everything.

"We met at embassy functions in Saint Petersburg," she said.

"What is your relationship with Konstantin Volkov?" He ground out the words, skewering her with a gaze that would freeze water.

"I have none. We met at a function. That's all," she lied, tamping down panic.

"You've been seen in conversation. What is between you and Volkov?" he persisted.

"Nothing. There is nothing between us." That much was the truth. Any "conversation" consisted of veiled threats and an attempt to get her alone. She had avoided him as much as she could. *What lies between us is not the business of the Marquess of Glenaire.*

The marquess's face became a mask of concentration. She could almost hear the gears turning in his clockwork mind weighing her answers.

"Do you have me watched?" she asked.

"My dear Miss Thornton. You will have noticed this is no simple house party. The entire Ottoman delegation is here, as well as a sprinkling of diplomatic officials from across Europe. We watch everything."

She had noticed. "The Ottomans," she murmured. Delicate diplomacy indeed.

"I don't know how Volkov got himself invited, or why," he told her. "But I mean to find out."

She would do the same in his position. She knew perhaps more than she should about Russian intentions.

"What did Volkov want with you here?" he asked.

"This morning he begged that I save a dance for him. I declined. He's a terrible dancer," she said. *Easy, Lily. It is always better to stick to as much of the truth as you can.*

"Tell me what you know. I will find out eventually," he said. His graceful, long-fingered hands, splayed over knees encased in fine black silk, drew her attention.

"Miss Thornton, what do you know?" he demanded.

"Did I say I knew something?" she asked, eyes firmly on his hands. She did not look up. He wore a large sapphire set in hammered gold on his left hand, its intaglio design an elaborate coat of arms.

Cold beads of sweat dripped down her back. What Lily knew might interest the Foreign Office, but she dared not mention it.

"I will find out eventually, Miss Thornton," the marquess repeated. He stood and took her hand to help her rise, drawing her attention back to his face.

A frisson ran up her arm at the feel of her hand in his. His knowing eyes never left hers when he bowed over her hand. *My, but the man is gorgeous! Impossibly arrogant, but lovely to look at.*

"Until later," he said, and he melted into the crowd.

Lily stared after him. She looked in vain for the circle of admirers she had worked hard to cultivate. *Damn you, Glenaire! I'll have to start over.*

A hand snaked out from behind her and clamped on her arm.

"My dance, I believe," Volkov said in a voice that just avoided being a snarl. He pulled her arm over his in a mockery of a gentleman's protection and held it there. "Smile, Lilias. Walk with me."

The iron grip tightened. She had no choice.

"Darling Lilias, it is good to meet you again," he said loud enough for bystanders to hear. "Smile!" he hissed.

Lily put one foot in front of the other and tried to do as he ordered. He leaned toward her, mimicking a lover's concern.

"Your father must miss you," he murmured in her ear. "Do you know he walks out every evening after dinner since you left?" *He has Papa watched—of course he does.* She shivered.

"What do you want?" she whispered back between clenched teeth.

"Why, the pleasure of your company. You've run from me all week. You will talk to me now."

Lily's knees threatened to buckle when he led her to French doors and out into the shadows.

Chapter Two

Lily's head slammed against a solid wall. After Volkov pulled her down the terrace, he had pushed her through an open door into a dark hallway.

"What did you tell him?" Volkov hissed.

"Nothing. I told him nothing." Her breath heaved. Volkov stood so close the familiar scent of bergamot and lime overwhelmed her senses. Once she had welcomed his touch, allowed him liberties. Now his very smell turned her stomach. Over the ringing in her ears, far from her revulsion and terror, Lily heard the faint sound of the waltz being played in the ballroom. Volkov's touch made her skin crawl

"Liar." He leaned closer, his face inches from hers. His breath reeked with whiskey and yesterday's dinner. "I warned you to stay away from Glenaire. Don't tempt me to change my mind about protecting your reputation. A few words in the right ears and your marriage hopes will die an untimely death." The last word slid slowly off his tongue.

Lily swallowed her rising gorge.

"What did you tell him?" he repeated.

"Nothing!" she insisted, her anger growing. "You both ask the same questions. He demands to know what I say to you."

She pushed against his chest, but the man didn't budge. "I gave him the same answer I give you: nothing."

"If my man in Thessaloniki is compromised, your father will pay with his life. Do you understand me? Fault will lie on your head. If you hadn't been so nosy, you would not be in this position."

"I've forgotten his name." She lied. Shame and regret overwhelmed her. She had allowed herself to be lured to Volkov's apartments. He had hinted at marriage. He had led her step by tempting step into sensual desire in a series of trysts until she lost all common sense.

"You know enough," he snarled. "You listened at the door."

"Yes, I listened." Thank God for the interruption. "I heard enough to know what a fool I had been to allow myself to be seduced by a man who wanted only what information he could suck out of me."

"Dear Lily"—Volkov smirked—"your tidbits about your father's dealings with the Ottomans proved useless. Information wasn't all I wanted." He ran a hand down her neck to cover her breast. "If you had stayed instead of slipping out my bedroom window like a thief, you would know how much more I expected from you."

She pushed harder, but he pinned her arms. When he leaned in for a kiss, she turned her head and kicked her knee up. He jerked away before she could hit his vulnerable parts.

Instead of cursing as she expected, he laughed. "If we had privacy, I would show you how much I like my women feisty. As it is, I'll leave you. For now."

Lily tried to slip out of his slackened grip.

"Remember your father," he murmured against her ear. "A gentleman who walks alone in a strange city? So many things could happen."

Lily's eyes widened in panic.

Volkov smirked. "Or to an unmarried and no longer eligible woman in London, for that matter. Though that would be a waste."

He pushed away. "Avoid Glenaire, Lily. Don't make me question your loyalty."

~

Richard stood in the open door and watched Volkov swagger down the hallway. Lilias Thornton sagged against the wall.

"Don't make me question your loyalty." What the hell did that mean? Loyalty to whom? The damned woman went off with that worm as soon as I warned her away.

Richard saw them leave across the crowded dance floor and made it to the terrace in time to see them slip into a darkened hallway. A couple, intent on romance, came out behind him and forced him to slow his pursuit.

By the time he turned into the door, Volkov leaned in like a lover to whisper in her ear. The look on her face when Volkov slithered away, made his guts clench. Whatever just passed between them wasn't gentle.

When he stepped inside, she jerked upward. Is she trembling? If I didn't know better, I would believe she's afraid.

"Volkov," he said.

"What of it?" she demanded, pulling herself upright and lifting her green eyes to his.

He saw defiance, yes, but he also saw fear.

"Did he hurt you?" The bastard.

"No." Her voice broke. "It is nothing. If you'll excuse me …"

"You're afraid."

The defiant chin shot up. "What exactly do you want from me?" *The chit has backbone. I'll give her that.*

"What does Volkov want?"

"Nothing. I keep telling you that."

"What I just saw didn't appear to be 'nothing.'" He moved closer. He saw her tremble and reached out a hand to steady her. *Fear without a doubt. Volkov will pay for this.*

"What aren't you telling me?" he asked softly. Russian machinations and Richard's overwhelming responsibilities faded behind concern for this frightened woman, faded but didn't disappear.

"Nothing you need to know. It is—" she hesitated. "Personal."

Nothing that man does is entirely personal.

"I doubt that. What Volkov does impacts England. What did he mean about loyalty? Where does that loyalty lie?"

She swayed a bit at that, and he reached out his other hand, gently holding her shoulders and pulling her closer until they were inches apart. A fine rose scent wrapped around his senses.

"With my family," she rasped, her eyes on his. "And with my country."

"Then talk to me about Volkov."

"I can't."

"You're afraid to."

She turned her head away, unable to look at him.

"He threatened you." He didn't need to ask.

She bit her lip. He thought she wouldn't reply.

"Not me," she whispered at last. "At least not primarily."

He waited. There has to be more. *Talk to me Miss Thornton.* The rose scent drew him in; he shook it off.

"Tell me what you know," he demanded. "Whatever it is, I can fix it. There is nothing I can't manage if I have all the facts."

Suddenly, she snapped her head up. "You want to know everything about Konstantin Volkov? Call my father home."

"What?"

"He'll come if the Foreign Office orders it."

"Thornton is in the middle of delicate trade negotiations," he began, thinking out loud. *If Volkov is involved, Thornton needs to come home. Another thought struck him.*

"You asked him to come, and he refused."

She didn't respond; she watched him steadily.

Richard stared back, eyes fixated on her mouth.

Dear God, her lip is quivering. Richard's entire consciousness narrowed to a need to soothe her quivering mouth. He leaned closer until his own touched hers. She startled.

"You don't need to fear me," he murmured against her lips. He felt her mouth soften. He explored her mouth with care, absorbed in the sensation.

The woman responded tentatively, moving under his lips, and he forgot his purpose entirely. Desire to comfort gave way to desire to take. Just a taste, a small taste of what I've wanted all evening. When the tip of her tongue touched his lower lip, he deepened the kiss, probing and demanding.

She shocked him with a response that matched his. A red cloud of desire consumed him. He slid his hands up her arms to cup her face. When she didn't pull away, he put one arm around her waist and pulled her until her body touched his, from his knee to his chest, her soft curves warm against him.

When Lily tried to push him away, Richard had to blink to clear his vision. He had her against the wall, her skirts bunched in one hand, her bodice askew. *My God, what madness!*

He pulled his hands from her bodice and leaned on the wall, one hand on either side of her, breathing heavily, his head hung low.

"I'm sorry," he began. He felt like a fool and hated it.

"You're just like him," she spat.

"I beg your pardon?" His loss of control had left him disgusted with himself, yet her accusation outraged him. "I'm nothing like Volkov!"

She pushed him away. "You're no better than Volkov. You will use any means to get what you want," she said, rearranging her dress. "You make me sick, both of you."

His irresponsible behavior left him with no response to that.

"Now I can't go back in there," she went on, looking down at her disheveled gown. "My entire reason for being here lies in tatters, and you, sir, are to blame. I trust what just happened, that much at least, will stay between the two of us. I can't afford the notoriety."

She started to leave but turned back and glared at him. "You owe me. Call my father home."

Her clear voice grated on his memory. "I can't afford the notoriety!" *How odd! Any other chit would try to trap me into marriage.*

He knew he ought to feel gratitude, but he felt nothing but anger. He had behaved like a damned fool. Watching her, wanting her all evening, offered no excuse. Richard Hayden never lost control. Never.

Damn the woman anyway.

Richard drew breath to clear his thoughts. He would call John Thornton home; she could be sure of that. And he would stay away from Thornton's tantalizing daughter, as far away as he could.

Chapter Three

By the time the footmen began clearing the soup course the following evening, Richard profoundly regretted not taking a firmer hand with the seating.

Will's Catherine, as hostess and Countess of Chadbourn, sat at the head of the table. Sahin Pasha, the guest of honor, sat to her right and Richard to her left. The countess commanded a remarkable range of knowledge. Having glossed over politics and recently published books, she engaged Sahin in a comparison of the flora and fauna of the English countryside with his native land. The bluff, avuncular man happily described flat farmlands and the rocky mountainous region of Cappadocia.

Their conversation progressed, as it ought. Richard's problem lay with the two young ladies next in line, given their places at his mother's request no doubt. The two had been after Richard like hounds on the scent all week.

Lady Jane Ashbourne sulked to Sahin's right, spouting banal comments about primroses and expressing horror of a world without them. She came just short of insulting their guest.

Lady Sarah Wharton preened to Richard's left. She ignored everyone around her while she kept up a dogged effort to engage Richard in a conversation about the probable social events in the coming season. Whenever he nodded politely, Lady Sarah took it as encouragement, and Lady Jane cast a sour frown in her direction.

From the far end of the table, holding court to the right of their host, his mother watched serenely, a satisfied smile firmly in place. He had no doubt who placed the two bloodhounds near him.

"But surely a landscape devoid of flowers must depress one!"

He looked across at Lady Jane—pretty enough, with good bloodlines, but utterly lacking in sense. As his hostess, she would cause an international incident within a year of marriage.

Lilias Thornton would know what to say. That thought came unbidden, as did the urge to look down the table at the woman herself who, lacking title or station, sat safely beyond the massive silver epergne that marked the middle of the table. Lilias sparkled up at Walter Stewart and his ilk, junior diplomats all, obviously enjoying the conversation. She would make one of them a good wife. The thought irritated him.

"I would prefer the beet root to the asparagus," Lady Sarah declared, not quite keeping annoyance from her voice.

Stop staring and pay attention to the chit next to you!

"Of course." He gestured to a footman. The footman brought the dish, and Richard did what manners demanded. A gentleman always offered the lady next to him her choice. He wondered briefly where his manners had scattered, glanced back at Lilias Thornton, and looked swiftly away.

He offered Lady Sarah her choice of fowl.

"The duckling, please," she beamed.

This one had impeccable manners. If she found the presence of a Muslim at her table troublesome, she hid it well. Lady Sarah possessed a suitable dowry and background for the wife of a future duke. Their fathers were cronies when not locked in rivalry. Perhaps I ought to consider her.

Moments later his mind wandered again. He caught himself glaring at Walter Stewart, who leaned too close to Lilias. *Raise your damned eyes above the woman's décolletage, Stewart!*

The next thing he heard came from Lady Sarah. "But your eminence, isn't Greece part of your homeland also? All those islands?"

Richard held his breath. He did not want a discussion of political tension at dinner. That could wait until the men were alone.

Sahin smiled as a grandfather might at a simple child. "Greece lies under the protection of the Ottoman Emperor for sure, my lady. It is as you say, quite beautiful."

Lady Jane wrinkled her nose. "How can it be Greece and Ottoman?" she asked.

Before Richard could respond, Sahin Pasha spoke. "How does your Scotland lie with in the United Kingdom?"

"My father calls the Scots barbarians in a wild land," Lady Jane sniffed.

"Not so!" Lady Sarah objected. Catherine, Sahin Pasha, and Richard all looked at her. Lady Jane glared.

"My cousin has a manor near the borders," Lady Sarah continued. "It is quite, quite beautiful. The company is cultured, even if the weather is not what one might like."

Richard looked at Lady Sarah more closely. Yes, perhaps I should consider this one. It would at least relieve me of my mother's machinations.

"Ah, but part of Greece's attraction lies in its weather," Sahin responded.

Richard let Catherine steer the conversation into the safer realms of temperature and thunderstorm. He glanced down the table again. This time he caught his mother's frown. She glared at Lilias.

When Catherine finally rose, Richard sat back in relief. He watched the ladies troop out, forced his gaze away from Lilias Thornton, and caught a martial look on his mother's face. Perhaps he should avoid joining the ladies altogether.

Lady Sarah Wharton took the place next to the Duchess of Sudbury on a brocade sofa. Lily watched with less detachment than she liked.

Other young ladies, including the sour-faced Lady Jane, clustered around, peeping like so many ducklings vying for place. Whatever else this house party intended, the competition for the Marquess of Glenaire waged fast and furiously. Yesterday that amused Lily.

Suddenly the entire marriage stakes wearied her. She longed to escape to her room. Petite, blond, and assured of her own worth, Lady Sarah represented everything Lily was not.

In three days at Chadbourn's house party, the girl had emerged as the catch of the season, and she clearly had the duchess's endorsement. Lily could have viewed her as competition, except Lady Sarah's quarry lay far above Lily's touch.

What would the little darling think if she knew her precious marquess had kissed me?

Memory of Glenaire's mouth on hers vibrated through Lily's body. She had been restless since she had let Volkov touch her intimately. Now the marquess set every nerve on edge.

She couldn't deny that she found him attractive, but, even if fear of Volkov didn't poison any attraction Glenaire held, the man himself would quash what pretense she might have made of seeking his attention.

"Yes, Sarah, do play for us," the duchess pronounced. Everything that woman says sounds like a pronouncement, Lily thought. She watched Lady Sarah spring into action, watched the duchess's beam of approval, and watched the others follow her with false smiles and calculating looks.

Enough! Lily rose to seek her hostess and take her leave, relieved to turn her back on the tableau by the pianoforte. She spied the Countess of Chadbourn at the far end of the room and stepped quickly in that direction.

"Miss Thornton! Do come sit," the countess greeted her. "We were discussing *A Modern Prometheus*. Have you read it?"

"Frankenstein?" Lily asked, diverted. "No, actually. Is it quite the horror people say?" An older woman moved so she could sit by the countess.

"Oh quite!" Lady Chadbourn said, "But the delicious part is speculating on its anonymous author."

"The preface is by that poet Percy Shelley," one of the woman put in, "but it seems unlikely he wrote it."

"I can see that he might prefer anonymity if he did," another said.

Lily's head spun. "An anonymous author could be a woman," she said without thinking.

The countess beamed at her. "My point precisely!" She leaned over and lowered her voice in mock secrecy, "Perhaps even a lady of standing."

"Should I be shocked?" Lily asked, eyebrows high, hiding her smile.

"Of course," the countess lied to general laughter.

"You walked over here with purpose," Lady Chadbourn continued more softly. "Don't tell me you plan to leave us so early."

The change in company tempted Lily to stay. She knew she ought to linger long enough to speak with Walter Stewart and continue her campaign to fix his attention. Tonight she couldn't bear it, not with Glenaire nearby. Walter Stewart would keep for London.

Lily opened her mouth to plead headache when a rustle of skirts around the pianoforte alerted her to an open door.

"I fear I must," she answered quickly. "We leave so early tomorrow, and I suspect a headache will keep me from sleep." If she didn't have one now, she would after an hour in the same room with Glenaire or Volkov, either one. She rose and accepted the countess's sympathy.

Lily reached the midpoint of the enormous salon when she saw Glenaire's tall frame fill the doorway and linger there. A hunted look swept across his face; a mask of indifference quickly shuttered it. Lily hesitated, pretending interest in a Dresden figure on the Adam mantelpiece in the center of the wall. She waited for him to move away from the door.

The duchess marched toward her son with a swish of skirts, and he moved forward from the doorway. He looks resigned to the inevitable.

A crush of gentlemen entered behind Glenaire to seek their companions. Lily thought that if she stepped softly she could slip past the marquess and his mother and get to the door without being noticed. She paused her escape at the sound of her name.

"I saw you staring at that Thornton woman," Lily heard the duchess hiss.

When she hesitated, one of the junior diplomats smiled at her hopefully and approached. He stood with his back to the duchess, blocking Lily from view. He began to complement her gown, a conversation that necessitated little beyond nods and blushes.

"I did not stare at Lilias Thornton," the marquess replied to his mother under his breath.

Lily smiled up at her admirer, one ear cocked to the conversation behind him.

"'Lilias,'" the duchess sneered. "Her very name has the reek of Scotland, as if that hair weren't enough. She is nobody and has pretensions above her station."

Lily's smile wavered, but she kept her admirer talking. Eavesdropping seldom blessed the listener.

"Her father is a well-regarded diplomat," the marquess responded. "Hardly 'nobody,' but you needn't fear. Miss Thornton has the least hope of becoming Marchioness of Glenaire, much less Duchess of Sudbury, of any woman here," he said.

Quite, Lilias thought. *The very least hope.* She made her excuses. One thought carried her up the stairs with unladylike speed. She needed to return to London, to begin her marriage quest anew, to regain her sanity.

She pushed open the door, determined to leave at first light. A folded paper just inside the room where it had been slipped under the door made her stop abruptly and grab it up.

She snapped the message open.

Perhaps we will meet in London. I will certainly see you. Be careful what you do and say, Darling Lily.

V

Lily fought back rising bile. *Volkov. How can I pursue respectable marriage with Volkov lurking in corners?*

She wished her papa home, she wished him safe, even as she knew wishes solved nothing. Panic flooded Lily's imagination with desperate ideas in torrents that eddied and flowed until one idea began to shape itself in her head. Neither fear of reprisal nor thought of propriety shook it loose. Prone on her bed, she thrashed about for another solution and found none. Finally, weary, she rose and began to write.

Moments later she dribbled hot wax to seal the missive.

The Marble Marquess isn't the only person who can be devious.

Chapter Four

Richard worked his way steadily through the contents of a bulging dispatch case the following morning. He had commandeered the Earl's estate office and his desk. He was not alone.

"You do this every morning?" Will asked, warming his hands on a cup of coffee. A dozen reports lay in organized array across the desk, with a pile of requests, forms, and other documents to be signed in front.

"Most days. There will be more in London. These are the most pressing." Richard spoke without looking up.

"The Ottomans are gone, thank God." Will sighed. "Now if I can just rid my house of the Foreign Office," he added slyly, "I can get back to my estate."

Richard grunted. "Your estate didn't suffer," he said without looking up. "It is far too well run to require your daily attention."

"My hands haven't been dirty in eight days," Will complained. When Richard glanced at his own meticulous manicure, the Earl chuckled.

Richard caught the grin and looked back at his work. "Only you would care," he said. The fashionable world didn't call Will the Farmer Earl for nothing. Family and fields made up his entire universe.

"Perhaps my children will recognize me when they see me again," Will went on, "now that the demands of King and country have been met."

"Your children weren't neglected. I know you climbed the infernal stairs to the nursery at least twice a day all week. Catherine more often."

"Scandalous as it may seem, Catherine nurses Emma herself," Will said. "It suits them both."

Richard had no comment on mothers and babies, the most foreign bodies on the planet in his estimation. He worked his way silently through a pile of papers.

"It would do you good to set up a nursery of your own," Will prodded.

Richard looked up at that. "If you mean, it's time I married, I've been considering it."

"Your mother certainly pushed a number of choices your way the past few days. Did one of them catch your attention?"

"Lady Sarah Wharton merits additional attention," Richard mused. He finished one pile and shifted another into its place.

"Really? I had no idea you were attracted."

"Attraction isn't relevant. She is a duke's daughter and an earl's granddaughter on her mother's side. She has enough wit to maintain diplomatic dinner conversation and sufficient polish to show well at functions."

"'Show well at functions?'" Will sputtered. "You aren't hiring an ambassador."

"She looks healthy enough. I presume she could provide an heir with little trouble," Richard went on, eyes firmly on his work.

"You aren't buying a brood mare either, Richard! Did she inspire any feeling in you at all?"

"She possesses all the right attributes to make bedding her pleasant enough, if that's what you mean."

"That is precisely not what I meant," Will said. "Do you care for her at all? Why even marry?"

"As you pointed out, it's time, and it's my duty. Marriage would also put an end to my mother's interference. She can go back to making my sisters miserable."

Will looked as though he had more to say, but a discreet knock interrupted them.

"Enter," Richard commanded, ignoring the owner of the office who sat next to him.

Roger Heaton, one of his operatives, entered.

"She left, my lord," he said.

"Lilias Thornton? I would expect so," Richard answered. "Most of the guests plan to leave today."

Heaton glanced at the earl; Richard motioned him to continue. "His lordship is trusted," he said.

"She borrowed a horse from the stables an hour ago," Heaton explained, "And left."

"Without her luggage?" Richard asked.

"Odd that. She ordered her luggage be delivered with her aunt to London. The aunt didn't seem to know much."

Dotty old Marianne Thornton wouldn't know anything, no matter how obvious to others, Richard thought.

"The old lady said something about her wanting air and joining the carriage along the way," Heaton went on.

"Perhaps it's true. Volkov?" Richard demanded.

"That's the thing. Left shortly before. On horseback, his one bag tied to his saddle. I thought you would want to know."

"A meeting?" Will asked.

"An assignation more likely," Heaton said. "Dalliance on the road. Volkov hardly took his eyes off her all week."

A vision of Lilias Thornton in Volkov's arms, in his bed, exploded in Richard's mind. Willing or unwilling, he found the idea disgusting. Cold fury, all the more potent for being controlled, took hold. He had warned her to stay away from Volkov.

She knows something. I'm sure of it. And Volkov has some hold over her.

"Do you want me to follow them? If so, I need to leave immediately," Heaton asked.

Richard had already risen. "No. I'll take care of Miss Thornton myself."

Heaton bowed out.

"I'll need your fastest horse. I need Mercury," Richard told Will.

A knowing look came over Will's face. "You're mighty anxious to intercept this Thornton woman, if you dare ask for my favorite mount."

"I know he has your heart. I'll bring him back safely." Richard stuffed the papers into the dispatch case. "I'll be back by late afternoon to finish this."

"I have no doubt you'll care for my horse. It's the Thornton woman's fate that concerns me."

Chapter Five

"What do you find so amusing, little one?" Sahin Pasha stretched his aging legs across the floor of a private parlor in an undistinguished inn, lifted a flagon of ale, and regarded Lily fondly.

Away from Chadbourn's manor and his official duties, the old man wore western clothes. Anyone observing the fit of his coat and his comfort would know them for his normal dress. If they ignored his dark skin, they might take him for a local squire. No one would identify him at first glance as the representative of his Sultan.

"Hmm," he repeated, "what amuses you?"

"You, favored uncle. Sitting in this very English Inn sipping ale," Lily replied. She had pestered him to teach her Turkish during long winter nights in Saint Petersburg when cards and conversation in her father's apartment gave the Turks solace from the cold and dark. She spoke it well, but tonight they spoke English.

"I like your English ale," the old man said. He hefted the tankard to demonstrate.

"I feel better just laughing with you," Lily said.

"You looked happy enough when I observed you with your court," Sahin told her. "I thought it best not to scatter your admirers with attention from an elderly eastern potentate."

Lily acknowledged the truth of that with a sad nod. "I've taken your advice and entered the marriage stakes."

He shook his head. "Marriage stakes! Wretched term. My country has more civilized customs. We protect our young women so older, wiser heads can ensure the honor of their suitors. You English parade your young women like horses for auction."

"It feels that way some days," she agreed. "So much posture and appearances and only my Aunt Marianne to look after me."

"The very neglectful aunt. It will not help your marriage prospects if people know you rode cross country alone for this very inappropriate meeting," he chided.

Lily's face heated; she stared at her tankard.

"Do you plan to tell me what troubles you, Lily? What drove you to this foolish undertaking?"

She looked up into sympathetic eyes, but words didn't come. Belatedly she remembered that Sahin's loyalty to his country came before his concern for an insignificant foreign woman. A man in his position did not let kindness outweigh duty.

"You know I fled Volkov," she began.

The old man nodded. "You remind me again why we Turks protect our women. The man should be shot."

"He did me no permanent harm!"

Sahin's implacable look did not soften. "So you tried to convince me. Did you speak with your father as I advised?"

"No," she admitted. "I couldn't. If I tell you something, can you promise to keep it confidential?"

"Something personal? Of course," he replied.

"There is more, things to do with politics." She cleared the lump in her throat.

"Ah. In that case, it will depend on what you say. I have duties to my office, you know that."

She clamped her jaw shut and stared into her ale. Volkov's plans were vile; Lily knew rather too well that revolution always exploded on the backs of the poor. She looked at Sahin Pasha, who had been a true friend, and felt shame for keeping the information from him.

"Perhaps I may help," Sahin prodded. "Your father, good man but neglectful I fear, is far from here."

If my man in Thessaloniki is compromised, your father will pay with his life. Lily's stomach clenched, remembering Volkov's words. See what comes of letting fear rule you instead of reason? Use your head Lily.

Sahin would see to it that Volkov's agent in Thessaloniki, imbedded in the court of the Ottoman governor of the province, met a swift death if word got back to them. What will happen to Papa then?

Sahin waited patiently, allowing silence to grow between them. "You rode recklessly to meet me, and now you will not speak. You need a protector, I think," he said at last.

Lily took breath to deny it, but words froze in her throat. She couldn't deny the truth of his assertion. "I thought perhaps ally," she mumbled.

"Perhaps you should speak to your Marquess Glenaire," Sahin said, pinning her with a knowing look. "One suspects he will have interest in what you have to say."

"I can't!"

"I have seen how that one looks at you," Sahin said. He watched her closely. "I don't believe he means you harm."

"He cares only for himself and for England," she retorted.

"I doubt if he knows the difference between the two," the old man chuckled. He leaned forward and took her hand. "You need a protector, Lily. You are foolish to carry burdens alone."

Lily wondered if he understood how a London lady might take the meaning of "protection." *He must know Glenaire's rank prevents him from viewing a minor diplomat's daughter as marriage material.*

Before she could reply, a door slammed open behind Sahin. Its violent explosion echoed through the room.

Sahin sat straight, instantly on guard; Lily looked up into the face of catastrophe.

~

Rage, when it collides with evidence of misconception, shatters into pieces. Richard felt his anger crumple into shards and reassemble into alternating waves of bafflement and irritation. Nothing was as he expected.

Lilias Thornton and Sahin Pasha? The old man could be her grandfather. Could she be Volkov's messenger? Where was the damned man himself?

The representative of the Sublime Porte, cousin and ambassador of the Sultan himself, sat looking like a dark-skinned version of an English gentleman at a rough table with Richard's quarry.

Lilias looks terrified. The blasted woman should be for leading me a merry chase.

Two rather large men he had passed in the taproom, who were, upon closer look, not the English farmers Richard had taken them for, moved to either side of him. At sharp words in Turkish from Sahin Pasha, they melted away.

"Ah, my friend, we just spoke of you. Come and sit," Sahin said.

Richard looked from Sahin's amused face to Lilias's stricken one. He sat, muddy and haggard, with as much dignity as he could muster, growing more irritated every minute. *How does this blasted woman undermine my common sense? I could throttle her.*

"Would one of you like to tell me what is going on here?" he demanded, with more heat than he intended. His famous sangfroid eluded him.

"My good friend, Miss Thornton, sought out my advice," Sahin told him.

Good friend? Vienna, Saint Petersburg, of course! Damn it! Why can't I reason properly where this woman is concerned? He chose not to examine his relief that whatever he interrupted was not a lover's assignation.

"You borrowed a horse, fed your aunt some nonsense, and rode like a mad woman cross country to ask for advice?" he demanded.

Lilias raised her chin. "And why did you do the same?" she retorted.

He sent her a glare that should have shriveled her.

"You thought I came to meet Volkov!" she exclaimed.

Heat rose up his neck. "I warned you..." He glanced at Sahin Pasha, who smirked back at him.

"As you see, I did not," she said primly.

"The Russian wolf frightens your Lily," Sahin said. "She is shockingly reluctant to tell me why."

She's not my Lily!

"You too?" Richard asked ruefully. "What do you know, Miss Thornton?"

She looked over at Sahin and at Richard and appeared to consider something.

"Damn it, enough secrecy."

"Did you call my father home?" she asked softly.

Richard ran a hand over the back of his neck and sighed. "Yes."

She brightened. Sahin leaned forward.

"At least I ordered it. The dispatch will take time to reach Saint Petersburg."

She hesitated.

She looks like a rabbit faced with a fox—or perhaps I should say wolf. Volkov certainly is one.

"He threatens your father, little one? I told you the man should be shot," Sahin said.

"Our couriers are faster than Volkov's," Richard said, praying he was right. "Even if he guesses you've told me, we'll get there first. I ordered a bodyguard to accompany him."

Still silence.

"Miss Thornton—Lily—is that what friends call you? Lily? I doubt if he will know. We have time to protect your father. Tell us what has you frightened." He glanced up at Sahin.

"Let us help you, little one," Sahin urged.

Lily let out a shuddering sigh. She looked at Sahin, avoiding Richard's eyes.

"You know Volkov pursued me in Russia."

The old man nodded.

"I allowed myself to be taken to his apartments," she mumbled, coloring deeply. Sahin shook his head sadly.

Richard's worst images flooded his mind. *I will kill the man myself. No wonder she didn't want to discuss it.*

"We were interrupted," she added in a rush.

Before or after the bastard got what he wanted?

"Go on," Sahin prodded.

"A knock on the door. He went to answer, closing the door to the —the room we were in. Some sort of messenger had arrived. I heard them."

"What exactly did you hear?" Richard asked; he tried not to think about the room they had been in.

"I didn't hear it all, but I heard enough. Volkov has an agent in Thessaloniki."

Sahin shrugged. "Agents everywhere. We know this."

Lily shook her head. "This one is imbedded in the court of the provincial governor. You have a traitor who will provide support to revolution. When the time comes, he will assassinate the governor."

Richard cursed silently. "At which time Russia will step in to assist the rebels," he said. England needed stability in the region. Greedy Russia threatened all of Europe.

Sahin looked grim. "Or to assist my government—at a cost. Either way, Russia wins."

"People will die in the streets," Lily said hotly.

"What else did you hear," Richard asked.

"Much sounded garbled, but I think Volkov acts on his own."

"The czar's foreign office doesn't know?"

Lily nodded. "Volkov wishes to be a hero. He has the idea he will announce his brilliance after the fact."

"Fool!" Sahin pronounced. He looked at Richard. "It appears our friends, the Russians, have more than one effort under way in Greece."

Richard nodded agreement. *Volkov acting on his own has even more to lose if Lily betrays him.*

"Did you hear the man's name?" Richard demanded.

She looked from one grim face to the other. "You must promise not to act until my father is safe," she said.

Richard nodded. He couldn't promise for the Ottomans. The old man shrugged.

"Your father has been summoned," Sahin said. "That must satisfy you." He leaned forward.

She told them what they needed to know.

Sahin rose to his feet. "I will leave the two of you to discuss Lily's protection," he said. "I must travel if I am to reach London tomorrow." He smiled fondly at Lily. "You did right, little one. I know this man can protect those you love."

"I hope so," Lily whispered to the old man's retreating back. "Volkov will be merciless."

Richard sat motionless. *I have a duty to protect her. A duty.* He knew and understood duty; he refused to acknowledge the underlying passion.

Lilias pressed both hands on the table and rose to her feet. "Too late now. Volkov will know I spent time with you," she groaned. She turned her eyes to his. Green, he thought. Green and so luminous they light the room.

The desire to protect overwhelmed him. Richard almost drowned in the flood.

Lily swayed forward.

Chapter Six

Glenaire's hand, which had shot out swiftly to steady her, lay hot on Lily's arm. She batted it away.

"Too late," she said. "Keep your protection."

He rose to tower over her. "You doubt me?" Glenaire sputtered; he pinned her with a glare. "Your father—"

"Yes, I know. You've taken steps. Will I be safe on the streets of London?"

"He threatened you also." It wasn't a question; his eyes burned, hot with rage.

She rolled her eyes. *Damn but the man is exasperating.*

Lily pulled her skirt, giving it a yank to free it from where it snagged on the rough chair. She needed to get out of there. The impulse to seek out Sahin Pasha had been, she thought, ill advised. Ill advised? It may end in disaster.

The marquess put out a hand again to stop her but stopped short of touching her. "I can protect—"

"What about my reputation?" she demanded. "Can you protect that? Volkov promised to destroy all hope of a suitable marriage." Despair enveloped her; she felt her body sag.

"I shouldn't have come," she breathed. "I should have avoided you all."

She pushed away from the table. "I have to leave. I can meet Aunt Marianne on the road. I can try to minimize the damage."

"I'll escort you," Glenaire said. From another man that would be a polite offer. From Glenaire, it sounded like a command.

"No need. I will send the earl's horse back to him."

He followed her past the taproom to the courtyard; she couldn't prevent it. "Wait here," he ordered, "while I get our horses."

Leaning against the wall, Lily squinted at an orange and red sunset. The air already grew colder and night would come on fast. Cold from the stones seeped into her. She tried to silence the drumbeat of worry. *Volkov will know. Father must be protected. Volkov—*

The Marquess burst from the stables in a rush, looking as if the Furies rode his tail.

"That damned old man outmaneuvered me," Glenaire spat, rushing past her.

"What do you mean?" She hurried after him.

"He took our horses," he growled over his shoulder without slowing. Lily skipped to keep up with his long stride. She followed him into the sort of public room no lady should enter; it reeked of ale and stale bodies. Horror over the consequences of her impulse to seek out Sahin ate at her.

"Rent two more," she suggested in desperation. "You can afford them. You can afford to buy them."

"Sahin Pasha beat me to it. He bought them all," Glenaire said over his shoulder. He strode up to the bar and demanded the innkeeper.

Sahin, favored uncle, don't do it, Lily moaned inside herself.

The old man wanted to delay Richard long enough to get couriers out of England on their way to Thessaloniki. They would outstrip her father's travel arrangements. She leaned one hand on a filthy table to keep from toppling over from the sick feeling in her stomach.

The innkeeper bustled over.

"What happened to our damned horses?" Glenaire demanded before the man even came to a stop.

"The mussulman gentleman told me you ordered him to take 'em, to help like. Have a powerful need for horses do the mussulman folk," the man said. He looked genuinely confused. He wrung his hands.

"What did the bastard pay you?" Glenaire demanded. The

innkeeper looked at Lily. He pretended to look affronted at the marquess's language for her sake.

"I have to leave. I can't stay here," Lily cried, panic rising.

"The mussulman gent told me you would be well protected, and so you will be." He glanced up at Glenaire. "Promised to send horses, he did. Only take a day. No more'n two, once he finds more. Fer now —" He wiped his hands on his apron, ready, Lily suspected, to extort large sums from two people he mistook for fools.

"You heard the lady," Glenaire growled. "She cannot stay here. You will send someone to Chadbourn Park to fetch a carriage. You will do it now."

"M'lord!" the man exclaimed. "It is come dark already. Send a man ten miles on foot in the dark? Even if a man don't lose his way, he could fall in a ditch or be gored by Harry Martin's bull. Safer in t'morning."

Neither Lily's pleading nor Glenaire's aristocratic bullying moved the man, who insisted, "T' lady and gent can stay til morning." When Glenaire threatened to bring the full weight of the Foreign Office, the man suggested Glenaire might meet the full weight of the village blacksmith by morning.

Dear God. I am trapped at an inn with the Marquess of Glenaire. Volkov will know. All of London will know.

"I HAVE TO LEAVE," Lily choked. "I can't stay here."

Before Richard could respond, she pushed aside the inn door with one hand and stumbled out. Shadows engulfed her, her graceful figure swallowed up in growing darkness.

The sight struck Richard dumb mid speech, eyes on the door and one finger pointing at the innkeeper. No one had ever walked out on him before.

"Best fetch 'er. Dangerous in th'dark," the innkeeper said.

"I'm not finished with you," Richard responded in a rush.

He strode to the door with the remnants of his dignity and broke into a run when he did not see Lily in the inn yard.

He bolted onto the road, short of breath, and scanned it in both directions for Lily without success. Across the open fields, a figure, faint in the darkening twilight, moved purposefully in the direction of Chadbourn Park.

It took him an hour of hard walking to catch her, delayed as he was by the need to pop back into the inn to fetch his saddlebag and berate the innkeeper. A rabbit hole, a muddy hollow, and a rather tenacious bramble had not helped either.

At least I haven't encountered Harry Martin's bull.

Every other step he berated the foolish woman for her determination to come to harm. In between he cursed himself for acting like the sort of fool who couldn't control his impulses. Once he thought he had lost her, and visions of her tiny body broken in a ditch hastened his steps until he saw movement ahead.

"Where do you think you're going," Richard demanded. Gasps for breath weakened the force of his words. Fear gave it an edge.

"To Chadbourn Park, of course, my only alternative with no conveyance. I plan to throw myself on the countess's mercy," she said without breaking stride. That woman is too damned energetic. She's out pacing me even with the train of a damned riding habit tossed over her arm.

"She can plot to save your reputation in the morning better than in the deep of night," he countered, keeping up.

"I have to get there before Volkov finds out we've both been gone all night."

"He's gone."

"What?" She spun around so fast he ran into her.

Richard put an arm around her waist to steady her. "He left this morning before you did." She didn't object to his hand at her waist; he left it there.

"Are you sure?"

"My man said he left first. I will verify that."`

Lily laughed, a deep rich laugh, no schoolgirl titter. She reached up and pulled a leaf from his hair. "How do you plan to do that?" she asked.

For a moment he stood transfixed, her breath sweet warmth on his cheek. The moment passed. Standing in the middle of a field in utter darkness, mud on his boots, and leaves in his hair, Richard felt vulnerable. He did not enjoy the sensation. He dropped his hand from her waist as if on fire.

"When we return, I will see to it," he ground out, resuming their hike.

She picked up the train of her skirt and stepped into place beside him. "So you agree. We'll return to Chadbourn Park tonight."

"No."

She sped up, moving deeper into the night. Richard matched her pace longer than he thought possible.

"Enough of this," he growled when he reached the end of his rope.

"I am not returning to that inn, my lord," she said, giving his title a twist of irony. He could hear the shiver in her voice.

"No, I don't suppose that would be practical either."

"What then?"

"We shelter for the night before we freeze and the sheep find our bodies cluttering their pasture in the morning." February winds cut through his greatcoat. How can she stand it, tromping along in that riding habit, the little fool?

"Sheep, my lord?"

"There are always sheep. This is Dorset."

As if at his command, twenty minutes of walking brought them to a sheep pen. Lily's outburst when she bumped into the rough stone wall in the darkness unleashed a frenzy of "Baa" from the pen's unseen inhabitants. The setting moon left them in gloom.

"Can you see a farmhouse?" she asked between chattering teeth.

"No, but I can barely see my hand."

"Look there," Lily said, "across the enclosure. Do you make out a shape?"

He took her hand; her fingers, icy even through her gloves, laced with his. Together they groped along the stone enclosure until they came to a rough wood structure. The stench told them it was no house long before they reached it.

"Storage barn?" she suggested.

"Shearing shed," he guessed. Will had gone on at some length about shearing one night. Richard wished he had paid attention.

He tightened a grip on her hand and looked in every direction. When he saw no glimmer of light or other sign of humanity, he tossed about for an alternative. This close, he could feel that she had begun to shiver violently. He needed to get her out of the wind.

"If the racket those creatures made didn't bring the farmer, he must be at some distance," he said. "This appears to be our only choice."

She tried to open her mouth, but her teeth chattered too rapidly to speak. If she meant to disagree, she failed.

If I don't warm her, she'll fall ill.

He pulled her into the shed, and into his arms

Chapter Seven

Warmth, wonderful warmth.

Lily burrowed deeply into it, shaking uncontrollably. Her nose nestled into the soft lawn of Richard's shirt, and she let the scent of sandalwood, shaving soap—the scent of man—fill her senses.

"Easy," he soothed. "Let me warm you."

His heavy greatcoat fell around her. In the protective cocoon of his arms, the odor of sheep receded, the ache in her legs eased, and her sense of threat in the darkness yielded to a sense of safety. She snuggled against him.

"Better?" he slid his hands up her back to her shoulders, as if to push her away.

"Some," she replied, cuddling closer. The hands slid back down, sending warmth through her. "I've made a mess of it, haven't I?"

He didn't answer.

"Too much a diplomat to agree with me?" she mumbled from deep in his coat.

"Too intelligent to state the obvious," he responded.

I acted without thinking. I put us both in jeopardy. I led him through muddy fields and sheep dung for heaven's sake. And Volkov will know. She shivered again.

"More cold?" he asked. He held her tight.

Volkov will know and Sahin will kill his agent. Papa!

The weight of it crushed her. Wet tears overflowed, ran down her cheeks, and soaked his shirt.

Richard jerked away. “Please, no tears,” he whispered. “It won’t help and—”

A sob escaped her and then another.

“Don’t!” She could hear his consternation and confusion in that one word, a man all at sea when faced with a woman’s tears. He pulled her close again.

Some things even Glenaire couldn’t control. A woman’s grief is one of them.

“Don’t,” he repeated more gently and lowered his mouth to hers.

He kissed her, she thought, to quiet her sobs as much as to comfort. It quickly flamed into something else.

She tasted salt in the kiss, her tears flowing into his mouth. His harsh lips softened, gently teasing and urging Lily to open to him. She did, falling headlong into the fire that had threatened to ignite between them for two days. One last coherent thought came to her: among the insane events of this foolish expedition, opening to Glenaire would be the most foolish. At that moment, she didn’t care. She wanted the comfort he offered.

He shrugged off his coat, brushing her hand aside when she tried to cling. “I need to touch you,” he rasped. “Let me get this out of the way.” He slipped off his tailored jacket and tossed it over the stall behind him. The jacket of her riding habit followed it, removed by his deft hands before she could protest.

Soon enough he’d wrapped his greatcoat around them both, his hands inside, gliding up her back to undo the ties of her chemisette, one after inevitable one.

Talented fingers slipped through the gap in back and caressed her through her shift, up, down, and up again to run his fingers along the edge where her skin burned at his touch. All the while his mouth moved down her neck to its juncture with her shoulder.

He tugged the front of her chemisette and followed it with his mouth when it slipped across her breasts to fall to her waist. His mouth clamped over one breast, wet through her shift, and sucked, gently at first and then hard and demanding. A sharp clenching deep inside overtook her. Lily found it hard to breathe. Impossible to think.

"Glenaire," she gasped.

"Richard," he murmured against her skin. He clamped one hand on her derriere and held her in place while his mouth found her other breast. She came up against the hard ridge of his arousal and slumped forward, leaning over his head.

I need to touch him. I need— She slid her hand down the neck of his shirt.

He shot up, yanking his shirt from his pantaloons. She pushed it up until she could kiss the places her hands explored. His hands—Ah, talented hands!—touched the sensitive skin above her shift, then inside to tease her nipples. When her hands slid to the waist of his pantaloons, he moaned deeply.

"Wait!" Cold air, sharp and icy against her overheated skin struck her damp breasts when he pulled away. Something rustled in the dark. She groped though the maelstrom of desire for her moral compass. She failed to find it.

He came back before the madness receded, swept her up in his arms, and captured her mouth. "Clean," he said against her lips.

Lily lifted her head, confused. He kissed her again.

"I found a bin of clean straw," he explained. She kissed him back, teasing the side of his mouth with her tongue. His mouth held hers when he lifted her off her feet and swept his coat from around her shoulders.

He spread the coat and lay Lily on it. In seconds he lay on top of her, his weight both warm and welcome. He pulled the edges of the coat around them both. His hands and mouth drove all thought but one from Lily.

More. I need to touch you more. I need to be touched. I need...

His mouth explored her, without the shift now, that garment pushed down to her waist. She gripped his hair with one hand and ran the other down the corded muscles of his back.

When a tug alerted her that he had loosened her skirt, she started to rise up so he could pull it down. Instead, he yanked it up to her waist, urging her to relax into the cocoon of his coat. One hand caressed her inner thigh, sending waves of heat through her womb. Her hands moved restlessly under his shirt.

Fingers fluttered through the curls between her thighs and caressed her where she already felt moisture. She reached for the fall of his pants, but he stopped her.

"Not yet," he murmured. "Almost."

One finger slipped inside her. Another followed. She drowned in a sea of unfamiliar sensation. His hands caressed until Lily clung to him, desperate and unable to contribute to his pleasure.

"Richard?" she murmured, her voice rising at the end. "Too much, too... Oh." Waves of pleasure left her blind. Mute.

When she returned to awareness, she felt him, hard and hot, press against her moist opening.

When did his pantaloons disappear?

He took her mouth and entered her a short way. When he pulled out, vague disappointment filled her. Could that be all? No. He did it again. And again. When he slipped in and out in shallow thrusts, her pleasure began to build again. Lily gave herself over to it until, in one hard thrust, he entered her completely.

Pain tore through her, igniting red sparks behind her eyes.

Lily cried out in pain.

Richard went rigid. He'd just taken her virginity with one vicious thrust and little care.

Damn it woman, why didn't you tell me you were untouched?

He forced himself to stay still, head down, panting.

I assumed, the business with Volkov—I assumed...

"I'm sorry, I'm sorry," she gasped.

Unwilling to withdraw, afraid to hurt her more, he focused on the sound of his own breathing.

"I heard the first time—" she began. "But I didn't—"

He started to withdraw. Her hand on his buttocks pressed him back.

"Don't stop, now," she murmured. "The damage is done."

Damage? Is that what this is?

"Really, Richard. I think you're not finished."

I damned well am not. The feel of her hands drove him mad. He began to move in her.

"Are you sure you're all right?" he rasped. He couldn't have stopped if he tried.

"I will be, Don't stop." She trailed a hand up his belly. The feel of it drove him to move again, gently at first until the madness overtook him, and he finished what he started.

As he fell, satiated, to her side, he heard her moan softly. He prayed the moan meant pleasure. He owed her that at least.

Damn, damn, damn.

"Why the hell didn't you tell me?" His words sounded curt to his own ears. *Why didn't I pay more attention?*

She didn't answer. He choked back a curse.

"Are you—" he began.

"Fine," she mumbled. She turned her face away. He let her. A moment later he curled himself around her from behind and pulled her close with one arm.

"Sleep," he said. "We have much to deal with tomorrow."

She lay very still. He hoped she slept. He did not.

What hold does this woman have over me? I never lose control. Never. But he had; he had ravished a respectable young woman.

Another thought struck him. I didn't even take precautions. Richard was no monk, but he kept his liaisons discreet. He used every precaution he knew to prevent fathering a child. So far he had been successful.

He had never approached a respectable young woman with so much as a stolen kiss.

Irrationally, he resented her for it. *Where was the damned woman's common sense?*

As soon as the sky lightened enough to see, long before dawn, he rose and began to assemble the remains of his clothes. He pulled up his pantaloons and picked up his shirt.

"Is it morning?" Lily's voice, muffled by his greatcoat, interrupted him.

"Almost. The earlier we get to the Park, the better."

He turned his back to her and examined his shirt. A particularly nasty stain covered the front. It would have to be burned.

"I need help," she murmured.

At least she isn't wailing.

He pulled the shirt over his head and turned to her. She lifted her shift back into place, covering her sweet breasts, but she groped in vain to fasten her chemisette. He would have her clothing burned also.

He knelt, closed the garment with a few short movements, and rose abruptly. He did not need the graceful slope of the back of her neck where she held up her glorious auburn hair to lure him to her. That dance had been done, binding him to her with silken cords.

He put on his jacket and handed her hers. The tailored riding habit did not look at all alluring. Yet, here he stood, his life in tatters.

They would marry of course. Not once in the entire night had he conjured a way out. They would marry. He pulled her to her feet and watched her fasten her skirt.

"We may still make Chadbourn Park before anyone rises if we set out now," he said.

"Except the servants," she retorted.

"They don't matter. We can contain the scandal." He picked up his coat and swung it around her.

She looked up then, hopeful.

"We will marry of course," he told her. "Quickly, but not so abruptly as to cause comments." He walked toward the door, expecting her to follow.

"I beg your pardon," she called out to him. "We will what?"

He turned on his heel. "Miss Thornton, you will be the Marchioness of Glenaire. That is far from ideal, and the difference in our state will no doubt cause talk. We will have to endure it."

"Why?" she demanded. "Why this 'far from ideal' demand? Has Lady Sarah refused you?"

"Don't be coy, Miss Thornton. You have led me into folly at every step. After last night I have no choice. I shall have to marry you. My family—"

"Your family would have kittens if I married you, which I will not."

"You have respectable, if not the highest, breeding, you will show to advantage when properly dressed, and you will do well as a diplomatic hostess. My family, I was going to say, will have to deal with it." He stalked away. "So will you."

"I will not," Lily shouted after him. He ignored her.

She isn't a fool. She will leap at the chance to be a marchioness. Does the damned woman think she deserves poetry also?

Chapter Eight

Arching one's back, Lily found, did little to stifle an ache when jostling along rough roads in a farmer's cart. She brooded in solitude on the back of Farmer Justice's wagon, legs dangling, her back to Glenaire who appropriated the rough bench up front. She added that to her list of grievances.

Chadbourn Park, they had been told, was not far "'f you take th'road that avoids th'village and up the back lane." An hour had passed during which Lily had plenty of time to nurse those grievances.

I will not tie myself to that insufferable boor even if he begs.

A vision of Glenaire begging brightened her spirits considerably. It did not, however, change her views. While she blamed only herself for succumbing to his advances—to her own turbulent passions, if she were honest—his insulting offer stuck in her craw.

This episode may bring disaster down on my head, but he's a fool if he thinks he can order my life. I will manage the thing myself no matter what he says.

The wagon bumped around a rutted turn and slowed. The outbuildings of Chadbourn Park emerged beyond the fields. People bustled about their business; a groom led a horse past. He looked at them with little curiosity.

We must look like the village beggars.

Glenaire jumped down and came round to help Lily. The farmer saluted them and went on his way with shouted greetings to acquaintances as he went.

"We're too late to sneak in unnoticed," she lamented.

"By servants perhaps, but I will not have the family see us in this state, nor my staff," he said.

Before she could object, he pulled her into the stone building that served as the earl's stables. When she could make out only one worker in the gloom at the far end, she seized what little privacy they had.

"Let me clarify this before we go any further," she hissed. "I will not marry you."

Richard opened his mouth to speak; she held up a hand to quiet him.

"The guests are gone. Your staff is discreet. The earl and countess will accept any story we tell them. Sahin Pasha took our horses. We immediately set out for the Park. We got lost. Period."

Glenaire listened, intent.

"Nothing. Else. Happened," she ground out.

"You could be a duchess one day," he retorted through clenched teeth.

"What makes you think I want that?" she demanded. "Not all of us live to be fawned over."

He gave her what she had come to think of as his "Lord of heaven and earth" expression, chin high, eyes sharp.

"You could be increasing," he said in clipped tones.

Heat crept up Lily's neck. *Pregnant? Pray God, no.*

"It won't matter," she lied. "In that event, I will manage the thing. You needn't concern yourself."

"I beg to disagree. In that unfortunate event, we will 'manage the thing' together. Do you understand me?"

The full force of his authoritative stance hit Lily in a wave, but she stood her ground.

"Perhaps. For now, however—"

"Richard, what on earth? You look like you've been dragged through the pig sty backward!"

"Sheep," Glenaire growled, his eyes on Lily.

Her heart skipped a beat.

"Just as bad," Will chuckled. The "worker" had materialized as a very amused Earl of Chadbourn. "You've done interesting things with that shirt," he said.

Lily tried not to think about where the shirt had been.

"No one would believe this if I told them," the earl persisted. "Glenaire, the Marble Marquess, has straw in his hair and mud on his face."

"You will tell no one," Glenaire said in quelling tones.

Will bit his lip, suppressing laughter, but sobered quickly. "We were worried when you didn't come back," he said while he surveyed Lily with open curiosity. "Stewart sent men to search. Is there a story here? I hope it's a good one."

Glenaire repeated the story Lily suggested with few words.

"You've been walking all night?"

"Until we found the Justice farm, yes," Richard said. His haughty expression brooked no contradiction. "We will, of course, want to hide the fact that we were gone all night if possible."

Will looked at Lily kindly and nodded.

"We need to get Miss Thornton into the house, seen by as few eyes as possible," Richard went on. "And into the care of your countess." He no longer called her Lily.

"Give me a moment. I'll find work for my people and clear out a path," the earl said. He left them alone.

Richard started to speak, and again Lily stopped him. "You will bring my father home," she demanded.

"I have already arranged it, as you know. I'll have Volkov watched. You needn't fear him," he responded.

"There will be no marriage," she repeated. "I will not have it."

"Very well, Miss Thornton. Let it be on your head, but you will tell me if there is a child. You have no choice. My child will not be born outside of marriage."

There are always choices, Lord High and Mighty. Not always good ones, but choices nonetheless. Most men would accept my decision with relief.

~

"I COULD DINE out on that story, you coming in looking like a bedraggled sheep-boy," Will hadn't stopped laughing at him all day. It had become one more thing to hold against Miss Lilias Thornton; she had made him a laughing stock.

Richard sat—bathed, groomed, trussed in a pristine suit—and sipped the earl's fine whisky. His hair had been cleaned. His nails had been filed. His clothes had been burned. A hefty bonus calmed his valet and removed all trace of the horrid night.

Not all so horrid. He shook the traitorous thought away.

"My couriers will reach London quickly, but I suspect Sahin Pasha sent his ahead on Mercury. They will be at sea to Thessaloniki by nightfall or tomorrow at the latest, tide and wind permitting. I am sorry about Mercury."

"We don't know that he's gone for good," Will pointed out. "I have hope Sahin will recall himself enough to return my property."

"Perhaps. He has other priorities." Richard tried to keep the conversation on the diplomatic mess, not his night on the road. "They'll kill the agent, of course, and possibly unleash more unrest. Russia may find the need to avenge their man."

"Or they may take care of Volkov for going rogue," Will suggested.

"Perhaps. It depends on how successful it turns out for them. In chaos they win either way."

"Catherine pronounced Miss Thornton fit. No harm came to her as a result of your misadventure," Will put in abruptly, searching Richard's face.

Richard broke eye contact and made his face a mask of indifference.

"Most of society would consider her compromised," Will ground on.

Indifference fled. "I consider her compromised. I made an honorable offer. She refused."

Will did not hide his astonishment, although Richard couldn't be sure if the offer or the refusal surprised the earl more.

For a moment Richard feared his friend would ask awkward questions. He glared until the earl looked away and changed the subject.

"Catherine quite likes the woman," he said. "She believes there will be little talk and any that arises easily squelched by the Countess of Chadbourn and the sister of the Marquess of Glenaire."

"Georgiana?" Richard asked, "I shouldn't be surprised. My sister has become the advocate of self-willed women everywhere."

"She gets no help from your mother, however," Will grimaced.

Richard's sister Georgiana and her husband, who were estranged from his parents, kept a house in London in addition to their home in Cambridge. Their salon had a wide list of devotees among the more intellectual set. The duchess preferred to think they did not exist.

Richard sipped his drink in silence. His mother's well-known prejudices did not require comment.

"I thought you would want to know. About Miss Thornton," Will said, watching him.

"We will, of course, arrange travel for the woman, but Miss Thornton is her own concern," Richard replied. He ought to feel relieved; it annoyed him that he didn't. "She will do what she pleases in any case," he said. *She'll try. We will watch her while she does it.*

Chapter Nine

"No, no, no. This is one case where bigger is better."

Lily listened to Catherine with sinking heart. In the weeks since the countess packed up Lily, her youngest child, the nursemaid and a train of luggage and swooped back to London to ensure that the Haut Ton knew Lilias Thornton to be her dearest of friends, Lily had learned better than to try to stop the woman's enthusiasms.

"I fear Catherine is correct in this case, Lily," Georgiana Mallet put in. Glenaire's sister had joined them at Chadbourn's London house to plot the campaign hatched by Catherine to "Pop Lily off in style." They sat around a gaming table covered with engraved invitations, lists, and scraps of notes.

"But we agreed I should set my sights a little lower than the upper ten thousand. I won't need to attend this ball."

"No dear," Catherine told her, "You set your sights there. We merely try to steer you toward success."

"I don't want or need a title," Lily said hotly. "So, why do I need to attend the Duchess of Pembrook's ball? It will be a stifling crush full of useless fribbles who wouldn't have me, and darling young ladies eager to cut me."

"Not all titled gentlemen are worthless," Catherine corrected tartly.

Not all men are gentlemen either. Perhaps I should give up on marriage. Any serious suitor will have to be told I'm not untouched. The thought depressed her.

"Generally, you may be correct about that sort of thing—not titled gentlemen but certain types of events," Georgiana said to Lily. "However—"

"Thank you," Lily interrupted. "I thought we had agreed to small dinner parties, literary soirees, and musicales. I won't go."

"Yes, but we must start large," Catherine insisted.

"First, because you must be noticed," Georgiana said, "and as much as I myself loathe the bowing and backstabbing, the first great ball of the season will get you noticed."

Lily grunted. She recalled Sahin's thoughts on the English marriage mart. *It's a horse auction, and I'm treated like a second-rate mare.*

"Secondly, you must cast your net wide. You can narrow your choices later," Catherine said.

"And third?" Lily demanded.

"Third, you might just have fun. You seemed to enjoy yourself at Chadbourn Park," Catherine said.

I did. Before Volkov caught me. Before Glenaire— She sighed. *Before Glenaire. If I attend this ball, he will be there, looking down his nose for signs of misbehavior.* Another thought caused her stomach to turn. *What if Volkov is in attendance?* She had seen no sign of him since her return to London, but she could feel watching eyes.

"I won't go," Lily insisted. She picked up the next invitation on the "maybe" pile.

Catherine looked hurt, but she pulled the invitation back from the "no" pile.

"Lily, Catherine went to great trouble to get you that invitation," Georgiana chided gently. "You must go."

When you use that tone, you are every inch Glenaire's sister. Glenaire! How can I face him? Lily had no answer to her own question, but she realized she had to face him, if only to seek news of her father. She looked from face to face, one set in determination, one hopeful. How can I repay their kindness with obstinacy? Her shoulders sagged.

"Pembrook's ball it is," she capitulated. "When is it?"

"Thursday next. You won't be sorry. I have it on good authority the Ottoman delegates have been invited, and the Foreign Office will season the attendees with their eager young men, your target audience," Georgiana said.

Lily already felt sorry. *If I see Sahin Pasha in public, I may cause an international incident. The Marble Marquess won't like that.* That thought perked her up.

~

"That's all?" the marquess demanded.

The dispatch rider, still in his road dirt cringed in the face of Richard's fury. He arrived unannounced at Horse Guards, went through the desk used to screen out frivolous requests and importunate beggars, and was dragged bodily into the marquess's private office overlooking Horse Guards Parade.

"No, I mean yes, my lord. This is the message exactly as John Thornton gave it to me. He didn't explain anything else."

Richard scanned the unsealed vellum again, but the message remained the same.

Ship floundered. We regret we are detained in Copenhagen pending repairs. Estimated departure 30 days. I will take the opportunity to explore Danish commercial interests and make use of the archives here.

J. Thornton

He folded it back and tapped it absentmindedly on his desk. We should have sent a more strongly worded warning. Still, the bodyguard knows his duty.

He laid the message down on the desk, calculating the time it took to send this message overland. He won't leave for another two weeks and then take three to four more to get here. John Thornton couldn't arrive in less than a month; six to eight weeks were more likely. He didn't appear to be in a rush.

I don't suppose the man bothered to send word to his daughter.

"Was this his only message?"

The hapless courier opened and closed his mouth like a carp. The man looked ready to drop. Richard reined in his temper.

"What I mean is, did he notify family in any way?"

"Oh! No, sir. At least I don't think so," the man said.

Damn. Until her father returns, the Thornton woman remains my problem.

"Go clean up and seek your rest." Richard punctuated his words with a shooing motion. "You made admirable time. I will see that your superiors hear about it."

The man turned to go, but Richard interrupted him. "Send in Mr. Heaton on your way out, if you please."

"Anything new regarding Volkov?" Richard demanded of Heaton five minutes later.

"No, my lord. He hangs on the edges of the Russian delegation. He gambles, but never to excess. He visits particularly sordid houses of—"

"Yes, yes, we know his vices. Has he approached Lilias Thornton?"

"No, my lord, no change since yesterday." If Heaton intended it as a rebuke, Richard saw no sign.

"We'd know if he did," Heaton continued. "Since we frightened that one ruffian off behind her lane two weeks ago, we've seen no other sign of anyone."

As I know perfectly well.

"If I may be so bold, my lord," Heaton began. "Have we had word about John Thornton's return?"

"A messenger arrived a short while ago. Not good news." Richard showed the young man the message.

"Does she know?" Heaton asked, concern obvious on his face.

"No. Her father left that to us."

"I'd be happy to call on Miss Thornton," Heaton said hopefully.

The damned puppy looks like a boy anticipating a sweet.

"No," Richard said. "I'll handle it. You may go." He watched the crestfallen young man leave and considered whether he should assign a different agent to the Thornton woman issue.

Don't be a bloody fool, Richard. Heaton would make her an unexceptional husband. At least he would if the puppy didn't bore her to tears, if he could be broad minded enough to overlook—

Richard frowned. His actions had, at the very least, complicated her marriage prospects. That thought hounded him out the door to call for his carriage.

An hour later, irritated and impatient, he let himself out in front of his sister's townhouse.

~

Lily Thornton had not been home. She had not been at Chadbourn House. The ladies, he was told, went shopping.

I'll be damned if I'm going to chase them all over Bond Street.

He could hardly impose on the countess, but he could stop unannounced at his sister's house and wait. If he were lucky, Georgiana would return home and Lily would be with her. Luck rode with him. He could hear the sound of women's voices even as he handed his hat to the butler.

"I'll see if Mrs. Mallet is at home," the man said.

"Of course she is," Richard said, brushing past him into the drawing room.

"The Marquess of Glenaire," the old man intoned behind him with pained expression.

Three faces turned his way, his sister's irritated, and Catherine's curious. Lily looked terrified.

"Don't mind my brother, Simpson," Georgiana directed her servant. "He believes manners don't apply to the Hayden family."

He ignored his sister. He hadn't seen Lily Thornton in four weeks. His eyes devoured her, taking inventory. She had her hair in some ridiculously complex knot. It hid the lights. He wanted the lights. She looked thinner. She looked pale.

Could she be with child? Then she would indeed be my problem.

The look in Lily's green eyes, wide with alarm, brought him to his senses. He straightened his spine, forced his eyes away, and squashed the flicker of hope that plagued him. *Absurd*!

Georgiana's raised brow looked like it owed more to amusement than impatience. My sister is too perceptive by half.

"Social call, Richard? Family matter?" she asked. He heard laughter in her voice. *Minx*.

"Business I fear. I went to call on Miss Thornton and found her here. Perhaps she could join me in the foyer for a few moments. That should be proper enough."

"I think not," Lily murmured. She gripped the arm of her chair. "There is nothing I have to say to you that my friends can't hear." All three women watched him expectantly.

"Perhaps, but there may be things I have to say for as few ears as possible." *She looks like she wants to bolt*. "Come, come, I won't eat you," he insisted. He regretted his choice of words when he saw her eyes widen.

"Very well," she said. She followed him to the foyer where he dismissed Georgiana's curious servants.

"We had word about your father."

Color drained from her. If he thought her pale before, now she looked positively wraithlike. She swayed backward.

Richard grabbed her elbow and rushed to assure her. "He is well."

She shook off his hand; hope flickered in her eyes. "Is he here?"

"No, delayed." *I've disappointed her*. He hated the way the light went out in her eyes.

"Still in Russia," she gasped. Her hand, pressed to her chest as if to steady her breathing, drew his eyes to her breasts.

"No, no," he floundered, pulling his attention back. "I'm making a hash of this. He left as scheduled, but the ship floundered. It limped into Copenhagen. They await repairs."

"Too close," she whispered.

"Pardon?"

"Too close to St. Petersburg." He watched her pull herself together. *Good girl. I can almost see her mind assessing the information.*

"He is well guarded." Richard prayed that was true. "Travel delays the Russians as much as us."

"Thank you for telling me," she said turning away from him.

"Are you well?" he asked her retreating back.

She turned and studied his face gravely. "Do you mean, have there been consequences? It is too soon to tell." Their eyes caught for a moment.

"You will—"

"Tell you if such a catastrophe occurs? Perhaps. Good day, my lord." She left with a swish of skirt.

Why does she have to be so damned prickly? Richard retrieved his hat, put it on with a disgruntled slap, and walked out into the late afternoon shadows.

John Thornton can deal with her. When he arrives, she'll be his problem, not mine. Not mine, he repeated as if to reassure himself and dampen any surge of disappointment.

Unless she's with child. He envisioned Lily big with child, and his lip quirked in the smallest of smiles.

Chapter Ten

Pembrook's ballroom radiated heat, noise, and the odors of seething humanity. Lily sat next to Roger Heaton and tried to formulate ways to discourage the man.

"Would you join me in a refreshment, Miss Thornton?" An unfamiliar baritone overrode pretty words from Roger Heaton, who had been attentive, too attentive, all evening. She allowed him only one dance, but he hovered all evening just the same.

"Refreshment?" the stranger repeated.

Lily hesitated another moment. The young stranger's dark face over a pristine, fashionably knotted neckcloth did not belong to an Englishman. She recognized him as one of Sahin Pasha's aides.

Heaton watched the man sharply; he put a protective—and in Lily's opinion, presumptuous—hand on her arm.

"Have we met?" Lily asked, removing Heaton's hand.

"We were introduced at Chadbourn Park," the man said with a rueful smile.

A lie, but a charming one. This is one of the "farmers" at the inn. *One of the horse thieves,* she thought.

She searched the room for Sahin Pasha and found him chatting with the Duke of Argyll. He did not appear to be aware of Lily's presence, but she knew better.

"Of course, I remember now," she chirped, carefully avoiding names since she had no idea what this handsomely dressed gentleman called himself. "I would indeed like refreshment."

She thought Heaton might try to stop her, but good manners

prevailed. She could feel his eyes following her. She liked Roger Heaton well enough, but she wasn't prepared to give him exclusive attention.

"What do you really want?" she whispered to her escort when they approached the refreshment table. He smiled down at her and melted away. She turned to find Sahin Pasha helping himself to cake. The sight did not astonish her.

"Ah, Miss Thornton," he crooned. "Always a delight." He took her plate and began to fill it with sweets.

"And you, too, favored uncle," she said. She made no effort to keep sarcasm from her voice.

"I know we parted on difficult terms," Sahin said.

"Difficult, favored uncle? You underestimate," Lily said. She leaned toward the plate and whispered for his ears only, "It might have been catastrophic."

"Was not your marquess protective?" She followed his eyes across the room where Glenaire stood next to his mother. She watched him lead Lady Sarah Wharton to the dance floor; she saw his mother's grim satisfaction. The girl carried herself with a perfect mix of confidence and fragility. Her coiffure and gown reflected the height of current fashion exactly.

They make a beautiful pair; Lady Sarah is born to his world.

"He isn't my marquess," she said, "But yes. The marquess protected me." *From everything but himself.*

"My apologies if I misread the situation," the old man said, watching the pair caught up in the dance. "Necessity drove me."

"I accept for myself, favored uncle, but my father—"

"Is he not in London, little one? I had hoped to see my friend, John Thornton, here." The old man shrugged. "Travel this time of year..."

"Alas his travel has been delayed for repairs in Copenhagen," she said. "The Foreign Office can only do so much." She took the dish of sweets she would never eat and lifted her skirt. "Now, if you will excuse me, I'll take my leave." They had begun to draw attention.

The old man nodded gravely. "I am in your debt, I fear. If you ever have need of my help, you know you can come to me," he said.

Lily circled the edge of the dancers and put the entire plate of sweets on the tray of a footman stationed by one wall. She wondered if she would ever seek Sahin Pasha's help again. The first time ended in— *In what, Lily? Disaster?*

Her stomach felt queasy, and she needed air. Pembrook's ball had been the sad crush she anticipated, but no crowd of suitors surrounded her this time. Only one name other than Heaton graced her dance card. She wasn't sure if she should be disappointed or relieved. She doubted that any of the callow young men would want a wife who had been unchaste.

What if there are consequences?

She thought she would seek out Chadbourn and his countess. The earl had come at Catherine's insistence. He loathed balls. Lily began to see his point. Georgiana had shamed Lily into coming but stayed away herself. Lily tried not to give in to resentment. She stood in a ballroom stuffed with London's highest society and felt more alone than she had her entire life.

She inched her way along the side until she came within feet of Catherine and the earl. She greeted her friend with a smile and walked forward, colliding with one of the dancers just leaving the floor.

"I beg your pardon," she began. A man's hand steadied her. She turned to find Glenaire's intense eyes seeking hers. She took a step back.

"Miss Thornton. I didn't know you were here."

Horsefeathers. You know everything.

"I came with the Earl and Countess of Chadbourn," she replied, giving Catherine a pleading look.

"We insisted," Catherine said, coming forward.

"And we're glad we did. Doesn't she look lovely?" the earl added. Lily thought laughter lurked in his eyes, but she couldn't see anything humorous. He seemed to be studying Glenaire.

"The dress becomes you," Glenaire said, searching her person rather more thoroughly than Lily found comfortable. His eyes came to rest just where her mother's pearls lay at the juncture of her neck and shoulder, a place his mouth had found frequently the night they—

I will not think of that, she told herself firmly.

"It suits you," the young woman on Glenaire's arm added. Lady Sarah studied Lily avidly and watched the marquess with a proprietary air.

Glenaire snapped his attention away from Lily. "Lady Sarah Wharton, may I present Miss Lilias Thornton. Miss Thornton's father is in service to the Foreign Office."

Lady Sarah nodded in acknowledgement and smiled. "It is good of you to take an interest in the people who serve under you," she said. Her smile held no sweetness.

"The dress does become you," Lady Sarah went on. "Most women could never wear that shade of green," she said.

"Lily is lucky it shows her eyes to perfection," Catherine rushed in.

"One finds that some people look well enough in gowns that are not quite the height of fashion," Lady Sarah crooned. "You are to be congratulated, Miss Thornton. Isn't she, Glenaire?" She sparkled up at him.

Lily's dress had come from Saint Petersburg by way of Paris. It had subtle sophistication and none of the flounces popular in London ballrooms.

Glenaire ignored the beauty at his side. Lily squirmed under the intensity of his gaze.

"Glenaire?" Lady Sarah repeated.

"Miss Thornton does not require the changing whims of fashion to look well," he said.

"Quite so," Catherine agreed. Lady Sarah's smile grew wider and less sincere.

"Your gown is exquisite," Lily said to Lady Sarah. She told the truth. It must have cost the moon. She will make a beautiful ornament on his arm if they marry.

Lady Sarah nodded her head as if to acknowledge the deference of an underling. *That one is born to lord it over us mere mortals. They make a perfect pair.*

A discreet tug on his arm, one Lily didn't miss, must have alerted Glenaire to his partner's impatience. He made his bows and walked away. They moved slowly enough that Lily couldn't miss Lady Sarah's question as they did. "Who is that woman? Is she someone who matters?"

"An empty-headed debutante," Catherine mumbled.

"Not so empty," Lily said. "She is quite bright, and she knows what she wants."

"I don't like her," Catherine said with characteristic bluntness.

"She's the Duchess of Sudbury's choice for Richard," the earl pointed out.

"Yes, but is she his?" Catherine asked.

"He has said as much," her husband sighed. "I don't think he feels much enthusiasm. That may be why he delays. He seems to be waiting for something."

Waiting for me, Lily thought. *Waiting to hear if he must do his duty to impending offspring.* What had Glenaire told Chadbourn?

"They make a perfect pair," she said out loud. "Lady Sarah was born and bred to be a duchess."

The earl grunted. "She'll turn out like his mother. He will hate it."

"I think not," Lily said. "He will merely work around it as long as she adorns his table, just as he works around his mother."

"All London waits for an announcement. If he stretches it much longer, he won't be able to get out of it," Catherine said.

If he waits for news from me, he is waiting in vain.

Lily pleaded headache and found herself escorted out in quick time by the earl and his Catherine, both relieved to be free of the heat, the gossip, and the ugly machinations of the social climbers. Lily followed in silence.

I need to tell him I'm not increasing. There is no point in waiting.

Chadbourn looked at her quizzically when he handed her into the carriage. She attempted a reassuring smile and came to a decision.

I will reassure Glenaire there is no baby—even if I'm not sure it's true.

Richard dismissed Pembrook's ball from his mind as soon as he ordered his man of business to send "Roses, yellow, two dozen should do," to Lady Sarah Wharton. He found it harder to dismiss Lily Thornton.

Lady Sarah's pedigree is sterling. He forced himself to remember that. His parents had certainly forced his attention to it at least twice the evening before. *Lily Thornton brings intelligence and an independent streak that would be attractive in sons,* his rebellious mind retorted.

He pushed women from his mind and attempted to concentrate on the massive walnut desk from which he presided over the far-flung affairs of England. Its carved handles and brass fittings usually gave him a sense of order. Neatly organized stacks of reports, dispatches, and work to be accomplished surrounded him. Today, his thoughts refused to cooperate.

Lady Sarah's perfect manners and social connections make her an ideal political hostess, he reminded himself. Again the second thought came unbidden. *Lily Thornton understands the subtle undertones of diplomacy. She knows Turkish and Russian, and I suspect her French is—*

He ran a hand over the back of his neck. *She won't have you, Richard. Be done with it.*

Castlereagh had demanded his analysis of the growing unrest in the Kingdom of the Two Sicilies. He stared at the untouched notes scattered across his desk. Word from Naples sounded dire. He wondered what Lily would make of it.

Enough! Make your addresses to Lady Sarah Wharton or don't. You can't seriously consider Lily Thornton as the future as Duchess of Sudbury, even if she would have you. A vision of his mother presiding over dinner at Sudbury House prodded him to look at his work. *Why not?* a traitorous voice whispered in the vicinity of his heart.

He pulled more minor affairs closer. Four embassies requested increased funds. An outpost in Canada requested troops, the seventeenth man in two months having gone absent and disappeared into the frontier. Their agent in the Duchy of Werltvelt reported dalliance between the crown prince and the consort of a neighboring baron. Could he suggest a devious solution? Troubling information that came from an interrogation at His Majesty's Prison at Millbank required a carefully phrased warning to the governor on Gibraltar. A trade report from the Sultanate of Johor on the island of Singapura arrived inconveniently late; a meeting with appropriate men of business had to be scheduled.

Beneath them all lay one small note on fine vellum. He snatched it up, broke the seal, and flipped it open.

To THE Marquess of Glenaire

My lord,

The business we discussed at Chadbourn Park had a positive outcome. No further action is needed.

Your obedient servant,

Miss Lilias Thornton

"A POSITIVE OUTCOME." *Can a woman tell as soon as two months?* Richard's unease turned to disappointment—an irrational, absurd disappointment. *Of course she can, you fool. Lily Thornton's folly spared her an unfortunate birth. Honor satisfied. Be relieved.*

He pushed away from his desk. *It was my folly*, he chided himself. He paced to the window, something he never did, and it irritated him. His own irritation annoyed him further. *Why can't I let it lie? I do not let petty emotions rule me*. His emotions seemed to have other ideas.

An ornate watch, pulled from a cannily designed pocket in his waistcoat, ticked steadily. One-thirty, still time for a "morning" call, he thought. I may as well use the time. I'm accomplishing nothing here.

The latest in his constantly shifting parade of secretaries came running at the sound of Richard's bell.

"I will be out the rest of the afternoon."

Too well trained to show any surprise he might have felt, the young man dispatched a footmen to call for the marquess's carriage. Richard retrieved his hat and tapped it on his head.

Perhaps I will call on Lady Sarah. She will have received my token by now.

The piles on his desk drew his attention. The far right, as always, indicated "Urgent Matters." The stack looked taller than usual. He remembered Castlereagh's demands and almost changed his mind.

"Tell Heaton and Stewart I may return this evening," he told the secretary.

After I visit Jackson's saloon to find someone who would like a thorough pounding.

"You needn't wait," he added.

Richard ignored the curious eyes of clerks, ogling the sight of the Marble Marquess leaving early, and walked directly to the main stairs.

Lady Sarah will be pleased by a call.

He stepped out into the sun to wait for his coachman.

Too pleased, he thought.

Lily Thornton's face continued to plague him. He couldn't dismiss the thought that she looked pale when he saw her at

Pembrook's—too pale. *If she isn't increasing, something else is wrong. Perhaps simply worry. She should be relieved.*

He hopped up into his carriage. *So should I.*

A footman took hold of the door to close it. "Where to, my lord?" he asked. I should direct him to Grosvenor Square, to the Duke of Lisle's townhouse.

"Gilbert Street," Richard said instead.

"Just off Bloomsbury Square?"

Richard nodded. The man called the directions to the coachman. The door closed. The carriage lurched forward. In moments Richard sped toward Gilbert Street, home to intellectuals and the professional class—home to Lily Thornton.

Chapter Eleven

Teacakes made Lily queasy. So did biscuits, toast, Aunt Marianne's pug, and the nosegays of lilacs and lily of the valley beautifully arranged on a marble-topped table near the window of Aunt Marianne's first floor withdrawing room.

She sat erect, attempted to sip tea, and smiled wanly at her visitors. Both Walter Stewart and Roger Heaton sent posies and gratifying greetings the day after the ball. When they came to call, their stay lengthened perilously close to the limit of good manners for a morning call.

Utter nonsense naming afternoon visits a 'morning' call.

For a moment, that absurd thought symbolized all the weary idiocy of the so-called marriage mart. Another wave of nausea taunted Lily; the entire tedious effort might come to nothing.

One other visitor cheerfully munched cook's lemon cakes and gave the appearance of contentment. She had met James Heyworth, newly elevated to Baron Ross, at Pembrook's ball. He had arrived, danced one dance with her, and disappeared into the card room. Now, here he sat in her drawing room. He brought no posies. He puzzled her.

The man looked whip thin. Either he exercised heavily or ate irregularly. His uniform, nicely brushed but well worn, appeared almost shabby. He wore a suit at the ball. Does he even own another? A narrow black armband tied haphazardly to one arm paid tribute to the recent death of his father; he did not have the look of a grieving man. The only time his cheerful countenance faltered came when

Walter Stewart congratulated him on coming into his title. That soured him; the barony did not appear to be flush with funds.

"Are you in London for long, Baron Ross?"

He looked momentarily perplexed. "I hope to be," he said at last.

How does one respond to that?

Stewart and Heaton eyed each other. Each, she suspected, hoped the other would leave first. Lily felt too weary to find that amusing.

"Was it difficult for you gentlemen to break free from your many duties?" she asked sweetly. She knew full well the Foreign Office did not necessarily keep business hours. She also knew young gentlemen who wished to get ahead worked long and hard.

Stewart looked uncomfortable, but Heaton smiled back. "For your company, Miss Thornton, one makes every sacrifice."

Outrageous. Get back to work you fool man!

"Lily, look. Another admirer," Aunt Marianne chirped from her chair in the corner.

Aunt Marianne's old butler bowed into the room. "The Most Honorable the Marquess of Glenaire," he intoned and bowed out.

Glenaire stood erect in the doorway, his blinding white neckcloth a marvel of engineering, the fine silk of his suit a remarkable expression of tailors' art. Cool blue eyes under perfectly groomed white blond hair surveyed the room.

Lily didn't rise; fear that a display of dizziness would make her look foolish pinned her to the chair. She fixated on the folds of carefully crafted French lace that draped from the marquess's cuffs over long-fingered hands.

His brilliant, beautiful hands.

He reached out one hand to greet Aunt Marianne with perfect ease, bowing over her fingers, and turned to Lily. She clasped her own hands tightly together to prevent any similar greeting. Glenaire's eyebrow rose slightly.

"Miss Thornton," he said with a nod. He did not say she looked well.

"My lord." She did not say, "Welcome."

His gaze held hers for but a moment before he turned to Heaton and Stewart.

"I see you gentlemen did not receive the message I left for you at the office," he said.

The two gentlemen shifted in their seat, murmured excuses, and rose. Both bowed over Lily's hand.

"We'll see ourselves out," Stewart said with an uneasy glance at Glenaire. Lily felt grateful she didn't have to endure lengthy goodbyes, but resented the marquess's high-handedness all the same.

"You've scattered my admirers again, my lord," she chastised when they were gone.

"Like geese, again," he agreed.

Their eyes caught in shared memory of their first encounter at Chadbourn Park—and what came next.

He did not, she noted, scatter Baron Ross, although he had skewered the baron with a pointed look.

"Hello, Richard," the baron said, still at ease. "Didn't expect to see you here." He snatched up another teacake.

Richard? Who dared call the Marble Marquess by his Christian name? Not another of Glenaire's spies, then. Does the man actually have normal friends?

"Jamie," the marquess nodded in greeting. "Enjoying the Misses Thornton's hospitality, I see."

The baron grinned back. "Their cook makes fine cakes." His grin rearranged itself into something like that of a naughty boy. "But I think it's time I take my leave," he said.

"Please stay seated, Miss Thornton. I will escort the baron out," Glenaire ordered.

Lily saw that Aunt Marianne had nodded off in her comfortable chair in the far corner. She rose carefully, took hold of the back of her chair, blinked to banish dizziness, and watched the backs of the two departing men through the open door of the drawing room.

The marquess tipped his head to listen to Baron Ross, who spoke softly. Once, she saw, the baron looked back toward the drawing room, his face set in compassionate lines, and turned to say something to the marquess. At the outside door, Lily watched as Glenaire laid a hand on the baron's back, a gesture of support to a friend unlike anything she expected of him.

Odd that. Perhaps Glenaire wished his friend sympathy in his grief. Except the baron had shown no signs of overwhelming grief.

When the baron turned his face to smile up at Glenaire, it held no sadness.

His smile looks genuine, and not some cheeky grin, she thought. And, unless I misunderstand, the man looks grateful.

As Lily watched, something passed between hands. Glenaire passed banknotes to the man discreetly.

I'm right. The baron does not eat regularly. He isn't the first member of fashionable society to rely on invitations just to eat.

The idea of Glenaire as a generous friend altered her image of the man. She would have to digest that new information later. The marquess himself watched her from the drawing room door.

"Do sit, Miss Thornton. You look as if you need to."

Lily slid back into her chair and closed her eyes. She opened them to a pair of blue ones studying her.

"My friend's assessment is correct. You are not well."

"It's nothing. A slight discomfort," she said. I pray it is something I ate. "Did you send him to spy on me?"

The firm line of his mouth bent subtly upward. "'Spy' is an ugly word. Jamie possesses too much sympathy and too little discretion," Glenaire said. "I give him little—," he spread his hands in an expansive gesture, "—errands, for want of a better word."

"So you can pay him," Lily finished. "Well done of you, my lord."

Glenaire's cool façade didn't alter; he didn't respond.

"I own I am fatigued, however, and I must ask you to—"

Both aristocratic brows rose. "Dismissing me, Miss Thornton?"

Lily held herself perfectly still and thrust out her chin. I need to get rid of this man before I fall over.

"Are you perfectly certain 'The business we discussed at Chadbourn Park had a positive outcome'?" he asked.

She stifled a groan. "A woman is always certain about these things, my lord."

He leaned forward abruptly. "Men, however, are never certain. Lily, tell me the truth."

So, I'm Lily again?

"Are you calling me a liar?"

He reached for her hand; she pulled away. He leaned back into his seat. "So I am to understand that 'No further action is needed'?"

"As I wrote, my lord," she said. "Was it not clear?"

"Will there be other repercussions? When you marry, that is?"

At least the damned man didn't say "if."

"My marriage prospects are my concern. I need nothing from you. I expect nothing from you. I want nothing from you."

Glenaire—oh hell, Richard—glowers like no other man I ever met. It is enough to strip the bark off a tree. She refused to wilt under it or look away in the long minutes that followed in silence.

"In the matter of your father, Miss Thornton, you do have concerns," he began. Her heart began to race. He went on before she could ask. "In matters of that sort, no news is often literally the best news, and we have heard nothing. I've sent men to watch every port between here and Copenhagen. If he is delayed again, or if Volkov's agents appear, I will hear. When I do, you will know."

"Thank you," she whispered.

"Has Volkov tried to contact you?"

"What do your spies tell you?"

"That he hasn't. He had someone watching, but we put a stop to it."

The dratted man doesn't even try to deny that he spies on me. Volkov too—good God!

"They are correct. I have seen and heard nothing."

She insisted on walking him to the door. *I want to shut the door on him, shut the door on the entire episode of the Marble Marquess in my life.*

"Good day, Miss Thornton. You will hear from me."

"Do send a message if you hear anything," she replied. *Send a message—don't come here again.*

She shut the door firmly behind him, turned, and deposited her sparse luncheon and tea into a potted palm, retching painfully for a few moments.

Ugh, but I hate that. Please, dear God, let this be something I ate. She clung to hope but found it harder to doubt every day.

I think, Lily dear, you are about to face the consequences of what happened among the sheep. She felt her marriage hopes die with sinking heart. *What will I do?* she wondered with rising panic. *I will have to leave London for certain. How can I do that until my father is here? Papa, where are you?*

A maid hurried to clean her mess. Lily thanked her, suggested they leave Aunt Marianne to her nap, and began to climb the stairs to her room, weary beyond speech.

Pregnant, Lily? What in God's name will you do now?

LILY SPENT two days tossing about for a solution to her problem, with no results. Confiding in Aunt Marianne, her father's ineffective spinster sister would be no help. She needed a distraction badly. Three evenings after the miserable visit from Glenaire, Lily judged herself well enough to go out. The Mallet's literary evening, she believed, would do nicely.

Lady Georgiana Mallet hosted a literary salon, noted for the quality of its speakers, who were as interesting as they were brief, and for the delectable refreshments prepared by the best French chef in England, on the second Thursday of every month. Her brother Richard never came. Lily felt safe attending.

She walked a few short blocks to the Mallets' townhouse, a

discreet footman in tow, and skirted the British Museum. Living close to that institution gave Lily joy; it often provided hours of engrossed fascination when she could forget about her father, about Volkov, about the fear of impending motherhood.

Any approach to unmarried motherhood she considered so far required that she leave London. She felt that loss keenly.

I will miss the museum and its library, she thought. I will miss the squares of Bloomsbury. She crossed into Bedford Square; the small patches of green surrounded by neat townhouses suited her.

She preferred the formal gardens of St. Petersburg or Vienna to wilder places, even the English countryside. *I will hate languishing in some obscure cottage in the wilds of Yorkshire or wherever I find refuge.*

The little fountain in the center of the square gurgled cheerfully as she passed.

If I married Glenaire, I could have London. The thought floated in unbidden, and she quickly pushed that temptation away. Duty made a poor foundation for a happy union. Marriage to a controlling and arrogant marquess, especially one who looked down his nose on her origins, meant a long life of purgatory. There has to be another way.

For now Lily had Bedford Square and its carefully tended flowerbeds. She would have it until her father arrived. She crossed onto Bedford Street west of the square.

Should I confide in Georgiana or in Catherine? She quickly dismissed that idea also. *However much they may care for me, Glenaire is one of them. He commands their first loyalty.* Involvement with her problems would put them in an awkward position at best. It would empower the marquess to bully her at worst.

A few short steps and she stood under the great curved door to the Mallet townhouse. Evening closed in and the windows above lit up with candlelight. The sound of happy conversation drifted down when the footman knocked. Lily smiled in anticipation.

Georgiana's salon never fails to distract me.

"Miss Lily Thornton," her servant told the butler. He stepped aside. The man would wait to accompany her home.

Weariness threatened her when she followed the butler upstairs to the drawing room. She gripped the railing and hesitated before stepping into the first floor hall.

She smiled wanly at the butler when he looked ready to catch her if she slipped.

Perhaps I should not have come.

She needed the distraction of friends. The door to the expansive drawing room lay open. The butler gestured her toward it. Andrew and Georgiana Mallet stood on little ceremony and required no announcement.

Lily fixed her smile in place and paused just inside. Georgiana, on a settee by the windows and already deep in conversation with one of the curators of antiquities from the museum, glanced up at Lily with a swift grin but didn't rush to her side.

Georgiana's husband Andrew approached unimpeded by his slight limp; his scarred face lit in welcome. War had left his body damaged, but his brilliant mind and kind heart intact.

I envy the Mallets their marriage, she thought. Her heart sank. That door may be closed to me forever.

"Don't look so sad," her host greeted her. "Come, help Winston defend his contention that the Russians are not so backward as some in this country maintain."

Lily looked toward Henry Winston, one of Cambridge's leading scholars on the Slavic nations who spoke to someone with his back to her.

Andrew led her in that direction.

"Andrew, come set this fusty man straight," Georgiana called across the room. He shrugged at Lily, gestured her forward, and turned to answer his wife's summons.

Lily took a step toward Winston. The man's companion turned, and she looked up into the penetrating black eyes of Konstantin Volkov. His lip curled in a cynical mockery of a smile.

"Miss Thornton," he said, "It has been far too long since we spoke."

Lily froze in place.

"You know our Miss Thornton?" Winston asked.

"I know her very well," Volkov said, his tone implying all the intimacy Lily hated. "We met in St. Petersburg. Miss Thornton loves Russia and all things there. Don't you, Miss Thornton?" the swine went on.

"All things there." *Does he know Papa left?* The pulse in her throat pounded.

"When last we met, we discussed your"—Volkov hesitated—"health. I trust you are well?" He looked at her as if she were a very tasty rabbit cowering before his vulpine jaws.

Lily opened her mouth to speak, closed it, and then opened again to say, "You will excuse me please, gentlemen."

She walked swiftly to the hallway, leaned against one wall, and gasped for breath.

Oh God. He has gotten to me.

The lights faded into darkness, and Lily slipped to the floor in a dead faint.

Chapter Twelve

"Where is the bastard?" Richard demanded.

"Not so loud, you'll wake her," his sister cautioned.

"Andrew, where is he?" he asked more quietly.

"Gone. Did you expect us to thrash him, bind him, and toss him in the dungeon? We had neither the means nor the authority to detain a foreign national. He had done nothing," his brother-in-law answered.

"Lily collapsed in a dead faint, and I'm supposed to believe he did nothing?"

"She walked out into the hallway and fainted. Volkov—along with the rest of our visitors—expressed concern and left politely. Why didn't you warn us about him?" Andrew demanded.

Richard forced his expression into bland control. "Volkov is a Russian agent we have watched. We have Lily protected. How could I expect him to find his way into my sister's drawing room? Why did you invite him?"

"We didn't invite him," Georgiana told him. "Our gatherings are informal. He came with Winston. Shall we warn him away—or warn Winston in any case?"

Richard gave it a moment's thought. "I think not," he replied. "Invite Roger Heaton. I'll make sure he attends every one of your salons."

He looked closely at his sister. "Better yet, cancel your gatherings. Should you be entertaining in your interesting condition?"

"Don't be a snob, Richard. I'm with child, not languishing with ague. Our gatherings continue," she replied tartly.

"In that case, invite Jamie while you're at it."

"Jamie?" Georgiana laughed. "Academic conversation is hardly his bailiwick."

"No, but he knows what to do in a crisis," Richard said. A slight smile failed to light his eyes. "Besides, he loves your chef's brilliant pastries."

Andrew agreed. "Jamie is a good man to have at our back. Why do you think Volkov came?"

"To frighten Lily, to remind her of his threats. My men can handle him." If they noticed his use of her Christian name, they didn't mention it.

"Apparently your watchers lost track of him today," Andrew scoffed. "Are you sure of them?"

Richard glared down his nose at his friend. "My men know their duty and do it well," he said. But they are damn well going to account for this lapse.

Andrew knew better than to contradict his brother-in-law directly. "Do let us know what you expect of us mere mortals in the meantime. We live to serve." He put his arm around his wife's shoulders.

"I'll see her now," Richard said.

"You will not," his sister retorted. "She's resting. With luck she's asleep."

"I said I would see her, not molest her."

Georgiana gave in. She opened the bedroom door on silent hinges to reveal Lily lying still under a coverlet by the light of a single candle.

Too pale. She looks frail.

He reached out to brush a lock of hair from her face, remembered his good sense, and pulled back. Lily didn't stir.

Leaning close, he could smell roses and the subtler scent of woman. The urge to protect gutted him. Too frail. Lily Thornton strides through life, a force of nature, she does not faint.

"Miss Thornton," he whispered to his sister who stood just behind him, determined to keep this discussion formal, "doesn't strike me as a female who makes a habit of swooning. Odd, don't you think?" He turned to look carefully at Georgiana, robust and rosy in spite of pregnancy, her second.

"He gave her a fright," Georgiana whispered back. "She also told me she had missed her tea. That could have made her prone to fainting."

Would she even tell me if she thought Lily was increasing?

"Is that all?" he probed.

His sister gave an unladylike shrug and a shrewd look. "That's all Lily shared with me," she said.

He stood for several long moments watching the woman on the bed, breathing her in, willing her to be well. When he finally turned, his sister and her husband eyed him keenly.

Georgiana shut the door behind him. "The best thing we can do is let her sleep," she said.

"That dotty aunt of hers offers no protection," Richard growled. "I doubt if she even knows about the threats."

"You have a guard on her house?" Andrew asked.

"On the whole of Gilbert Street, but we can't watch her everywhere. She would be safer at Sudbury House." The Duke of Sudbury's mansion in Mayfair boasted a thick stone wall and sufficient beefy footmen to guard every door.

"Mother would eat her alive," Georgiana said, "assuming she didn't cut you to pieces for moving a single young woman—and one she would consider of less than desirable lineage at that—into the sacred family compound."

Richard did not often have what he considered a foolish thought, but moving Lily Thornton into his mother's house qualified as one of his rare ones.

Lily drives me to insanity. So does my mother.

"Can you keep her here?" He looked at Andrew. "She should be housed in a home with a competent male in charge. That aunt of hers is worthless."

Andrew appeared to consider the consequences. Georgiana didn't wait. "We could if she permitted it, which she will not do. Lily values her independence fiercely. I admire that in her."

"Increase your guard," Andrew said. "Assign an escort."

"She's been eluding Roger Heaton for a week. I'll have to try another," he said.

"She'll hate that," Georgiana said.

"She won't know. An escort will serve. Miss Thornton will have to put up with it."

Miss Thornton what?

Outrage pulled Lily from the dejection that had weighed her down since her humiliating collapse in the Mallets' hallway. Young men she had considered admirers spied for Glenaire. Disappointment piled on discouragement.

She had felt his presence by the bed. She knew when he leaned in close. For moments, she felt safe and protected, but then she heard his voice—his toplofty, commanding voice.

Damn his arrogant hide.

She sat abruptly and began to look for her slippers, grateful for the sound of retreating footsteps.

I'll go home as soon as the high and mighty Glenaire leaves. I'll go home and—. And what Lily? Wait for Volkov to attack? Drat them all! She scooped up one slipper and began fastening the ties around her calf.

What difference does it make, Lily? You aren't exactly marriage material in your current state. Go home and stay there. Let them all cool their heels in Gilbert Street.

Her resolution lasted ten days before boredom drove her to

accept Walter Stewart's escort to view Sir George Beaumont's collection of Flemish paintings. Soon she shopped with Roger Heaton, ate ices with Stewart, and attended theatre with Heaton, on alternating occasions. Neither man ever positioned himself farther than ten feet from her. Neither mentioned orders. Neither acted particularly lover-like either, to her relief. Once or twice the even less lover-like Jamie Heyworth escorted her.

At the end of a month, over ice at Gunther's, she lost patience with the pretense.

"Has Glenaire had news of my father?" she blurted to Heaton, her escort du jour. She had no sympathy with his stricken look nor respect for his inarticulate reply.

"Come, come. You know we should have heard by now. What does the marquess say?"

"We continue to hope that no news means all is well. Repairs can drag on," Heaton said.

Lily knew that to be true. Once they had put up on Malta for four months waiting for repairs so they could complete a journey to Rome. Her mother had been alive then, and the time had been happily spent. Not this time.

"Waiting batters one's spirits," she sighed.

"I know. Your desire to see your father is natural," Heaton said.

Do you know how frightened I am? Has he told you what Volkov threatens?

Every passing week put her in greater jeopardy of discovery. Discovery of her condition by the gossips would ruin her socially. Discovery by Glenaire would destroy her freedom.

They finished their ices in awkward silence. Heaton helped her to her feet and walked her to their waiting carriage.

"Don't worry about your father, Miss Thornton," he told her. "If you know we are watching for Volkov, then you know we will take care of you." He said it with smug confidence. Lily didn't share it.

"Thank you, Mr. Heaton. You're doing your best, I am sure." Her escort preened.

Glenaire assumes his good intentions are enough also. *If Papa suffers, I hope the marquess finds the well-known end point on the road of good intentions. I hope he rests in hell.*

That thought steeled her nerves all the way home. When the pompous young man handed her from the carriage in front of her Aunt's townhouse, a worse thought struck her.

If Glenaire's efforts don't bear fruit soon, I may be forced to leave London before Papa arrives. Where will I go then?

Chapter Thirteen

Convivial company spilled out of Richard's sister's house and out into the street shouting their good nights and continuing their obscure academic arguments in pairs and threes as they dispersed to the their own homes. Lily wasn't among them.

The hour loomed late, too late for a newcomer, but Richard believed he had timed his arrival perfectly. He waved the butler aside and climbed the stairs.

"You're late, brother," Georgiana said. She made no effort to hide her amusement at his appearance. Richard never attended her salons. "Did you have an earlier engagement?"

His eyes found Lily and held. Her color appeared better; she sat straight, not as weary as before. He traced the slope of her neck and followed the garland of forget-me-not and ivy embroidered on the neckline of her muslin dress with his eyes. He felt his body react to the sight and frowned at Lily. That dress is too damned transparent by far.

"Stop glowering at my guests!" his sister snapped. "Sit before you frighten us all."

Get a grip, man. Stewart does his duty. All is well.

"Sit down and stop towering over us," Georgiana went on.

He spotted a sturdy chair, half hidden by the bookshelves. No footman leapt to assist. *Typical. Georgiana's household management has gone ramshackle since she married Andrew Mallet.*

He pushed it toward the group clustered by the open window and peered at Stewart. *Does he have to lean so close to her?*

"As you see, Mr. Stewart obeys his orders," Lily pointed out tartly. She smiled at the younger man. "And he held his own against Professor Appleton on the importance of our presence in Malta."

Walter Stewart colored; he did not speak.

"Good work, Stewart," Richard grumbled. He sounded grudging even to his own ears. "The hour grows late, and you have committee work tomorrow. I will see Miss Thornton home."

Stewart hesitated momentarily, glancing at Lily and back at Richard.

I said leave, damn it. Richard held Stewart's eyes until the man looked away and rose to make a courteous goodbye to his hosts.

"Well, at least one member of the Foreign Office has manners," Georgiana drawled, bringing a grin to her husband's face. "That was not well done of you."

"What? He managed his assignment to escort Miss Thornton. I relieved him," Richard said.

"His assignment? Am I furniture? A report? A piece of baggage to be transported?" Lily said hotly. She looked angry; he liked Lily angry. Anger gave her color; her chest heaved. He liked it very much indeed.

Enough Richard! He pulled his eyes from her heaving anger. "Nonsense," he said, looking at his brother-in-law but addressing Lily. "You know the danger. The Foreign Office is responsible for Miss Thornton's protection." A fact that may surprise the foreign secretary.

"Checking up on us, Richard?" Andrew asked.

"Most affairs have guest lists. Your salon is, as you said, informal. I wanted to be sure Volkov didn't slither in again."

"Roger Heaton told me you had word Volkov has left London," Lily said.

Roger Heaton talks too much.

"But not England," he told her. He wasn't going to tell her Volkov merely went to Portsmouth, sniffing about the docks and taverns for information.

The confusion in her eyes stabbed him. "He made no attempt to travel to Russia," he said.

"Or Copenhagen?" she asked softly.

"No, not that either." He wished he could wipe the worry from her face.

"Why didn't you just come earlier? You could have helped Stewart defend the concessions we won at the Congress of Vienna," Andrew said.

"Vienna settled everything—and nothing. There is nothing to discuss with amateurs. I had another engagement as your wife suggested."

"Do tell," Georgiana prodded.

"If you must know, I attended a dinner party with the Duke and Duchess of Lisle."

"Sarah Wharton's parents?" His sister laughed. "Are we to wish you happy?"

"Not yet," he said, glancing at Lily.

"Mother must be impatient," Georgiana said.

Richard grunted. "She will have to wait. I know my duty to the estate."

"London watches you avidly," his brother-in-law said.

"London will have to wait also. It's time for me to escort Miss Thornton home."

She looked like she might object.

Don't be a fool, Lily.

She didn't object until they descended to the Mallets' front door and he gestured to the door of his waiting carriage.

"No, thank you. I prefer to walk, my lord. I'll bid you good night here." She turned to go.

Richard directed his coachman to wait in Bloomsbury Square and caught up with her in two strides. *Stubborn woman.*

He winged his arm at her, but she hesitated before taking it.

"I suppose I have no choice," she said when she reached accept his arm, her tiny hand white on his black jacket. She walked in silence.

"You are well?" he asked.

"Quite," she replied.

They crossed to Bedford Square.

"The overly warm weather doesn't bother you?"

She shook her head.

Her hand, he realized, trembled where it lay on his arm. A fierce desire to protect seized him. He placed his other hand over it.

"My lord?"

"You trembled."

In the distance, his carriage turned away from them. They walked into the narrow confines of Gilbert Street, draped in darkness. Her home lay four doors down.

"I did not," she protested. "Even if I did—"

A shaft of yellow light from a window lit her face. She looked up, momentarily inarticulate.

Can she see desire on my face?

"—what concern is it of yours?" she finished in a whisper.

"Your well-being is very much my concern, Lily. Very much indeed." *It shouldn't be, but it is.* He searched her face in the dim shaft of light. He saw confusion in her eyes; he watched her tongue dart out to wet her lips.

Fascination with that mouth held him even while he used his free hand to pull her around into shadow.

She had ample time to protest when he lowered his mouth toward hers. Ample time. She did not.

One kiss. One taste before I tie myself to Sarah Wharton. He clamped down on his raging desire. *One gentle salute, a farewell.*

Lily froze momentarily but didn't pull away. At his persistent urging, she opened her lips slightly and allowed him access. For a long moment, the taste of her satisfied him. When her hand crept up his neck and into his hair, however, the need for more overwhelmed him. He pulled her closer, tasted deeply, and slipped his hand to her breast.

Lily wrenched herself away at that with a groan.

"What do you think you're doing? What, dear God, do you think I am." She turned on her heels and walked toward her house.

"Lily, wait—" he said, catching up in two long strides. He grabbed her arm to turn her. She tried to shake him off. *Damn it, Lily, you seemed willing enough.*

"Wait for what? For you to bring my father home? For you to maul me again? Leave me be."

He dropped his hand.

"Go to Lady Sarah," she went on. "Make your addresses. London will fall at your feet. Just leave. Me. Alone."

He had no answer for that. No apology either. *What does this confounded woman do to send my wits begging?* For a brief moment, he considered offering for her again, but she would only throw it back in his face.

Instead, he bit back an angry retort and handed her to the door. She didn't look back when the servant let her in and closed the door behind her.

He stood on the pavement staring at the closed door. *She's right, though. Nothing good can come of this. Offer for Lady Sarah Wharton and be done with it.*

Lily stood in her darkened bedroom and pulled the curtain aside. Richard still stood outside her house watching the door as if she might emerge from it. He shook his head.

He walked across the street and moved unerringly to the dark recess of a door near the corner. A man stepped out of the shadow and leaned forward for a word.

As if satisfied, Richard strode down Gilbert toward Bedford Square.

She sat on her bed in the gloom and weighed her options.

Papa could be marooned in Copenhagen for months. He is probably making free with the libraries there. He probably assumes I manage fine on my own. He probably feels no need to hurry.

There would be no rescue by her father; Lily's luck had run out.

She was three months along. *I can't wait any longer.*

Chapter Fourteen

"We cannot divert one of our packets for one man," Lord Castlereagh sputtered.

Castlereagh had little time and no patience for what he considered minor affairs. He had been Secretary of State for Foreign Affairs since 1812. He was shrewd, ruthless, and unendingly pragmatic. Richard admired the man but didn't always agree with him.

"If we responded to every Englishman's family inconvenience, the entire Foreign Office would turn into a fraternity of errand boys. No, you may not have the Gibraltar Packet."

Castlereagh is right, of course. He usually is.

"Who did you dispatch to Thessaloniki?" The foreign secretary demanded.

"Archer. We've had no reports."

Castlereagh grunted, cocked his head to the right, and tapped his thigh with one hand impatiently. "We need information, damn it!"

Richard didn't bother defending what they both knew to be a simple fact of their life. Dispatches took time.

"Information. Our stock in trade," Castlereagh growled. "Someday we'll find ways to get more of it faster. For now, fast horses, fast men, fast ships."

Richard didn't interrupt the old man.

"What I need from you, Glenaire, is your analysis of the risks posed by revolt in Naples to our colony on Malta. I read Maitland's report, but I need you to factor in dispatches from the ground throughout the area, particularly about potential piracy activity. Have you gotten the reports I requested from returning naval captains?"

"Some," Richard replied. "I should have the rest in a few days."

Castlereagh pointed a finger at him. "Any information Thornton could have given us from Russia will have gone cold. He can make his way home as best he can."

Lily will have to endure the delay. Her precious Papa is safe enough in Copenhagen.

"Yes, my lord," Richard said. "I'll take my leave."

It had been over three months since he promised her he could retrieve her father. Heaton said she had begun to openly complain about the delay. She would have to endure it.

I will not put my career on the line for Miss Lily Thornton, he thought grimly. England needed stability in Greece, quiet in Naples, troops in Canada, trade in India. Apparently, it did not need John Thornton home in a hurry.

He wrote a quick note to his business agent. The man had decent taste; he would know what sort of ring would impress the lady. Richard could absorb the cost, whatever it was.

Having managed that piece of business to his satisfaction, Richard wrote a brief analysis of troop morale in Canada.

He finally returned to his notes about the Mediterranean waters. Castlereagh's fears lay on vague, but likely true, concerns. Richard reviewed his notes about the Barbary pirates. Since the Americans' efforts and Decatur's victory at Cape Gata, the seas had been safer. Safer but not secure. Chaos in Naples may encourage the damned pirates again. Damage to shipping hurt the economy, and the threat of ransom weighed on the foreign secretary. Richard's jaw clenched at the thought of their last discussion about it.

"We can't pay blood money," Castlereagh had insisted. "It only encourages the trade." He planned to notify their embassies and outposts accordingly. Richard's retort that the poor souls sold into slavery might view it differently fell on deaf ears. The old man must know slave auctions are as lucrative as ransom. Letting English souls fall into Barbary slavery is unconscionable. He wondered if he could find sufficient argument buried in this heap of notes.

He was still at his desk when word came from Heaton.

Sir

Miss Lilias Thornton has given us the slip. Thought you should know soonest.

R Heaton

Castlereagh's report on Naples would have to wait.

It was ridiculously easy, Lily thought, to give those fools the slip. Desperation drove her errand; she didn't need Glenaire's spies to follow. A quick and overly blunt reference to one's bodily needs, a convenient back door, and swift feet did the work. It may not be so easy next time.

The diaphanous scarf she had stuffed into her reticule covered her hair and face sufficiently. Adjusting her walk to that of an old woman helped also.

The servant at the door, very tall, very dark, and unsmiling had gestured her to a seat in the outer hall. He wore English-style clothing. The white of his shirt contrasted with his dark skin. He took her card and returned moments later with pursed lips and a disapproving frown to escort her to a man whose frown looked even less approving.

"So little one," Sahin Pasha said, "You have come on an errand even more foolish than your last."

"No one saw me come here."

"Your Marquess of Glenaire implies he sees all."

Lily smiled at that. "He likes to believe that. His minions should pay closer attention. I slipped away from them easily. No one saw me."

"We shall hope that is true," Sahin said. "What then brings you to take this risk?"

Lily looked around. Two men stood by the door. One was the man from the entrance.

"You may speak freely, little one. One man," he gestured to a fierce little man to the left, "neither speaks nor hears. He merely guards. The other," he shrugged, "is a eunuch. Protector of women, you understand?" He indicated her escort.

Lily understood. Her reputation could be protected, at least in Ottoman terms.

So proper. How will he react to what I have to say? She dug deep for courage. Sahin Pasha's words at the Pembrook ball came back to her—*I am in your debt, I fear. If you ever have need of my help, you know you can come to me.*

Lily managed to speak by breathing deeply. "You will recall that you are in my debt, favored uncle. I need to collect."

She had his attention. The old man nodded and waited for her to go on.

"My father has been delayed," she said.

"We know this, little one."

Just say it, Lily!

"What is it I can do for you?" Sahin persisted.

"I need employment," she responded.

He didn't try to hide his astonishment.

"It is not customary for young women to seek employment even in this barbaric country."

"I need to leave London, favored uncle," she said. "Soon."

"Is it the Russian again?"

"Only in part." Lily took a long shuddering breath, the kind that shook her whole body. She glanced back at the man who can't hear and the man who—*If his job is to protect women, what will he think of one who has allowed herself to get with child?*

She slid back to face Sahin.

"Remember your debt, favored uncle, when I tell you this," she said. Sahin made a gesture with his hand as if to brush it aside.

"I am with child," she said, softly but distinctly.

Sahin sat back, grim faced. "This is a terrible thing, little one. Especially since your father is not here to protect your honor."

Lily struggled to swallow her fear, to control her expression.

"Who is this dog who did this to you?" Sahin demanded.

Heavens! What would he do? A knife in the ribs?

"I will give him a choice, little one," he said gently, as if he read her mind.

"Choice, honored uncle?" Lily asked, momentarily confused.

"He can agree to a respectable marriage with no harm to your name, in which case he will keep his head, or—" He shrugged. He didn't need to spell out the alternative he had in mind.

"Please no. Oh God, no. I do not wish to marry him, uncle."

"Foolish. Without marriage you have no protection."

"Marriage to that man would condemn me to misery."

"You are a defiant one, little one. You should do your duty to the man and this child."

Lily raised her chin and shook her head. "No marriage," she said.

Sahin Pasha looked thoughtful. "Is it possible I own some responsibility for this catastrophe?" he asked shrewdly.

Lily dropped her eyes. The old man is too perceptive. She focused on her toes where they peaked out from her gown and bit her lip. She would not help him puzzle out what happened.

Sahin waited a long time, but she didn't budge. At long last he sighed. "How is it you think I can help with this 'employment'?"

I have no idea. Despair washed over her. Idiot. Women have even less freedom in his country than here. What were you thinking, Lily?

She tried frantically to recreate the notions that drove her here.

"I thought," she began, spelling out the only strategy that had presented itself in long days of searching for alternatives, "you might suggest a place where I can teach. I will call myself a widow, have my child, and earn my keep."

"And then?"

"In a few years, with my father's help, I can return to England, a widow with a young child. It would work if—"

"—if you had 'employment,' a refuge, among people easily fooled."

"No! I don't mean to fool anyone, I just—I have told you the truth, favored uncle."

The old man nodded. "Yes. Truth is good."

Neither swish of fabric nor footstep warned Lily. The tall, dark man behind her moved to Sahin's side. He made obeisance and spoke in rapid Turkish. Sahin appeared to object. Lily strained to hear. She understood the language. Sahin's visits to her father helped pass long winter nights in Saint Petersburg, and it entertained him to teach her. The men's soft whispers, however, made it difficult to sort the words. The tall man's responses sounded respectful but emphatic. He glanced at Lily, spoke a few more words, and returned to his place.

"My debt weighs in your favor," Sahin said. "Ahmet reminds me that I must help you find a solution. He has suggested a way."

Lily's hopes soared. She felt her heart beat in her throat. She glanced up at the one called Ahmet and quickly back to Sahin.

"My aunt is Valide Sultan. Do you know what that is?"

"The Sultan's mother, I believe."

"Usually, although not currently. She is a woman of great influence and power, the head of the sultan's household. She administers the entire household, the Seraglio, hundreds of people. You understand?"

"What has this to do with my problem?"

"My aunt devotes herself to good works, most particularly education. The Sultan, or in reality the Valide Sultan, requires that every man and woman in the household be literate."

Lily sat up, attentive. "Hundreds of people? The household? You called it the Seraglio?"

"The Seraglio, yes, a complex that requires considerable administrative skill. It is vital, you understand, that no scandal upset the smooth running of the household."

Lily nodded.

"I will take you to my aunt. You will tell her everything. What happens after that is up to the Valide Sultan."

"Time, favored uncle. I don't have time to wait."

A slow smile spread across Sahin Pasha's face, reached his eyes, and warmed. "God is with you, little one. We have packed up our delegation. We leave in two days."

"Two days?" she gasped.

"If you wish our help, you must take it now. If you choose not to, I will consider our debt filled."

"Very well, favored uncle. I will come with you in two days."

"Your father?"

"I'll leave word for him and pray he reaches London to get it."

"He may follow you, as is his right. I won't hide you."

"I wouldn't want you to."

"And your marquess? Will he pursue you?" The shrewd old man held her eyes.

"He is unlikely to expend effort for a troublesome woman." *And he isn't my marquess.* "Besides, I believe he is about to become betrothed."

"I see," Sahin said sadly. "I regret—but no matter. It is good he will not pursue."

Stepping out the back of Sahin's London townhouse, swathed in her scarf, Lily hoped he was correct. A dark-skinned servant slipped silently out behind her. She wanted to protest but knew it to be futile. Sahin, in his way, could be as stubborn about her need for protection as the marquess.

As to his lordship, a niggling doubt about his willingness to pursue her would not stop teasing at her mind. Glenaire might not care about her personally, but he did hate to have his will thwarted. She pitied Roger Heaton.

Chapter Fifteen

"Any half-pay corporal, any semi-intelligent boot boy could have stayed with one small woman. A sickly schoolgirl might have done a better job. A—" The list of those who performed better than Heaton had gone on for some time, and still Richard's anger boiled over.

Why can't the damned woman do what she's told? That Thornton woman has cut up my peace since—

"Find her, Heaton. Find her before the sun goes down."

"Yes, sir, we have men—"

"Yes, yes, you have squads of our men looking. Not good enough! Don't try, man. Succeed. Find her!"

Heaton left too beaten down to register relief.

Where the hell are you, Lily? That snake Volkov is loose and— What if she went to meet him? To beg for her father?

Richard felt ill. He did not like the feeling. He grit his teeth and sat down. The naval reports on the waters around Naples and Sicily lay on his desk.

I have too much work to worry about one foolish woman determined to put herself at risk.

He sorted the papers into stacks: one for naval reports; one for dispatches from his agents on the Italian peninsula in Malta and on Sicily; one for those actually inside the Kingdom of Naples. Yet another, dark with age, came from the ambassador in Washington. It quoted verbatim Stephen Decatur's reports on his destruction of the

Barbary fleet off Algiers and the concessions he wrenched from Algiers and Tunis.

Lily would find this interesting, he thought. He dropped his head back and stared at the ceiling. *Lily Thornton, with her fine mind, ought to know better than anyone how dangerous Volkov could be. Why can't she think sensibly?*

He reread Viscount Exmouth's report on the bombardment of Algiers and the concessions England extracted in 1816. He pulled the current analysis from Maitland, England's governor general on Malta, to the front and read it through. The man sent one brief page to tell the Foreign Office no danger existed, patent nonsense. The corsairs scaled back their raids but never ended them entirely. Richard flipped it over twice as if he could find better intelligence. The words swam together, and Lily's face, pale and frightened as he saw it the night he found her with Volkov, came into focus.

She knows, and takes risks anyway. What is driving the fool woman?

He pushed Maitland's assertions aside and began to read dispatches from Naples, listing each known fact on one list and speculation on another. It would take him hours to go through the mountain of reports in detail. Perhaps then he would have some idea what to suggest to Castlereagh.

Malta matters to England, matters greatly. Lily Thornton doesn't.

He tried to focus on the first dispatch, but his own harshness shamed him.

She doesn't matter to England, but she matters to her father. Her aunt. Her friends.

He scribbled lists for precisely eight minutes before he threw down his pen. He looked at what he'd written. Tripe! He balled up the paper and through it across the room, instantly felt childish, and picked it up to spread it open. The Marquess of Glenaire never stooped to childish acts.

He stared at the paper a moment longer, his mind on Lily Thornton. Work had become hopeless, another charge to put at Lily Thornton's door.

If those puppies can't do what I told them, I will have to do it myself.

He called for his hat and his carriage. Castlereagh's report could wait another afternoon. The woman would be taught she could not evade surveillance.

LILY almost reached the rear of Aunt Marianne's house through the mews before an arm snaked from the shadows. A hand clamped down on her shoulder, jarring her to a stop. Her heart stuttered and gave a leap of fear.

Volkov?

"What have you been doing?" a familiar voice demanded.

Relief filled Lily at the sound of Richard's voice; warmth pooled inside her at his touch. *Traitorous body.*

"None of your business." The words came instinctively to her mouth, but the stench of horses and dirt wafting from the mews undermined any force she may have given them. Her recently sensitized stomach clenched.

Traitorous body, she thought, in so many ways. The ebb and flow of fear, the strength expended to meet Sahin, the weakness of her pregnancy, and the feel of Richard's hand overwhelmed Lily's senses. Blood drained from her face, and her knees buckled.

Strong arms caught her up until she looked into the face of a very irate male, inches from hers. "Damned foolish woman," he grumbled, taking her back stairs with ease.

Lily's aunt employed a tiny staff. The sight of a marquess carrying their mistress's niece through the tradesmen's entrance sent them all into a frenzy. Only sharp words from the marquess himself gave order to their efforts: one to fetch her aunt, one tea, one a coverlet.

He laid Lily down on the settee nearest an open window and stood with his hands behind his back.

"You needn't glower so," Lily said. "And you did not need to frighten our staff. I could have walked." She tried to sit up; he pushed her down.

"You are pale."

"You gave me a fright. What did you expect?"

"Lilias Thornton is not a weak-willed ninny who goes faint."

"You, sir, are not the expert on what Lilias Thornton does or doesn't do." She sat up. When he put out a hand to stop her, she held one of hers up in front of her and dared him to try. He pulled back.

"Why were you lurking in the mews behind our house?"

"Waiting for you. I suspected you would sneak in."

"Your man could have confirmed it. I waved to him at the corner of the street," she said. She stared, chin high, and refused to apologize.

"I told you not to go out without escort," he said.

"Even the Marble Marquess does not always get what he wants."

Marianne Thornton fluttered into the room to stand wringing her hands at Lily and bobbing a crooked curtsey at Richard.

"Your niece felt faint," he said. "She is much improved." He gestured to the corner of the room. The far corner. "Could you allow us a moment?"

"Of course, of course," the woman said breathlessly. She patted Lily's hand. "I'm glad it was a false alarm, dear." She fluttered off.

Richard spun back toward Lily.

"What have you been doing?" he demanded.

"I believe you asked me that once. I told you it is none of your business."

"Whom did you meet?" he pinned her with his eyes. She didn't look away; she didn't answer.

"Volkov?"

"Good God, no," she choked. "Why would I want to be anywhere near that man?"

Richard let out a breath. He stayed where he stood but seemed to back off. "Not Volkov," he said more quietly.

"Of course not," she answered. "Do you take me for a fool?"

He does. He thinks me foolish.

"Who then?" he asked less forcefully.

"A friend." She looked directly at him until he looked down.

"Someone safe?" he asked.

"I said friend, so yes, safe."

"You should have taken Roger Heaton."

"I grow tired of your watchdogs, Richard, those eager puppies. We've exhausted the weather, the gossip, and fashions, every damned polite topic I can dredge up. I tried foreign affairs. Stewart is coming along, but Heaton—for a would-be diplomat, he has no sense of reality. He is simply not devious enough." *Unlike you. Or I.*

He unbent at that and pulled a chair closer to her. "He is able enough to do what I ask him, and what I asked him to do is keep you safe."

"I am safe as you can see."

"Volkov is a threat to you. Until he does something overt, we can't arrest him or expel him."

"Do you know where he is?"

He nodded.

"In England?"

Another nod.

If I can elude you, he can too.

"Until my father returns safely to England, you dare not expel him. Bring my father home, Richard."

He opened his mouth to reply, but she held up a hand. "Shortage of trees for masts. No ships available. The man hates overland travel. I know. What news of Thessaloniki?"

"Little. Rumblings of unrest, but no specifics. No sudden beheadings in the Pasha's court, at least word of none has reached us."

Shivers ran down her arm when he picked up her hand and held it in his.

"There is no change and no reason to believe you are any safer from Volkov. Take Heaton or Stewart when you go out." It wasn't a request, but softness crept into his voice and Lily couldn't resent the implied command. She couldn't tell the truth either.

"I will take one of my champions whenever I go about London," she agreed submissively. She didn't mention Falmouth, the sea, or Constantinople, about which she made no such promises.

He looked at her as if trying to sort through her words for some escape clause. "There's more you aren't telling me," he said at last. "I can't fix anything without information."

She kept her silence. His eyes had softened; their intensity touched her deeply.

"My life isn't yours to fix, my lord," she said at last over the lump in her throat.

"'My lord' is it? Very well, 'Miss Thornton.' I will continue to see to your welfare whether you wish it or not." He leaned a bit closer, eyes moving toward her mouth. "I worry for you, Lily," he whispered. "Don't frighten me again."

Lily's mouth fell open. She thought for a moment he meant to kiss her. She thought for a moment she wanted him to. She pulled herself upright and looked away.

"I apologize for causing distress," she said. "That was not my intent. I'm used to seeing to my own welfare. Your concern, while sweet, is not necessary."

He snapped upright. "My concern is damned well not 'sweet,' madam. My concern is for England's welfare, and you find yourself embroiled with dangerous forces."

"Life has risks," she said, desperate to change the subject. "I will risk a walk to Chadbourn house tomorrow night."

"Too far. Ride. Take Heaton," he retorted.

"Will you attend?" she asked.

"I'm engaged to attend the theatre," he responded.

"With Lady Sarah Wharton." It wasn't a question.

"Who I choose to escort isn't your concern."

"You will suit each other," she said. She meant it.

He bristled at that, but said, "I believe so. She is of good family."

Lily nodded. "Lands, polish, and breeding that is well beyond adequate—all that is needed in a marchioness," she said, throwing his assessment of her breeding back at him.

The marquess looked momentarily puzzled as if he couldn't be sure whether or not she had insulted him. Lady Sarah could have him. Lily had her own life to live.

"I wish you well, my lord," she said.

"And I wish you safe," he responded, rising to leave. "Stay with Heaton when you are out."

"I already promised, didn't I?" She couldn't meet his eyes. "Roger Heaton may escort me about the city."

But no farther.

Chapter Sixteen

The maneuvers—small but effective—that Lady Sarah carried out in order to time her entrance to his parents' box at the Royal Theater, Covent Garden, exasperated Richard. They arrived late but still early enough to be seen by all.

Generals launch campaigns with less planning.

Her erect posture, serene countenance, and gown, carefully chosen to reflect light from the newly installed oil lamps, showed to perfection in the flickering lights of the theater. Tiny diamonds discreetly nested in her suitably demure pearl necklace glowed in that light just as she must have known they would.

Every eye in the pit followed her graceful descent into the Duke of Sudbury's box on Richard's arm.

She sees me as nothing more than an ornament to perfect the image she wishes to project—Lady Sarah Wharton on the arm of a duke's heir. Any heir would do. Richard winced. He thought he ought to give the girl more credit, but the thought persisted. She can't help it. She's caught up in my mother's schemes.

Avid glances from the other boxes took in the powerful and highly titled companions around them: the Duke and Duchess of Sudbury, the Duke and Duchess of Lisle, and Castlereagh—the Marquess of Londonderry, foreign secretary, Richard's superior, and one of the most powerful men in Europe.

Tactical error, Richard. Not one but two dukes—both parents and the foreign secretary? May as well send notice to the papers.

He attempted to ignore prying eyes. Taking notice of the masses, he had been taught, gave one an air of vulgarity. He handed his companion to a seat next to Lord Castlereagh and sat on her other side.

At least Her Grace is content to take a back seat for once.

His mother held court behind him, dripping with the Sudbury sapphires. She appeared content to let her protégé bask in the light while she entertained the girl's ducal parents.

The dismal mood that had troubled him for weeks descended again, threatening to crush him. He must marry; he owed it to his name and lineage. Lady Sarah met every criterion he sought in a future duchess: breeding, manners, looks, money... She came close to perfection. He simply couldn't bring himself to like the match. Irrelevant, he tried to tell himself, duty doesn't require pleasure.

Still he couldn't warm to the idea, and nothing in the mediocre performance distracted him. Once he caught Castlereagh casting an assessing glance at the lady. While Richard didn't require the foreign secretary's approval to marry, that approval would smooth his career. From the man's face, it appeared there would be no objection.

The performers droned on, and Lady Sarah made every pretense of watching the play. Unless someone watched as carefully as Richard did, they missed her covert glances at other boxes. With the slightest tightening of lip or elevation of brow, her face reflected approval here, clear disapproval there, and the occasional outright condemnation somewhere else. Drama would never hold this woman's attention; society with its castes and intrigues always would.

What, he wondered, *will we ever find to discuss over breakfast? Not the theatre.*

He saw with sudden clarity that it didn't matter. They would rarely share breakfast. She would break her fast in her boudoir and be above stairs until time for afternoon calls. He would rise at seven as always, take a vigorous walk or ride, dress, and be at his desk before the clerks.

Marriage to Lady Sarah would not disrupt his ordered life. That ought to be enough. He suppressed the niggling thought that it might not be.

Applause cut in to his morose musings. He rose, grateful for an excuse to get away.

"Shall we stroll along the promenade?"

She glanced once around to make sure eyes followed her every move and once back to his mother, who nodded her approval with regal dignity. "I would be delighted to, my lord," she said.

The upper hall behind the box seats quickly filled with people equally eager to stretch their legs and just as avid to be seen. Richard's companion strolled with grace and dignity, occasionally nodding a greeting.

She's damned careful whom she acknowledges and whom she does not!

Poor Martha Rutledge, whose older brother teetered on the brink of Newgate for debts, got the cut direct. Richard nodded gravely at the woman behind his companion's back.

He noted the greetings Lady Sarah reserved for the sons and daughters of the higher peers. Lesser nobility got cold nods.

Baroness Widener merited barely a nod. What will she make of my friend Jamie, a mere Baron Ross. It feels, he thought, rather like walking with my mother, an activity I rarely like. He had experience ignoring his mother. *Can I ignore a wife as well?*

They were almost back to the box when the unexpected sight of his sister Georgiana and her husband gave him a spurt of joy that made his face wrinkle into a smile, the first unforced one of the evening.

"Richard! We noticed you making use of the familial box," Georgiana exclaimed.

"My lady." Her husband bowed correctly to Lady Sarah.

Richard felt her go stiff at his side. She did not return the greeting.

"At least one of you remembers manners," Richard told his sister with a nod at her husband.

"What do you think of Miss Boothe's Cymbeline?" Georgiana asked. She, at least, actually watched the play. Her enthusiasm amused him.

Andrew laughed. "Don't answer her, Richard. The Bard has had enough insult for one night." Richard noticed his friend's surreptitious glance at Lady Sarah standing stiff and silent.

"She is rather awful, isn't she?" Richard agreed. "I expected you two to be at dinner with Chadbourn and his countess."

"Professor Brauner gave us his seats," Georgiana told him.

"No fool, he," Andrew said. "Must have known it would be bad."

His wife poked his ribs. "Tickets are a rare treat for us," Georgiana went on. "Catherine urged us to attend Cymbeline and come late."

"We're going there now. We've had all the theatrical histrionics we can take," her husband added.

"Don't let me keep you from it," Richard told them. His companion remained mute; her hand bit into his arm.

"My lady," Andrew bowed his exit and offered his arm to his wife. The look they shared when they walked away gave Richard a pang.

When did lovers' looks begin to strike you as anything but maudlin. Haydens despise middle class notions of romance, remember? Get a grip, man.

"Your mother does not receive them." His companion hissed beside him.

"I, however, do," Richard retorted, turning to face her. "I'm fond of my sister and her husband."

Lady Sarah pursed her lips and forced a smile. "But he is a schoolmaster's son, you must see that," she explained. Having made her point, she nodded with satisfaction. "We really must get back to their graces. Lord Castlereagh will wonder what has become of us."

She speaks as if she thinks I am a particularly dim schoolboy. I won't tolerate it when we marry. He offered his arm without attempting to argue. *If we marry*, he added silently.

He led her back, wishing to ignore the conversation. Lady Sarah had other ideas. She leaned close in a pretense of intimacy and whispered, "Richard, surely you must see. She is" she stumbled over the word—"*enceinte.* A decent woman would be in the country if she found herself in an interesting condition." She blushed scarlet.

Richard had to admit his sister looked rather obviously with child, and he wished Georgiana showed a bit more discretion in that regard, but he viewed it with resigned good humor.

In the brief privacy afforded by the entrance to their box, his companion had one last salvo before he could speak. "Your mother will not like that you allowed a person in that condition to address me. I certainly don't. Kindly consider this for the future. I cannot like it."

If you are my wife, you will entertain my sister and her husband, and you will like it.

Lady Sarah stepped into the box, saving him the need to respond.

Thank God.

In the vast expanse of the Royal Theater, Richard felt the walls closing in, snapping shut like a trap door. He thought again of the look the Mallets had given each other. They left to join Chadbourn and his countess, two other besotted fools. He longed to go with them.

He thought again of Lily. *She won't have you, you fool.*

No other candidate for Marchioness of Glenaire struck him as any better than Lady Sarah. Do I have a choice?

No one ignored a summons from a duke, not even the Marquess of Glenaire. Richard certainly didn't ignore a summons from an influential member of the foreign affairs committee.

He cooled his heels at White's though he'd rather have been working. He thought of the work piled up on his desk, and the wait sat badly with him. The polished wood, the well-worn leather, the smell of cigar closed in on him where he stood in the foyer like a boy awaiting the headmaster.

The old despot only makes me wait to put me in my place. The only other man in England who would dare treat Richard that way, his father, sat in aristocratic splendor at Sudbury House. They both pretend to rule the universe while abler men keep Europe stable and at peace.

Unfortunately, the Duke of Lisle was also Lady Sarah Wharton's father. He strongly suspected the duke didn't plan to address affairs of state.

The faintest rustle of activity among the club servants announced the arrival of an elevated member as clearly as if they had shouted it. Richard rose before the old man even walked across the room.

"Your Grace," he bowed correctly. "You wished to see me?"

The duke waved a hand with two fingers extended in casual salute toward a hovering servant and sank awkwardly into a broad leather chair; one Richard suspected no other member dared use. The servant hurried off. He needed no more information to fetch the duke's preferred brandy and sweet nibbles.

The old man pulled his gouty foot to a footstool and settled his girth comfortably before gesturing Richard to sit.

Heat burned in Richard's chest and died in his iron control. *Don't let the man flummox you.*

Brandies arrived. Servants left. The duke sipped slowly in silence. Richard controlled his racing mind by calculating the number of reports on his desk, mentally dividing them into different numbered stacks and assigning a level of importance to each. He could wait as well as the duke and longer.

"You probably wondered why I asked you to meet me," the duke said, words rumbling out like gravel down a rough chute.

Asked? I know a summons when I read one.

"I assumed you wish to know more about instability in Naples," Richard answered smoothly.

"Naples? Unstable? Nonsense. We defeated the damned Corsican."

You would know better if you bothered to read the briefings we send to the House of Lords. Richard clamped his lips tight rather than respond to what he knew to be ignorance.

Lisle pointed an impatient finger at Richard. "I asked you here about my daughter."

"Lady Sarah is well, I trust. Last night—"

"Last night I expected you in my study. The girl and her mother did, too," the old man sputtered, spittle dropping to his cravat. "Hell," he went on, "half of London did."

"I was unaware we had an appointment of some kind."

"Damned well should have. You've been paying court the entire Season. Parliament closes for the summer soon. City is emptying. The girl is in fits and has started wondering when you're going to declare yourself."

"If I've given her reason to expect—" Richard began. *Given her reason to expect? You let your mother crown her duchess-in-waiting; you let her dragoon you into escorting the chit everywhere; you fell into that piece of theater in the box last night.*

"Do you mean to say you paraded her in front of the ton—in front of Castlereagh—on your arm last night and you didn't think it gave her expectations?"

"I have an interest, certainly." Richard chose his words carefully. "I considered asking to speak to you, but the hour was late." And I wanted to get to Chadbourn's before his dinner guests departed.

"So you are going to ask for the chit or not?"

Words stuck in his throat. He thought of the extraordinarily expensive betrothal ring sitting in a vault at his bank. He thought of the smug look—no question she looked smug—on Lady Sarah's face when they promenaded past other debutants. He thought of his parent's expectations about their due. He thought of duty. He thought of England.

Richard opened his mouth to ask Lady Sarah Wharton's father

for her perfect, well-bred, wealthy hand in marriage. The words would not come out.

"Speak up, man! You've all but driven away her other suitors."

"Lady Sarah is exquisite. Any man in London would be honored to have her."

"We don't want any man. We want a duke's heir. There was an earl on the hook, but m'wife tells me he is much too old. Viscount Osborn has made tentative overtures. He's well-to-pass and heir to an earldom. He might do. Would come up to scratch right enough."

He makes her sound like a statue at auction. It struck him she seemed cold enough, and chided himself for it. *Not fair, Richard. She possesses both beauty and manners. She would not only ornament your table but also serve adequately as an ambitious diplomat's wife. You saw that at Chadbourn Park; you planned to pursue the connection then.*

Thoughts of Chadbourn Park brought the feel of Lily Thornton's body pressed against his, unbidden, to his mind; the feel of her mouth burned his memory.

Lily Thornton is no statue.

The duke waved for another brandy. It appeared by his elbow in moments. Richard looked down at his own drink, almost untouched. He downed it in a single gulp.

That damned Thornton woman would never make an appropriate marchioness, much less a future duchess. Do your duty, man, and get it over with.

She had been gone by the time he got to Chadbourn's. It had been foolish to seek her out, and he admitted to himself he had gone there hoping to do just that.

She made it clear she doesn't want you. What are you waiting for?

"May I call on you next week?" he asked at last.

"Another damned week? You aren't exactly impassioned."

"I thought you sought a well-titled connection, not a damned besotted lover," Richard spat.

The old man chuckled. "Just so," he said. "Just so. You can have a week, Glenaire. No longer or Osborn will have stolen the match on you."

I doubt it. Your Sarah won't settle for an earl's heir if she can have a duke's. He made his leave, determined to sort his disordered thoughts.

One week. Perhaps if I lay out the advantages and disadvantages on paper, my decision will become clearer. His steps slowed as he passed through Saint James Park on his way to Horse Guards. *Perhaps in a week I will have dealt with Lily Thornton once and for all.*

He approached the end of the park and stopped, so lost in thought he dropped onto one of the benches lining the walk.

Lily. I owe her protection. I promised it. I promised her father home safe. The image in his mind shifted from Lily, frightened yet determined, with Volkov, to Lily, soft and warm from loving, in the dim shade of a sheep barn. Sheep barn! He smiled at that. *What I owe her is marriage. Why won't the damned woman see that?*

Chapter Seventeen

Subterfuge can exhaust a woman. Aunt Marianne didn't raise an eyebrow when Lily told her that the trunk she had packed the morning after her meeting with Sahin Pasha would be shipped to the country for storage. Their ancient butler looked merely puzzled when she handed the same trunk to a coal merchant at the tradesmen's entrance. He most likely attributed the man's dark skin to his business. Her maid, however, questioned the need to keep a carpetbag filled with necessities for overnight.

"Mrs. Mallet's time is uncertain. I want to be prepared to accompany her should it begin," Lily told the girl. She wished that were the truth. The girl didn't question; she didn't look convinced either.

If Richard's men question the servants, this one will give him an earful. With luck she would be gone by then and out of reach.

"When does Mr. Stewart arrive, ma'am?" the girl asked. "Shall I do up your hair?"

Walter Stewart. Damn. That one is a tad sharper than Heaton. She had forgotten the schedule. Nothing for it but to endure the afternoon call, plead headache, and slip out with Sahin's pseudo-tradesman at dusk.

"No, I think not. A simple knot will do." The maid frowned over Lily's choice of unbecoming gray, but she let the girl dress her before she dismissed her. There would be time enough tomorrow to learn to do for herself.

Lily sat at her vanity and pulled her hair back, whipping it into a casual knot. She loosened it for effect. Best look the part. A little powder enhanced her pallor. She made a pained look into the mirror. Loss of weight, underlying pallor, and the powder made her look genuinely ill. It will do.

Deep clouds blanketed London that afternoon when Lily stood at the window looking out at Gilbert Street. All nature conspires to match my mood, she thought. And Stewart is late.

She looked around for something to occupy her wait, picked up Aunt Marianne's needlework, and tossed it aside. The dear, sweet woman had taken to her bed with "the vapors," to Lily's relief. Deceiving her aunt depressed her most. *She deserves better, but what she does not know, she cannot tell.*

The papers, ironed and correctly presented, lay on a table by Lily's favorite chair. Most households for women did not receive newspapers. Lily insisted on it. She sat and began to read, quickly scanning the little international news that made it into London's rags. An item in the gossip columns caught her eye.

Lady SW attended the performance of Cymbeline last night on the arm of Lord RH the M of G. Their box included LC and two dukes. Can the long anticipated announcement be forthcoming this morning?

Has Richard offered at last? The Marble Marquess and the Ice Queen. Perfect. She tossed the paper aside and leaned her head back. Will this day never end?

Footsteps in the foyer broke into her thoughts. Stewart at last. She sat a little straighter, thought better of it, and relaxed her posture. She pondered how best to put a wan expression on her face when a voice broke it.

"You look ill." Not Walter Stewart. Blue eyes bore into her. Richard. Damn.

"I am not 'at home' today." Servants, she saw, had left the door open.

"Yet here you are. I left orders my men were to be admitted at all times."

"I left orders to admit only Walter Stewart today."

"Yet here I am." He stood in front of her, hands behind his back, glowering down.

"I have a headache," she told him. "I planned to tell Walter I would stay in today." She forced herself to keep her eyes on his, willing him to leave.

The moment dragged on, something hot and crackling in the air between them, until he looked away, turning to face the window.

"I came to discuss something."

Lily did sit straight up then. "My father?"

"No, no." He looked back. "I didn't mean to frighten you."

"What then?"

He paced to the window, leaned on the sill, and looked back at her. "You look ill."

"I told you, I don't feel well. Why are you here? Not that certainly." *Get on with it and be gone.*

Richard paced back in front of her, turned and began to fidget with a Dresden shepherdess on Aunt Marianne's mantle. *The Marquess of Glenaire does not fidget. I can't fathom what he means to say.*

"Am I to wish you happy?" she asked, glancing at the discarded papers.

He shot her a pained look. "No. Not yet, but that is part of why I'm here." He walked closer and stretched his hands toward Lily where she sat. "What happened during our stay at Chadbourn Park—"

Lily squeezed her eyes shut. *Not that. Please not that again.*

"—compels me to remind you what lies between us."

"Nothing lies between us."

"So you say. Nevertheless I am obliged to offer you marriage. That is the least that I owe you after what I took."

"My lord, you took nothing I did not give freely. You owe me nothing. We settled that at the time. You offered marriage." *You demanded.* "I refused."

"But you are my responsibility."

Dear God, he wants to take me on as a burden to be borne as he carries England on his back.

Richard began to pace and point out the advantages to Lily: money, position, title. He outlined marriage settlements.

"We will, of course, live in London primarily. My work demands it. If you prefer the country—you don't by chance prefer the country do you?" he swung around to ask.

She gaped back at him, unable to answer.

"Marry me, Lily."

Tell me that you love me. Tell me you want a partner. Tell me you want me to join my life to yours. He did not.

"No, I—Richard this is nonsense. I will not marry you."

"Why not?"

Why not? What kind of suitor, once rejected, asks why not?

"Your family will not approve, for one thing."

"Of course not. Your family background, while adequate, will not add to my consequence, and your fortune, to be kind, is modest. What they want is of no consequence."

Your dragon of a mother is of very great consequence indeed. She would make us miserable.

He rushed forward, not waiting for a response, and took both her hands. "What happened between us demands—"

"Nothing. It demands nothing. I have not suffered for it. I am not shunned. I am not with child." She almost choked on the lie. She pulled her hands away. One went instinctively to her belly where his child even now grew, where she felt it move the day before.

He offers safety and comfort, Lily. Doesn't your baby deserve that? Marry him. Accept his offer.

Safety and comfort called out to her, but when she closed her eyes to wrap that sense around her, a vision of long years, she and a child trapped in a loveless marriage, relegated to the far corners of his life, took its place. Immense loneliness pushed all other feelings away.

When she hesitated with her answer, Richard resumed his pacing, his scowl deepening.

In that universe I would be on my own, more lonely in that marriage than I am now. If I must be alone, I can bear it better on my own than I could manage inside such a marriage.

"My answer doesn't change. I will not marry you," she said at last. What he offered would not do. It would never do.

"Nevertheless, I am not free to look elsewhere with that between us," he insisted.

She did choke then. "Are you asking my permission to offer for Lady Sarah?"

He stopped in his tracks, snapped upright. "No. Of course not."

"Ask for her. Everyone expects it. I wish you well of each other. We are finished." She hoped the steel in her voice and in the look she gave him would move him.

Eventually it did.

"Very well, Miss Thornton, I will not trouble you again. Be aware this is the last time I will offer you the protection of my name." He waited, expectant.

"Keep it," she answered, "Offer it elsewhere."

He made his bow in silence, grim faced.

Lily began to shake when the door closed. Weeping seized her, and she doubled over. She wept until it threatened to make her sick; only fear for her baby gave her control.

Papa, forgive me, but I just turned down a duke's heir. I must leave with Sahin Pasha, she sobbed. Pray God I get away unseen.

The Malta report failed to distract Richard; it also failed to engage his attention. He stayed at his desk late into the night after visiting Lily, picked it up repeatedly the day after, and still it lay in pieces around his office one more day after that.

This is not how I work, he thought, pushing the report back one more time. Women make me crazy. The sooner I offer for Sarah Wharton and get my life back to normal, the better.

He picked up a group of forms and requests requiring signatures, signed eight, and sent five more back to underlings with sharply worded notes. The clock chimed half past eleven in the morning.

The day gaped in front of him. For an odd moment, his entire life gaped in front of him. *Damn,* he thought, tossing aside his pen. *When did you become melancholy? Will would laugh at you for this.*

The earl could lighten anyone's mood, but Richard remembered he planned to leave for the country the next day. I need to see him one more time before he escapes to his turnips and his children. The walk may do me good.

It didn't. He arrived at Chadbourn House in a worse mood than he left Horse Guards.

"What has you so blue-deviled?" his friend asked over a heartier meal than Richard would have gotten at Sudbury House. They ate informally in the family's sunny breakfast parlor.

"I am not blue-deviled. Not all of us are blessed with a frivolous nature," Richard said, even though a black mood lay behind his visit.

"So you say."

"I've decided to offer for Lady Sarah."

Will grunted. "You don't look happy about it. Trap is yawning?"

"No man goes to it willingly."

"Some of us do." The earl smiled beatifically. "It depends what bliss awaits." He raised his eyes up, but whether to heaven or his bedroom, Richard couldn't say. When he looked back at Richard, he sobered.

"What of Lily Thornton?" he asked softly.

"The Thornton woman is not my problem! 'We are finished,' she said. I'll be damned if I act like a mooncalf over that woman. Lady Sarah is. I have three days until Lisle's deadline."

Will's eyebrows shot up. "You make it sound like an execution! Don't do it."

"I need to get it over with," Richard told him, "before this marriage business interferes with my work any further."

"Nothing interferes with your work."

Richard ignored that salvo. Perhaps coming here wasn't a helpful idea.

"What's new with you?" he asked.

"Very little. Catherine is anxious to get home; she's too busy packing to join us. Children are more easily managed and certainly better enjoyed in the country. Have you seen Jamie lately?"

"Not for two weeks. Why? What is our newly elevated baron up to?"

"I don't know, That's why I asked. He's been even more blue-deviled than you for over a week, something deep and not at all like him. He turned down a dinner invitation. He never turns down a free meal. I went over to his rooms yesterday to see about him."

"And?"

"Gone. Scampered without paying his tab. No one could tell me where."

Richard reached inside a pouch cunningly sewn into his waistcoat and pulled out a tiny fold of paper with notes in his most crabbed handwriting. He scribbled another note. "I'll look into it," he said.

"I hoped you would. Finding people, including lost majors and barons, is a bit of a specialty for you." He raised a teacup in salute.

"My agents found you well enough that time in the Peninsula."

"They got Andrew out of that hell of a French prison, too. You never told me how you managed that one," Will said, looking at him under lowered lashes.

"I never will, either." The two men grinned at each other in the pleasure of a long-shared friendship.

The conversation turned to the earl's impending trip, to crops and livestock, Will's dearest endeavors. Richard let it, content to lay his own baggage down for a bit.

"Pardon me, my lords," a liveried footman broke in. "There is a gentleman here to see the Marquess of Glenaire."

"Show him in," the earl said.

Walter Stewart bustled in moments later.

"Thank goodness I found you, my lord," he said without preamble. "She's gone again." He didn't need to elaborate on "she."

"Where?" Richard threw down his napkin.

"That's just it. We don't know. Don't know when either."

"Tell me," Richard demanded through clenched teeth. Damned foolish woman.

"When I saw her two days ago, she pled headache and declined to go out. Heaton went yesterday, and they told him the lady was 'indisposed.' He didn't push it, thinking to allow the lady her privacy."

Richard suppressed a groan. Heaton's stunning lack of guile infuriated him. "And?"

"I got the same story this afternoon, but I didn't like the sound. Turned out the blasted aunt hadn't spoke to her in two days. She returned a tray night before last and told them not to bring more until she specifically requested it. The story didn't sound right. I made the old woman go up and check."

Richard knew what came next, but he asked, hoping he was wrong. "Go on, go on, man."

"Room empty. Bed never slept in. Must have left that same night."

"Servants?" Richard rose to his feet.

"Yes, sir. Questioned them all. Most are a worthless collection of elderly retainers who neither see nor hear what is under their nose. Her maid had some information to offer. She said Miss Thornton had taken to keeping a carpetbag packed with overnight things. She said her mistress had been 'as nervous as a bug on a hot brick.'"

Richard called for his hat and gloves.

"And our men?" Who will find themselves looking for work alongside Roger Heaton before today is out. He held out a hand to the footman who handed him his things.

"Reported nothing. No visitors. No sign of Miss Thornton. No comings and goings except for merchant deliveries to the tradesmen's door, of course."

One of which left with Lily Thornton. He paused at the door to the breakfast parlor, another thought making bile rise in his throat.

"What's the latest on Volkov?"

"No good news there, either. I checked back before I tracked you down. He's gone."

"Gone?"

"Last seen at a tavern in Portsmouth. We had a man on him, but we've had no report in three days."

Richard cursed loudly. "Retrace Volkov's steps. Get our best agents on it." He started for the door, remembered his host, and turned to see Will watching him with concern.

"Sorry to leave so abruptly. I need to see to this myself."

"Find her, Richard."

"We'll find Volkov. If Miss Thornton foolishly declines our protection, we will let her go without it." Walter Stewart didn't try to hide his shock nor Will his disapproval. Richard ignored them both and stalked to the door.

Lily Thornton made it clear I'm not her keeper. So be it.

Chapter Eighteen

Doubt clung to Lily like the mold and damp that assailed her nose and congealed on her skin. Tepid tea did little to settle her stomach. Dockside inns were ever such. The diplomatic delegation sailed from the naval port, and Portsmouth held no exceptions.

As a diplomat's daughter, she had seen more than her fair share of such establishments in many ports of call. Before, her papa's bluff good humor always distracted her with his fantastical tales of coming sights and sounds. "An adventure, Lily, a magical time, have you but the eyes to see it!" he would say with a twinkle in his eye and dramatic gestures. Not so this time.

She took another sip of tea, grimaced, and stared at Ahmet—tall, black, and silently efficient Ahmet, dressed now in Ottoman dress. He was, after all, a eunuch, a man who could be left alone with a woman. Sahin Pasha assigned him to assist Lily along the way. Assist or guard? She couldn't be certain. Nothing felt certain.

She pushed her cup away and fidgeted with her reticule, anything to block out the reverberating question. *Am I doing the right thing?*

"The lady is restless," her companion remarked, his voice rich and rough, echoing up from deep in his huge chest.

"We've waited long."

"Tedious, yes, but necessary." The voice was rough but gentle, and his eyes, now that she looked closely, looked sympathetic. Lily merely nodded in response. A moment passed.

"Do you regret your decision? Do you question whether you have done the right thing?" he raised an eyebrow, but a gentle smile took any sting from his words.

She shook her head. "I've considered the alternatives," she said.

"All of them?"

All except marrying an arrogant marquess who would disdain my background.

Before she could answer him and put a lie to her thoughts, a messenger came.

"We leave now," Ahmet said. "If you wish to turn back—"

"I don't." She rose and sped to the door, anxious for air.

Ahmet led her down the quay toward their waiting ship. She put one foot onto the gangplank to step up. A shout rose over the general noise of the docks. Lily turned her head toward the sound.

One man pushed another and ran between buildings but not before Lily got a look at him. She glanced at Ahmet. His alert expression sent a frisson of fear through her. Did he see what she saw? For a moment, just a moment, the man who disappeared looked like Volkov.

She climbed the gangplank and stepped onto the deck. Only one thought reverberated now.

I'm doing the right thing.

~

A MESSAGE reached Glenaire's office the following afternoon.

YOU MAY CALL upon me at the fashionable hour tomorrow afternoon. The matter will not wait seven full days.

Lisle

HER EARL must be getting impatient.

His parents expected him at the ducal mansion that evening. Richard's routine included a monthly meeting to go over estate with his father, followed by dinner over which his mother harangued him about his unmarried state. His parents' expectations in this matter were locked in stone. Richard generally found it easier to simply comply. Lisle will have to wait his turn.

By the time he climbed the marble stairs of Sudbury House, he knew the words of Lisle's message by heart. His seven-day reprieve had ended. He assumed the duke and duchess already knew about it also. He didn't need his father's dictates to tighten the noose around his neck. He got them anyway.

I'll marry the chit, he thought irritably. *She'll do. His Grace can cease the lecture. Even Lily Thornton expects me to marry Lady Sarah Wharton. I damned well resent being strong-armed by two dukes and a duchess over the thing.*

"Once you've safely secured the lady's hand," His Grace droned on, "we'll pressure Lisle for those sweet acres bordering Mountview, the ones with the decent little house. It is one of his minor estates, part of his mother's dower, but free now. We'll get it written into the settlements."

The Sudbury estate doesn't need any more blasted land. Richard knew better than to voice that notion. A ducal family could never hold too much land.

"Her dowry will be substantial," the duke went on, certain his son would obey without question. "You must set up in something more suitable in town, of course. That hole in the wall of yours will not do once the lady takes her place in society." Richard's snug little townhouse, the hole in a wall, far outshone the houses of ninety-nine percent of the population of England, Scotland, and Wales. It would make an Irishman weep with delight.

"Good," he said, "for a moment there I thought this contract would be all gain to us."

His Grace pinned Richard with his eyes. "The chit will be a duchess. No small prize that. We won't sell it short."

"Sell it."

I thought she was the one on the cattle market. Am I to be trussed and branded before sale also? Bile rose and a sour taste took hold in his mouth. *Will she do? Will the whole damned deal do? Any more on Sarah Wharton and I'll run screaming into the night.*

"Show me again the numbers for the Northumbrian holdings," he said to distract his father.

An hour later the two men made their way through the cavernous Sudbury House toward dinner set up in the blue salon, and Richard tried to see the logic of the thing. He began to catalog the advantages of marriage to Lady Sarah when they left the estate office.

Beautiful face—if you like marble. Lily bloomed with life.

He shook his head and followed his father down a hallway lit with dozens of beeswax candles.

Impeccable bloodlines—that run a bit close to aristocratic inbreeding.

He looked at the back of his father's balding head. Lily's heritage would add intelligence, courage, and strength to any alliance. Pedigree isn't everything. That idea went against everything he had been raised to believe and took him off guard.

The duke winced a bit while he climbed the ornate marble stairs to the second story. Richard noted the signs of age coldly. He knew his father wouldn't welcome any mention of weakness.

The Whartons are wealthy—there is no arguing that. Perhaps she will do.

Richard considered the impact of one more minor land holding and found it negligible. They turned at the landing.

Poised and confident in social and diplomatic circles.

He could be certain Lady Sarah would decorate his arm and not embarrass him in public. What about in private? He couldn't picture bantering ideas about the affairs of state with her. In his mind, Lily Thornton laughed at him.

What about in the bedroom? No matter how hard he tried to squelch it, all he could see was Lily, passion raw in her eyes. *She won't have me! he reminded himself ruthlessly and clamped his jaw so tightly it hurt.*

They reached the withdrawing room where the family gathered before dinner.

The Wharton chit is well schooled in the duties of a duchess—

The haughty face of Her Grace, his mother, glared back at him. "You're late," she snapped. "We do not tolerate such behavior in this house."

Richard trooped in to dinner with his parents and youngest sister. They walked sedately in strict order of precedence. They sat in their usual places in the same order, just as they had from the time Richard reached adulthood and was permitted at table. Her Grace nodded, and serving began, formally and in silence. He stared at his soup.

"I spoke with Lady Sarah Wharton, this afternoon. We discussed preferred living arrangements. The girl has perfect taste," his mother pronounced. "You will turn over all decisions about such matters to her."

"We are not betrothed," Richard said, as blandly as he could.

Her Grace ignored him. She ignored all truths that did not meet her desires. "The matter of neighborhoods can be easily resolved. The wedding, of course, will be at Saint George, Hanover Square."

"We have not yet—"

"Yes, yes." His mother waved an impatient hand. "Don't keep Lisle waiting tomorrow."

He put down his spoon and stared at the table without actually seeing it.

She will not do. He knew it in his marrow.

Well schooled in the duties of a duchess—

Realization filled him. He didn't want a duchess. "I'm not going to marry Lady Sarah Wharton."

"Don't talk nonsense," Her Grace spat. "Restrain your tendency to low standards, Glenaire. "Lady Sarah told me you forced her to greet that schoolmaster's son and his wife at the theatre. We do not receive them."

His wife—your daughter. Her Grace chose to ignore that fact also. She couldn't bend Georgiana to her will and, therefore, decided she did not exist.

"She will not suit," Richard said.

"The Mallet woman?"

"Lady Sarah Wharton. She will not suit."

"She suits us perfectly," his mother sputtered.

Richard rose to his feet. "You don't have to marry her." He put down his serviette. "I'll take my leave. I will send notice to Lisle. They can accept her earl." Silence followed him to the door. *I've bungled the thing from the beginning. There must be some way to change Lily's mind. I'll find her; I'll do better. If not, I'll find another woman I can stand to live with, but it won't be Sarah Wharton.*

He didn't want a duchess. He wanted a wife.

Chapter Nineteen

Walter Stewart accompanied Richard to a modest cottage on the outskirts of Greenwich four days later. Richard loathed the errand.

If it distracted me from Lily, this damned trip might have value, but it doesn't. At least it frees me from seeing all the messages from Sudbury House about my "ludicrous behavior."

A groom engaged in removing the knocker from the door and hanging a black mourning wreath tried to deny them entrance.

"Tell Mrs. Clarke the Marquess of Glenaire wishes to pay his respects." The man pulled his forelock and went inside to comply.

"She may deny us, my lord," Stewart mused.

A woman whose husband died with his throat cut in an alley while doing England's bidding might well choose not to see the man who sent him there. *Damn Volkov.*

"She has the right," Richard answered. *I hope she refuses us. These things are always messy. Still, to avoid the call would be cowardly.*

"Volkov killed him on my watch. It is for me to see to his widow," he went on.

"Are we certain it was Volkov?" Stewart asked.

"Clarke had him in sight. We know he followed him after he sent notice to us from the tavern."

Stewart nodded glumly. "About the widow, my lord, won't the service arrange a pension?" The young man shifted uncomfortably.

"Of course," Richard answered. But an inadequate one. He

couldn't count the number of pensions he supplemented from his own pocket.

To Richard's disappointment, the widow didn't deny them. She served them tea and burdened them with John Clarke's dedication to England, pride in the Foreign Service, and personal devotion to the Marquess of Glenaire.

"John worshipped you, my lord. He would be proud to know you sit here with me."

Richard forced a smile he hoped hid his consternation. "We regret the cause of this visit, ma'am." He cleared his throat and withdrew a packet of paper, anxious to cut the visit short.

The arrangements required little explanation. Mrs. Clarke clutched the papers to herself.

"I knew what he did put him in danger," she breathed. "Though he made light of it. He always said if anything happened to him the marquess would see to me." She began to weep silently. "You didn't fail him."

I failed him when he went after Volkov alone. Richard needed air suddenly—badly. He rose to leave.

"I know you must leave," the widow said with a loud sniff to hold back tears, "but I must know. Please tell me."

"Ma'am?"

"How did my John die? Did he suffer?"

"He died of a single knife blow, swift and easy, Mrs. Clark. He didn't suffer." The lie slipped off his tongue with practiced ease; the truth stuck rock hard in his chest all the same.

"It is well you didn't tell her," Stewart said when they were safely gone. "No woman should know about such things."

The doctor's report had gruesome detail on every line. The man's throat had been cut, his belly breached, his body mutilated. Either Volkov lost himself in rage over being thwarted or he wished to send them a message.

"Volkov is an animal. We will find him," Richard said. He had ordered the casket sealed before being sent to the widow for burial.

The two of them walked downhill in sunshine so bright it glinted off the Royal Observatory like a beacon, shone off the trees in beams of green, and shimmered on the Thames where it lapped restlessly in its banks.

"About that, sir. I came here this morning to tell you. A man matching his description sailed for Alexandria yesterday. Our man in Falmouth is certain it is him."

"Alexandria?" Or any port in the Mediterranean. If they stop in Gibraltar or Lisbon, he can change ships to anywhere in the world.

"Yes, my lord. And sir, there is something else."

The marquess turned his head to raise an impatient eyebrow but kept walking.

"Lily Thornton," Stewart said.

Richard could feel his cheeks stiffen from the force of his clenched teeth.

"You didn't forbid me to follow up, so I thought—"

"What did you find, Stewart?"

"In London, nothing. We've kept watch, and she never came back. I thought that since we're scouring the ports for Volkov—" he gave a dramatic shrug.

Volkov and Lily.

"She left with him." Richard's heart stuttered, and he skipped a step.

"No, no! At least I don't think so," the man walking beside him went on. "We're fairly certain Volkov left on the Oceana for Alexandria. But I had people scour recent passenger lists. A woman about Miss Thornton's description left five days ago for Malta on the Captain James."

"Her description?"

"Single woman traveling alone with just the one servant. I took the liberty of interviewing some laborers at the dock. They remembered because she came all swathed in shawls. Tiny thing, like Miss Thornton, and the servant was big. Memorably tall."

"'Just the one servant,'" Richard mused. "Too tall to be Volkov?"

"That's the thing, my lord. The laborers thought he was a Muslim, or some exotic from the East."

Richard stopped short. "Are you sure?"

Walter Stewart looked back at him without answering.

"Of course you are or you wouldn't have told me." They resumed their walk.

"Can't be one of Sahin Pasha's people," Stewart said. "The lot of them embarked from the navy docks in Portsmouth for Constantinople the same day."

Volkov had contacts in the East. He could hire a thug to—what? Guard? Kidnap? Imprison?

"Sorry I couldn't find more, my lord."

She wouldn't go with Volkov voluntarily. I saw her face at Chadbourn Park. The man terrifies her.

"She might have gone off on her own, you know, my lord," Stewart continued.

"Yes. She would do that," Richard answered. *Why can't she just stay put where she belongs? Where I can see to her protection.*

They reached the quay. Richard put one foot on the steps to a waiting river taxi and turned to Stewart who waited expectantly above him.

"I'm going back to London," Richard said. "There's nothing left to uncover here. Return to Falmouth and see if you can find someone who can place Volkov on the Oceana for certain." He stepped into the small boat.

"And Lily Thornton, my lord?"

"Unless you discover she went with Volkov, she isn't the Foreign Office's concern." *Mine perhaps, but not yours.*

The oarsman pulled out into the stream, and the slap of the oars pulled him back toward London, back to the affairs of state. *Where are you, Lily? What have you done?*

If he couldn't reach her, he couldn't change her mind. He leaned back and squinted up where stars that ought to shine lay hidden behind city smoke and foul miasma. Lily wanted to manage her own life. He ought to leave her to it.

Let her try it anyway.

~

Three days at sea and Lily's uncharacteristic mal de mer continued unabated. Pregnancy had stolen her sea legs as well.

Ahmet looked down his substantial nose at her, his now familiar sympathy shining in his eyes. "You wish to rest?"

She shook her head. "Could we try something sitting still for a while?" She refused self-pity. *You brought this on yourself. You got what you asked for.*

The delegation assigned Lily a tiny cabin apart from Sahin and the rest of his entourage, one just large enough for lessons in court protocol. Ahmet had been assigned to teach Lily what she needed to know to impress the Valide Sultan.

He had demonstrated how to bow out of a room for the past half hour. Lily thought she might have it; she knew for certain the bowing contributed to dizziness. The ways of the Ottoman court remained strange, but Lily persisted. The more I learn, the better I will be able to get along.

"I assume we should also skip the protocols for the serving of food?" Ahmet asked rhetorically. Amusement lurked in his eyes.

Lily felt herself pale. "Please," she managed, swallowing hard.

"Let's review the hierarchies inside the women's quarters then." He began to drone on, listing the hierarchy beginning with the lowliest servant girl or Kalfa.

When he began expanding on the rights and privileges of the various ranks of imperial wives from the Iqbal, who may be favored with the sultan's attention but have no children, to Haseki, who would be awarded her own quarters and servants once she had given birth, Lily's head began to spin. Higher still was the Kadin, who had given the sultan a son. The concept of such a marriage and the structure of privilege felt as strange to Lily as the words themselves. *Where will I fit? As Kalfa, no doubt, or worse. Surely not wife.*

"Repeat the words for me, please Ahmet."

"You learn quickly, Lady."

She smiled wanly. "Languages come to me." Language, she knew, held the key. She could carve out a place for herself as a teacher only with perfectly fluent Turkish.

Kalfa, Iqbal, Haseki, Kadin, Kafir. Kafir—infidel.

"Kafir? That is me. Do you object to teaching a kafir, Ahmet, and a woman at that?"

"I live to serve women," the man said with a smile. "As to the rest," he shrugged, "You learn quickly. It is my privilege to teach."

She smiled back. "So shall I. It is my wish to teach."

"Then we both serve the women of the sultan's household, no? Shall we continue?"

Ideas felt less strange with repetition. The rigid order of precedence reminded Lily of the house party at Chadbourn Park. Chadbourn's guests had gathered before dinner and promenaded in rank order to their seats. The seats had been laid out according to the rules of etiquette and rank. The two worlds had more in common than someone might suppose.

The Seraglio need not be strange. One need only learn the rules to get along. Lily would do it. She had no other choice. She had burned her bridges behind her. If Richard found her background lacking, he would find the scandal of life in the Seraglio insupportable. He would never have her after this.

Chapter Twenty

A nervous clerk greeted Richard at Horse Guards.

"Fair put out he sounded."

"Castlereagh always sounds fair put out. What exactly did he say?" Richard demanded.

"You are to call on him immediately. And you—beg pardon, my lord, but these are his words—'damn well better have your analysis of Malta in your hand.'"

The agitated clerk blinked up at him, anxiety giving him the fidgets. Richard dismissed him with an abrupt gesture.

Malta. Did she sail to Malta? How unsafe are those waters? He looked at his unfinished report. *If you concentrated on your damned work, you would know.*

Messages lay on his desk, more complaints from his parents and what was sure to be an ugly message from Lisle. He went to answer the summons from the foreign secretary and returned with Castlereagh's anger burning in his ears, irritated with himself over his failure to complete his analysis. He had accumulated notes in fits and starts by collating observations of sea captains with agents on the ground, but allowed interruptions—and Lily Thornton—to disrupt the work. It remained to pull it together for Castlereagh, the prime minister, the cabinet, and, ultimately, the prince regent into a report that could enhance his reputation. He began to write the final report.

. . .

WHILE AMERICAN efforts have subdued the worst of the Mediterranean pirates, waters of the sea between Sicily and the coast of Africa remain unsettled. Unrest in Naples exacerbates the situation so that our forces on Malta—

MALTA. The woman Stewart described embarked to Malta.

Lily of all women should know how perilous the Mediterranean has become. Did she go willingly? He doubted it. Either someone coerced her or something horrific drove her to take off on her own. Either way, Volkov is behind it. He picked up his pen.

—OUR forces on Malta could feel the impact of shipping disruption.

HE BEGAN to list actions to be taken, numbers of marines to add to Royal Navy vessels, escalated improvements to the port fortifications, and beefed-up frequency for the Gibraltar packet.

The Gibraltar packet. They are the fastest ships we have. I could leave from Portsmouth on tomorrow's tide.

If he left immediately, he could get home to pack a few items and just make it on a good mount. From Gibraltar, passage to Malta would be easy.

Nonsense. One does not just hare off without planning. Besides, she has at least a week on me—closer to two.

Richard shook the very thought from his head. He owed Castlereagh this report and his father the courtesy of a reply.

Words flowed onto paper rapidly, if not coherently. They skimmed along the surface of the topic. They never plunged to Richard's customary depths. They flew toward a conclusion.

Richard frowned at it. The report would be presented in the highest circles. Totally inadequate for the audience. He had built a career on exactness in all he did, on the quality of his work. I need to rewrite it.

His eyes lost focus. His words lost meaning. His mind returned again and again to the Gibraltar packet, drawn like iron to lodestone. The seas around Malta churned in his mind, and the dangers haunted him.

Something drove her away, something so strong she knowingly put herself in danger or, worse, was forced into it.

In one swift motion he completed the manuscript with a message for Castlereagh, who wouldn't like it much.

Intelligence inadequate. I leave for Malta on the tide to see it for myself.

He had to leave London within the hour to make it. He sealed the report in a sleeve and called for a clerk.

"Send this to the foreign secretary in three hours. Not one moment sooner." The bewildered clerk merely nodded.

His career would be in tatters before he returned. He realized with growing elation that he didn't care. He picked up his hat and walked out the door.

I'm going to find her on Malta and, if I have to, shake the truth out of her. If I find Volkov too, he's a dead man, whether she went willingly or not.

The port of Algiers filled the air with odors great and small. Rotten fish and offal, the familiar rot of any port, contended with exotic spices and the cloying scent of dozens of unknown flowers. None of them sat well with Lily's churning stomach. In a month at sea, her nausea had not abated. Pregnant women, she now knew for certain, did not travel well. That afternoon their ship bobbed at anchor, a condition infinitely worse than forward motion.

Solid ground lay feet away. She had gone above decks to stare longingly at the teeming docks, but she had been forbidden to disembark.

"Covered in veils you would still give yourself away as the English you are. Has no one mentioned to you the slave markets of North Africa?" Sahin had demanded.

Slave markets. The thought made Lily shudder. The horror of Barbary slavery was the stuff of schoolgirl nightmares. Unlike other nightmares, it was all too real. Still, dry land called to her. She had hoped he would give in and send a guard with her.

Before she could object he added, "These streets are not safe for any woman, even with a bodyguard."

He had looked at her sadly. "Once inside the Seraglio, you will move freely only within its walls—broad, ornately decorative walls, but walls all the same. This is the life you have asked for, Lily."

The life you asked for. Lily lay on her narrow bunk in a cabin no larger than a linen closet and contemplated her decision.

She cupped her hands protectively over the baby growing inside her and fought remorse. Everything in her upbringing told her she should have accepted the marquess. Her conscience told her so.

"That's just it, little one," she said into the gloom, rubbing her abdomen. "If I marry him, your father will always be 'the marquess,' never Richard." Never beloved, not out loud.

Aboard this ship, she kept them both safe. Inside the walls of the Seraglio, they would be safe. She refused to regret it.

"When your grandpapa comes, he will take us back to England in time, safe and above contempt." She hoped it would be so. Her hopes lay in her knowledge of Sahin, who failed her only once, and in her loving, though often neglectful, father. She prayed her hopes were not in vain.

Another wave of nausea overtook her. To control it she stared at the ceiling and began listing her qualifications as a teacher: languages, education, and arts. When the interview came with the Valide Sultan, she would be ready.

~

Richard crawled into Malta on a small boat with peeling blue paint, filthy sails, and the reek of fish.

The Spanish fisherman he hired in Gibraltar gave him an ironic salute when he disembarked and mockingly patted the purse safely stowed in his pocket.

The grizzled old thief had demanded top coin when he realized how badly Richard wanted immediate transportation. No more formal passage to Malta could be found that departed sooner than a week; Richard agreed to the fisherman's extortionate terms.

It would take days to get the stink out of his clothes. For once he didn't regret traveling without a valet. His man in London would die of heart palpitations at the sight.

Thirty minutes later Richard presented himself to Sir Thomas Maitland, governor of Malta on behalf of the British throne. The unannounced appearance of the Marble Marquess, dirty and disheveled on his doorstop, stunned the governor. He gaped for a full minute before he barked orders to his staff for "bath water and plenty of it" and ordered lodging for his distinguished guest.

Richard bit back the one question he came to have answered and let a flurry of excitable Maltese servants carry him off to newly aired rooms.

It took Maitland's staff an hour and a half to assist the marquess with his bath, locate the correct amount of citrus oil to counteract the effect of fish, and truss him into an ill-fitting, borrowed suit.

They hustled him off to the formal dining room where he sat with disgruntled impatience at the governor's dinner table with a minor attaché, two colonels, an expatriate baroness, and the Anglican bishop of Malta and his wife, all of them eager to meet the Marquess of Glenaire. If Richard found the company less than sterling, the table setting and the cuisine matched that at the houses of the highest society in England. As it should for the cost of maintaining this pestilential place.

Most of the company cared little for the reasons behind his arrival, wishing only to bask in the presence of the Marble Marquess, luminary of foreign affairs and of the court. Maitland, however, obviously burned with curiosity.

"To what do we owe the honor of your visit, my lord?" he asked over the soup course.

"We are particularly interested in the safety of our shipping in these waters," Richard explained, staying as close to the truth as possible. *They'll think me a fool if I tell them I'm pursuing a woman who doesn't even want my attention.*

The governor general looked for a moment as if he might question the need for the foreign secretary's second to personally research in the field. He did not.

"Were my reports not received?"

"Your reports," Richard improvised, "were intriguing." *And damned vague.* "I became curious to see for myself."

Maitland looked skeptical, but he let the issue of his reports drop. Richard's dinner mates plunged into a lively discussion on the topic, each giving a firsthand—although, based on his research, inaccurate—account of the situation.

By the middle of the main course, conversation moved on to much more delicious gossip of amorous intrigue on the island. Over a particularly tasty duckling and beetroot dish, Richard finally saw an opening.

"My men reported a concern recently. Perhaps you can clarify something for me," he said, drawing all eyes, eager to help their high-ranking guest.

"We had word of a young woman traveling alone this way, a tiny young lady, accompanied only by a bodyguard or servant of Eastern extraction." He spelled out the dates. The guests looked at one another, puzzled. "With all of the instability, the Foreign Service has concerns about a woman alone. She sailed on the Captain James out of Boston."

Maitland's face lit up. "Ah, Miss Dalca, Maria Dalca. She is well. You may rest at ease."

"She arrived here safely?"

"Yes," the governor beamed. "But we only had her company briefly. She is bound to her home in Maldavia after schooling with her English grandmother."

"You spoke with her?"

"Briefly. Polite enough chit. Terribly accented English. Shows some polish from her time in England. Small. Lovely girl with volumes of dark brown hair."

Brown hair. Not Lily.

"Excellent. My men worried for naught," Richard murmured.

"Brown hair," the baroness chuckled coyly. "Perhaps."

What the hell does that mean? Was her hair brown or not?

"She transferred to a Russian vessel and sailed for Thessaloniki where her aunt will meet her. Whether they travel overland or continue by sea to Constantinople and the Black Sea I cannot say," the governor rambled on, filling in details about how much his majesty's government had been glad to help her on her way. Richard heard only two words.

Russian. Thessaloniki.

Chapter Twenty-One

Soon after Richard reached Malta, Ahmet ushered Lily, awkward and clearly with child, into a small audience chamber, and all her preparation flew out of her head.

The door whispered shut behind her, leaving her with only one other occupant in the room, a small woman with regal bearing who turned and unwound veils from her face.

"Mrs. Thornton, is it?" the woman asked in good but heavily accented English.

Lily froze. "Mrs." The first lie.

"Come, come. My nephew tells me of your troubles. Let us be frank here in this room at least," the Valide Sultan said. She examined Lily with unblinking eyes and beckoned her forward.

"Not 'Mrs.', Highness. I am not married." Truth felt right, but Lily trembled. "And, yes, I have troubles."

The woman smiled suddenly, a warm, sad smile that soothed. "I can see that," she said ruefully. "When is this little person to make his appearance?"

"More than four more months, Highness, almost five."

"Trouble, indeed," the older woman mused. "And dangers to your father also press in. My nephew told me something of it. Your loyalty speaks well for you."

"Thank you, Highness. I have not heard from my father in months."

The Valide Sultan nodded and took one of Lily's hands sympathetically. "My nephew also tells me you were of service to our country and that he may have caused your troubles."

Lily's face grew hot. "Not that! Sahin Pasha treated me with respect always." This woman can't think I'm carrying Sahin Pasha's child! "My problems are of my own making." That certainly rang true. "What Sahin Pasha meant, I think, is that he may have put me in an awkward position and I—"

"You let your heart rule your mind. Foolish."

Lily dipped her head. A graceful finger slipped under her chin and pushed her face up to look at the sympathetic brown eyes of the Valide Sultan. "Foolishness is why young women must be protected. My nephew knows this, and he failed you."

The woman switched abruptly from English to excellent, unaccented French. "So, tell me, how do you plan to repay my household if I offer you refuge?"

"I can teach," Lily answered in the same language.

The Valide Sultan smiled. "What can you teach?"

"Reading, writing, and speaking in five languages," Lily said in Turkish.

The older woman's smile broadened. "How is your math?" she asked.

"Mostly tied to bookkeeping but excellent," Lily answered. "I am well read in the sciences, also—geography, history, and politics."

"Politics! The Seraglio seethes with it. My ladies must know science and where it leads us. They must understand the geography and history of our empire and of other countries as well."

"Your women study these things?"

"All members of my household are required to read and write. The ladies of the harem learn more. Those with an aptitude read widely and learn as much as they can."

"I had no idea—hope, but no idea."

Valide Sultan gave a dismissive gesture. "Westerners think we are illiterate puppets, locked in prison. They know only what their small-minded diplomats tell them."

"Pig-headed men," Lily agreed.

The two women grinned at each other.

"We will do well together, Mrs. Thornton."

Lily's brows rose. "Mrs.?"

"Honesty is well enough between us, but it is better if I do not know," the Valide Sultan said, suddenly all business. "Unmarried pregnancy is a great disgrace. If I am known to condone it, it will reflect badly on me. Among the others, you will be an unfortunate widow."

Lily nodded numbly in the face of the woman's grim pronouncement.

"The consequences could be grave. You might be put out on the street."

Lily swallowed. She could only nod again.

"Good. Now, women enter this place in many ways from many places. Once here, they become Turk. They are given Turkish names. Your name shall be Zambak."

"Zambak?" Lily mused, "Lily?"

"Exactly. We will hide you in plain sight until your father comes to claim you. He will come, no?"

"May God hear your words, Highness."

She thought of England then and her home in London. She thought of Richard. She opened a space in her heart and locked England, her father, and Richard Hayden away. She prayed silently for the baby she carried.

Lily turned to leave, but the Valide Sultan had one more thing to say.

"Know this, Zambak. If you are found to not be a widow, I will deny any knowledge of the deceit. You will face the consequences alone."

~

Four days of inspecting the vaunted towers that ringed Malta taught Richard two things. First, Malta's historic fortifications, built by the Knights of Malta during the seventeenth century, were numerous, massive, and crumbling. Few looked suitable for modern gun emplacements, and the sheer number required a larger force than the crown had seen fit to assign. He also learned that, however brilliant Maitland might have been as a land soldier in Ceylon and Spain, naval strategy escaped him.

About "Maria Dalco," he learned nothing. Maitland met her only the once, found her "plain as a post," and ignored her ever after. Richard doubted Lily could ever make herself "plain," but he couldn't dismiss the possibility.

Maitland's aide responded to Richard's discreet questions with, "We saw nothing unusual. Why is she of interest to the Foreign Service?" *Shrewd observer, that one. Avoid him now but make note for the future.*

None of the troops, even those around the harbor itself, laid eyes on the woman. It had been foolish to ask, particularly the day Maitland overheard him and raised a questioning brow. I need freedom to poke around on my own.

It took him three more days to arrange a meeting between Maitland, one British admiral, and a group of captains that included a captain of an American merchantman. Richard arranged the effort to accomplish two things: allow the naval forces to explain their view of Malta's defenses and to distract the governor for a day so as to make himself free to investigate something other than stone and cannon.

As soon as the discussion between colonels and captains came to its predictable boil, Richard took his leave, climbed the long granite staircase to the guest wing, and rummaged through his things.

The clothing he had arrived in lay under citrus-scented linen. He couldn't easily scour the docks looking like a London beau. His impulse to order the excitable Maltese footman assigned to him to not burn the clothes proved correct. Though aired, his suit still smelled of fish. He discarded the coat. That will be burned. The stained shirt needed only a tear and some garden dirt to give him an adequate disguise; the trousers looked unspeakable without assistance.

He took the servant stairs and avoided being seen by anyone but a startled parlor maid. He slipped out through the French doors of the governor's private breakfast room without notice. The docks lay a quarter mile downhill.

Taverns lined the lanes around Malta's port. Like seaport taverns anywhere, they teemed with seamen and dockworkers deep in their cups. The latter were his quarry. His disguise may have passed, but his upper class accents would give him away in English. He tried his imperfect French. It seemed to work.

"Lots o'fancy folk come through here," he said to a burly dock-worker. "Bring trunks with 'em, do they?"

"Great fancy pieces. Scurry about like ants shouting at a body not to drop 'em," the man answered. He gave his name as Spiru.

"Did you hear about that puffed up marquess, though?" another broke in. "Let some fisherman cheat him into sailing two days in the hole with stinking fish. Mario at the big house says his clothes stunk all the way to the attic."

The entire tavern rocked with laughter. Richard looked down at his shirt and joined them. The damned thing cost more than this man makes in a year. The absurdity of it tickled him, and he laughed harder.

As he hoped, a raucous discussion about the foibles of the rich and favored broke out, with tales of eccentrics, bullies, and dandies in abundance, but no single woman.

"Your Mussulmen travel just heavy as your Englishman," Spiru said at last.

"Yes, but they keep their women quiet," another retorted. Richard remembered his name as Gorg. "English women fairly flay a man's skin off his back if he's rough with their precious trunks."

Richard saw his opening to ask about women travelers, but before he could push his luck, a booming voice echoed through the tavern. "Work to be had, lads," he shouted, and the tavern emptied out.

Spiru slapped Richard on the back and led him toward the disembarking ship. Before he had time to think, the Marquess of Glenaire found himself unloading cargo from an Egyptian vessel. Pride in his own fitness, honed in hours at Jackson's Pugilistic Club, faded quickly when his shoulders began to ache. He saw Gorg and Spiru exchange an amused glance and redoubled his efforts.

In spite of the ache, Richard felt elated. When his friends went to war, he served from a desk at Horse Guards. Will told him he saved more lives than the lot of them put together, but Richard never saw it, never had the heat of battle. When he dispatched Andrew to France, Richard had the worry but not the elation of actual danger. When his agents took the field, he sat at a desk, sifting and sorting and finding truths other men missed, protecting England with a machine-like mind and cool judgment.

Physical exertion is damned liberating. He thought of the months he spent buried in Britain's paperwork. He thought of the months he faced his parents to be spoon-fed his father's goals for the estate. He thought of the months he sleepwalked through the boring rituals of London society.

Better than good. I haven't been this energized since the Congress of Vienna.

Richard helped Spiru heft a final box onto a lorry, straightened, and rubbed his shoulder.

"Now there's a fierce one," Gorg said.

"Fierce?" Richard asked.

"Always come with the big guards. That 'un's a Berber," Gorg answered. He pointed to a tall dark man in a turban glowering down on them. His charge, a cluster of heavily veiled women, stood by the railing.

"Do you ever seen one travel alone?" Richard asked.

"Not often. Had one a month ago. Little thing in English dress with a bodyguard as big as that. But the woman was small. Somewhat stout. Brown hair all piled up like it might give her neck an ache," Gorg said.

Stout. Not Lily. All this way and it wasn't Lily.

"Not like the other one."

"What other one?"

Chapter Twenty-Two

The Seraglio, Lily discovered, teemed with babies, small children, and their mothers. One pregnant woman provided no distraction. A newly arrived widow, and an English one at that, did.

Her lecture on the Russian court overflowed with eager young women, most of them more curious about Lily than the topic. "Lecture" may have been too formal a word for a talk given in a room with blue tiled walls and lined with cushions where giggling students reclined. Some of them nursed their babies.

"You have been to Russia, Zambak?" one wide-eyed girl asked. She looked to be no more than sixteen.

Lily inclined her head to acknowledge the truth. "My father served in Saint Petersburg."

"Did you meet your husband there?" the girl asked.

The husband. Lies pile on lies. I have none and probably never will.

She struggled to formulate an answer. She and Valide Sultan agreed their story needed to be simple. She married a man in the British Foreign Service. He died en route to Constantinople, leaving Lily without protection. The women of the Seraglio understood what it was to be without protection.

"No, I met him in England," she said.

"Do not tease Zambak about it," an older girl scolded. "It makes her sad to talk about such things."

"I'm sorry, Zambak, for your sorrow," the girl apologized. She brightened abruptly. "But soon you will have your baby. If it is a boy, it will be a reminder of him."

A sudden sharp memory of Richard, fierce concern for her in his eyes, stabbed her. The arrogant fool cares for everyone as if they were his own. She knew she admired that even as she wished more from him.

"See, foolish one, you make her even sadder," the older girl chided. "Her son will never know his father."

Boy or girl will never know. Never. Even if we return to England, it can't happen.

Hushing quieted even the most curious of the girls. Sympathy looked back at Lily from around the room.

"Tell us again about Russia's policy in Poland," one of them asked, diverting the conversation back to their studies. Most of them had proved more astute than Lily would have expected. She tried to picture Lady Sarah Wharton curious about Russian intentions in Poland and could not.

They streamed out into the sunlight when Lily finished. She gathered up notes, wrapped the still unfamiliar shawls around her shoulders, and followed them. She thought she might seek a fountain she had discovered near the women's quarters. Fountains here did not dance; scarcity of water made that foolish. They were, however, beautifully decorated. She thought to sit for a moment and bask in the coolness before she filled her water skin.

A messenger intercepted her halfway there. The young eunuch made obeisance and gave her the message.

Sahin Pasha wishes to speak with you. It is not permitted that you meet alone. Come to the audience chamber by the old gate at sunset.

Valide Sultan

Sahin? She had been there a month with no word from him.

What now? Perhaps he has word from Papa.

Her heart began to race.

~

The head on the pole looked down at Richard with empty eye sockets, long since pecked empty by crows. From the look of the thing, it hung there several weeks before he reached Thessaloniki. If its location in front of the gate meant to squelch the rebels, the grumbling in the streets indicated that it had failed.

The decaying horror told Richard even less than it had the day he arrived, still puffed up with the excitement of disguises and assumed identities four days before. A coup had been thwarted. This man, most likely Volkov's agent, paid dearly. Whether Volkov skulked nearby, whether he came to Thessaloniki and departed, or even whether he came at all, the sunken face could not say.

Richard passed the sight, pulled his tattered hat down across his eyes, and elbowed his way through the crowd in the square. In twenty paces, he heard a half dozen miserable grumbles and at least one outright treasonous threat. He ignored them.

A message led him to a tavern that was seedy even by port standards. It lay streets off the main square. A quick scan of the place showed him his contact had not arrived. He took a seat where he could watch the door and called for ouzo.

Richard paid the barkeeper, drank deep, and slunk back in morose silence. The distraction he had enjoyed in his disguise on Malta faded in this third rate Greek port of call where the identity he assumed required him to stay in a bug-ridden inn like any good merchant would. The novelty had worn thin to the point of fraying.

What the hell am I doing here? In one month I've abandoned everything I worked for, the life I planned, and everything I thought I held dear in pursuit of a woman who made it clear she does not wish my protection. What is this madness?

A stocky man with full beard and hair around his shoulders

entered, bringing Richard to attention. The furtive little man behind him put him on his guard. The knife in Richard's belt under his loose jacket felt comforting against his back. The one in his boot felt even more so.

The bearded one saw him and gestured to the other with his head. The two sat in front of him, glancing around all the while as if watching for the sultan's agents.

"You, merchant, are trouble. I want paid now," the bearded one said.

"Who is your friend?" Richard asked.

"No one I want to know. Pay me now, and he may talk."

Richard pulled a leather pouch from under his jacket, weighed it in his hand, and held it up. "What we agreed on, not a cent more. I should take coins out for—" He meant to say "being late," but the bearded one grabbed the coins and bolted for the door.

"You better be worth it," Richard told the man left behind.

"Do you value your life?"

Richard nodded as much to keep the man talking as to agree.

"I am your one warning. You ask too many questions."

"Too many for whom? Russia or the Ottomans."

"Both."

So there are Russian agents on the ground. That answered one question.

"I leave them to their conflict. My interest is in a woman."

The furtive little man looked back, his face a mask of indifference. "Women come and go."

"One passed through here. Maria Dalco. I've been told she met her 'aunt' and sailed on." The statement got no reaction. "Another woman, possibly English, sailed with an Ottoman party. She may or may not have disembarked." The man sat stone-faced.

"Do you know of either?" Richard demanded.

The man shook his head. "What do we care about women?"

"Volkov cared for the one I seek."

Fear, clear and unmistakable, flashed across the man's eyes.

"What is that to me?"

"Do you know which of these two he may have followed?" Or coerced, or led, or— Richard shuddered to think what else.

"I know nothing of this," the man said. "You may not care about the works of Russia and the Sublime Porte, but they may not be so indifferent about you. Have a care. Your questions poke at a viper pit." He rose to leave, but he leaned on the table first. "I would depart Thessaloniki. Quickly." He left before Richard could stop him.

He walked back past the seat of Ottoman power with its grizzly decoration hanging on the pole in front. He couldn't tell what Russia planned, not officially, and he couldn't be sure whether or not the unrest was as dispersed and leaderless as it seemed.

Richard was out of patience, out of ideas, and out of questions. He only knew one thing for certain, Volkov's man died an ugly death. Volkov had threatened the same fate for Lily's father, if not Lily herself once, if that happened.

I have to find her.

He had no idea if she had really gone to Constantinople or why. He could go back to London with nothing and admit his stupidity or push on to Constantinople.

Gathering his belongings took moments. An hour later he walked toward the docks to look for transport on a coastal vessel. His cash dwindled, but he could get more in Constantinople. No more disguises.

A new thought occurred to him. Witnesses in Malta said the English woman with the Ottoman party appeared to be surrounded by eunuch guards. If Lily had put herself in Ottoman company, she went with Sahin Pasha—voluntarily or unwillingly. The crazy old man may have some notion of responsibility for her. It would be like him to stash her in the sultan's Seraglio itself.

He stepped onto a brightly painted boat with a smile on his face.

Chapter Twenty-Three

A vast complex of buildings made up the Seraglio, the sultan's walled "household." Covered fountains, fabulously ornate meeting rooms, offices, storerooms, bathing facilities, nurseries, and dormitories for high-ranking wives lined its tiled lanes. Sunshine and flowers wrapped themselves around beautiful, often brightly painted, buildings but failed to lighten Lily's burdens.

The Valide Sultan greeted Lily in the Courtyard of the Concubines as she indicated in her message. "You look rested, Zambak. Life here suits you." The older woman gave her a gentle smile. She moved with grace as well as purpose, pulling Lily along by the force of her personality.

"It does, Valide Sultan," Lily said. *Perhaps.*

The Seraglio suited many women. Lily found their company stimulating, as if she lived in the middle of one of Georgiana Mallet's salons filled with intelligent conversation and good food.

If only I weren't so achingly lonely. For Papa. For English conversation. For— She squashed the thought.

"You do well. Your teaching has been a blessing to many. Your description of the palace of the czar sent Guldem into raptures," she said without breaking stride.

"It is not so splendid as this, Highness," Lily said with an expansive gesture.

The older woman's approval glowed from her smile.

They entered the same audience room where she had interviewed Lily four weeks before. Ahmet followed discreetly. When he would have entered, the Valide Sultan indicated with the graceful wave of her hand that he was to stay outside. "She will be safe with me," the woman said. He frowned, but obeyed.

Sahin Pasha waited for them across the room, seated cross-legged on cushions covered in fabric the same color as the geometric designs that covered the walls.

"Greeting, honored uncle," Lily said, making obeisance.

"Come, sit, little one, and we will talk."

Lily made herself comfortable on a divan near Sahin. The Valide Sultan settled herself at a discreet distance, near enough to hear but far enough away to demonstrate that she would not participate in conversation.

Figs and dates were offered and shared; a long moment passed. Lily waited for him to speak as manners dictated.

"You look well, little one," he began.

Lily shared a smile with the Valide Sultan across the room. *They are at pains to compliment. I must have looked a horror when I arrived.*

"I am well fed and safe, honored uncle. I am grateful to you."

"Is it as you hoped, Lily?"

"It is as I expected...more than I expected," she said.

What does he want from me? He can inquire after my well-being without coming here.

"You are curious about this meeting," he said, concern pushing good humor aside. "I will not make you wait. Messengers have come." Concern gave way to a worried frown.

Every fiber in her body went on alert.

"My father?" *Not Richard. Please not Richard.* The vehemence of her concern for the marquess stunned Lily. *Why should he be in danger and why should it shake me so?*

"Our agent in London tells us he has not yet arrived there. We hope he is safe in Copenhagen."

Lily prayed that was true.

"I came with a warning, however."

She sat straighter, alert, and calmed herself.

"We have lost track of Volkov."

"You had him watched, honored uncle?" Of course they did. *Don't be an idiot.*

"After we confirmed his treachery in Thessaloniki and dealt with the traitor—"

Lily shuddered, all too aware of what "dealt with" meant. She had unleashed it on him; she hoped it was swift. She feared not.

"—we intended to make Volkov aware his actions would not go unpunished. He evaded our people in Naples when they got close."

They intended swift death for him also. He would run like a scared rabbit.

"Evaded, honored uncle?" she asked out loud.

"He ran from Portsmouth. We tracked him to Naples, but he escaped."

"North or south?"

"If he is after your father as he threatened, we or your marquess will catch him. He is well guarded." The old man shrugged. "We sent someone to Copenhagen also."

Lily nodded, relieved. "He threatened to kill me, too," she murmured. Both hands went instinctively to her belly and the precious burden she carried. Pregnancy had filled her with more fears than she had ever before imagined. She felt her skin go clammy.

"If he finds out where you are, which is unlikely, he might come here, but that is even more unlikely."

Of course it is unlikely, Lily. Don't be a ninny.

"I am safe here," she said.

"Inside the Seraglio, yes. It is the safest possible place. My warning is this: obey the Valide Sultan. Stay within these walls. Keep Ahmet or another eunuch near you at all times. Never put yourself in the reach of strangers."

"Of course, honored uncle!"

The old man seemed pleased. "No more foolish adventures, Lily," he admonished.

Walking back, the Valide Sultan praised her answer. "I know you will do this, Zambak. Your intelligence drives your actions, not impulse like some silly girl."

"Thank you for your confidence, Highness."

"I have hopes for you here."

"Hopes, Highness?"

"You have witnessed the complexity of my household. Administration requires skills—motivating people and seeing to their needs, managing finances, planning, and, of course, politics."

"Politics?" Lily couldn't keep the surprise out of her voice.

"This is the sultan's household. The affairs of empire are discussed in his offices, at his dinner table, in his chambers. I need women with a head for such affairs who are able to listen and influence. I have hope for you."

She bid the Valide Sultan good day and turned toward her quarters.A vision of long years in this place stretched out in front of Lily.

A few years only, I beg. Papa will come for me, and I'll go back. Go back to what? Life alone with my baby in a remote English village, near people who cannot add months? The Seraglio offers a sort of power and autonomy once you accept the basic structure. Would it be so bad to stay here?

Lily's hopes for a husband had faded with the marquess's offensive proposal. Richard's face, intense, determined, and arrogant, while he demanded—not asked, but demanded—marriage haunted her. She forgave him class snobbery. His assumption of male superiority stung, however. What man wants a partner for a wife? What man will offer for a "widow" with a child anything other than a place as his brood mare or nursemaid?

She turned into the bathing facility. Women and their young children clustered around a pool laughing and playing.

You have it better than many women. Here at least you and your baby are safe. No one will find you here.

~

The coastal boat smelled better than a fishing boat, but its company proved less savory. The boat stopped frequently, in and out of small coves, picking up packages and people.

Richard acquired a black eye before he arrived in Constantinople. He lost a shirt, a flagon of rum, and all of his money. He found freedom. For the first time in his life, the burden of responsibility and expectations lifted, leaving him with no cares but his own desires.

Lying on his back one night, he studied the endless stars and wondered if Lily watched them, too. It came to him then that he might love her. What else would explain this madness?

He began to laugh. *You always said love belonged to fools, and you've become one.* He laughed out loud until a fellow traveler threatened to blacken his other eye.

But love? he wondered, suddenly sober. *I never believed in it. I want her. I want her so badly that I offered marriage twice, even after she threw it in my face. That ought to be an end to it.*

He closed his eyes and tried to let the rocking of the boat lull him to sleep. *Why can't she accept that I care what happens to her? Isn't that enough?* He drifted to sleep knowing he would never understand women.

The boat put in to the foreign section of Constantinople, a blessing but a minor one. Crowds of peddlers thronged new arrivals in front of the colorful walls of old fountains and new mansions. The place seethed with humanity. A half dozen languages assaulted his ears at the same time; odors new and painfully familiar assaulted his nose; a confusing knot of narrow lanes, fanned out in several directions, assaulted his vision.

Did Lily pass through here? Proper ladies would put handkerchief to nose and demand immediate transport to a "good" (by which they meant European) house immediately. Lily would revel in this; she would refuse to hurry until she absorbed her fill. A wide grin stretched his dry lips. *When we're married, I'll bring her here.*

For now he had business. He asked directions to the British embassy. After two false starts and a long detour, compliments of a fig vendor with a particularly nasty sense of humor, he walked up to the British embassy.

A rail-thin boy in soft cotton trousers and hemp sandals stopped his systematic sweep of the steps to look at Richard with narrowed eyes.

"No beggars," the boy said firmly. He returned to his work.

"I'm not a beggar!" Richard bit back the impulse to announce his name and title. This savvy little laborer had taken in his appearance; he would laugh at some shabby beggar claiming to be a marquess.

"You Englishman?" the boy asked.

"I am."

"Office by side. His m'jesty's subjects get help there."

Well. A marquess is certainly a subject of the king. The boy's exercise of pompous authority amused him.

"Do you think I could get help?" he asked.

The boy appeared to think it over. "Possible," he said at last. "No beggars though."

The warning had teeth. When he tried his luck at the office, the clerks were equally unimpressed. Richard finally insisted that he knew Sir Robert Liston emphatically enough that a skeptical young man agreed to send a message to the ambassador.

Thirty minutes later the man himself arrived, hurried and annoyed. "Who the devil claims—Glenaire!" He stared at Richard in open-mouthed astonishment.

Richard rose, chin high, with as much aristocratic presence as he could muster in a stained shirt and undersized trousers.

"Sir Robert," he said, "I need your assistance."

Liston's eyes roamed over Richard. His wrinkled nose and pained expression left no doubt about his opinion of the marquess's appearance.

"Come then. We'll see if we can find you a tailor," he said, glancing back to see if Richard followed. "And then we're at your service. This must be a tale worth hearing."

"With all due respect, my errand is urgent," Richard said, coming up beside him. "I need access to the Seraglio."

Liston turned on his heels. "The Seraglio? All due respect to you," he retorted, "but no foreigner has access to the Seraglio. No one. Ever. Under any circumstances."

"There is a woman there, and Englishwoman," Richard told him.

"An Englishwoman?" Liston asked, astonished. "Who on earth?"

"It's a long story," Richard said, continuing up the stairs. He was increasingly sure she was there. Nothing else made sense.

I'll see her if I have to batter down the walls of the damned Seraglio myself.

Chapter Twenty-Four

A different Sahin Pasha than the sophisticate who had graced London's ballrooms in the spring greeted Richard and Robert Liston. Clad in oriental splendor, he reclined on cushions in bright silken patterns surrounded by silk-clad servants.

"Welcome, Sir Robert. I see you bring my friend the marquess," he said with no attempt to hide the amusement that crinkled his eyes.

The old reprobate! No amusement softened Richard's bitterness. "Where's Lily?" He demanded.

Sahin gestured to the seats near him. "Such manners, my lord! Come. Sit. Eat."

Liston reclined on a divan to Sahin's left. Richard remained standing. He looked around desperately.

"I sat on your uncomfortable English chairs all spring. Come, come. Sit in comfort."

Liston shot Richard a pleading look. He sank down onto the seat to Sahin's right.

"Where is Lily?" he repeated through clenched teeth.

At Sahin's gesture, platters of dates and honeyed sweets appeared alongside a pot of steaming Turkish coffee. The ringed fingers of a servant poured the drink into tiny glasses and faded away.

Sahin and Liston drank. Richard took a sip and grimaced.

"You will adjust," Sahin chuckled. "Eat some baklava, sweet to counteract the bitter."

"Lily," Richard prodded before taking a bite as directed. His eyes widened when the taste of honey exploded in his mouth.

"Such intensity! You should have protected her, My Lord Glenaire."

"We had her under protection!" Richard snapped.

"Yet she came to me for assistance. Who can probe the mind of a woman?" Sahin mused.

"Is there a story here I should hear?" Liston asked.

Sahin gave him a succinct overview of Volkov's threats.

"I've come from Thessaloniki. You dealt with your traitor ruthlessly—"

Sahin shrugged. "It is always so with traitors."

"—putting John Thornton in danger, not to mention Lily herself."

"You understand, Sir Robert, why I felt obliged to offer the woman protection when she sought employment in the Seraglio."

Damned poor choice of words. Visions of Lily entertaining the old man made Richard sick. He set his tea down with a thump. "What do you mean by 'protection,' and what exactly is Lily's 'employment' there?" he demanded.

"Your tone implies insult, my lord," Sahin replied hotly, his benign façade slipping briefly to allow the hard core underneath full view. In the flicker of an eye, the avuncular diplomat came back into focus. "In spite of your western stereotypes about our domestic arrangements, she is perfectly safe. She shares the riches of her mind with the women of the Seraglio."

"She's a teacher?" Liston asked, obviously intrigued. Richard, for his part, simply gasped, incredulous.

"Exactly." Sahin beamed. "By all accounts, an excellent one. My aunt, the Valide Sultan, is well pleased. She begins to have plans for Miss Thornton."

"The Valide Sultan is a powerful figure, Glenaire," Liston said. "The mother of the sultan, a woman of influence."

"Alas the current sovereign's mother is no longer with us. The position is held by his aunt, who by chance is also mine," Sahin told them. "I assure you, Miss Thornton could not be in a safer place."

"I demand to see her."

"Demand? Such a harsh word. Where is the Marble Marquess's famous sang-froid? His vaunted diplomacy so much in evidence last spring?"

Richard clamped his jaw shut.

"Can a meeting be arranged?" Liston asked.

"Do you expect me to believe you can't arrange whatever you please?" Richard cut in. "I will see her at the British embassy." I want her where I can protect her.

Sahin ignored Richard. He answered Liston. "What we can arrange and what Miss Thornton may want may not be the same." He turned to Richard, all pretense of friendliness gone. "There are audience rooms attached to the outer walls of the Seraglio that may be safe. The streets of this city, alas, are not. Whether Miss Thornton wishes to risk either is up to her."

"Are you telling me she won't see me?" Richard rose halfway from his seat. Liston cautioned him back with pained looks and a subtle hand gesture.

"Speak with Miss Thornton," Liston said smoothly. "Tell her that, while His Majesty's government trusts that the Sublime Porte treats her with all due respect and provides ample protection, concern for her welfare demands that we speak to her ourselves." He held Sahin Pasha's eyes.

Richard held his breath. The two other men ignored him. Sahin Pasha broke the gaze first.

"As you wish, Sir Robert. I will ask Miss Thornton to indulge you in this."

Richard felt his shoulders relax. He took a deep breath.

"Whether she wishes to see his lordship," Sahin went on, indicating Richard with a shrug, "is for her to determine." He looked over at Richard with stern disapproval.

Richard nodded in response.

In a flash, a sly look supplanted the disapproval. "Although such a meeting might prove entertaining at that."

What the devil does that old man mean by that salvo? Richard didn't care. *We'll see who's amused after I talk with her.*

Lily fretted in yet another anteroom. Word came that Sahin Pasha again requested an interview. The Valide Sultan professed to know nothing. This time, however, the woman left her as soon as they arrived in this anteroom. Ahmet, stern beneath his turban, stood next to her. He spoke no words of encouragement.

She smiled up at him; his expression did not soften. *His worried face does little for my peace of mind.*

She had been called to a room on the outer walls this time, the sort she knew opened out into the public parts of the palace. She puzzled over the meaning of such a venue but ceased trying.

You've become immersed in palace politics, Lily. You try to parse the meaning of every little detail, looking for machinations that might not exist.

Lily glanced down ruefully at her enlarged belly. At just over six months, she had begun to feel unwieldy.

What do you think Sahin up to now, little one, hmm? He does not seem to leave us in peace.

The door whispered open, and a female slave bowed out. Lily entered an audience room, much like any other. The only obvious difference was that, this time, Sahin Pasha stood just inside waiting for her, blocking her view of the room. No obvious signs of ritual hospitality were in view.

He stepped forward and took both of her hands.

"You look well, little one. Your situation agrees with you." He winked at her.

My "situation?" That's one word for it.

"What is it, honored uncle? Word about my father?" she asked.

"I fear not, little one. Your government believes him safe with his studies in Copenhagen still."

She studied his face. Something lurked behind his kindness. Sahin dropped one of her hands but held the other.

"Your government, regretfully, feels less certain about your well-being. They have made inquiries."

Lily felt sick. Sahin, who blocked her view of the room, moved to her side, still holding one hand. Her heart soared and did a flip. Richard.

A vortex of thought and emotion surged through her. *He came!* Confusion followed elation. *How? When? He's thin. His hair is too long. He looks—*

Blue eyes, wide with shock, stared back at her. Richard stood immobile, his face frozen in stunned disbelief.

She swung round to face Sahin. The old man's lips twitched; sly amusement lit his eyes. *You manipulative old man! You let me walk into this with no warning. Richard, too, from the look of it.*

When she looked back, Richard had not moved. His eyes had lost the glaze of shock, however. What she saw instead shook her to her core.

Still as a statue, he gaped, grief and longing stark on his face.

"Richard, I—" *He must hate me.*

His eyes moved from her face to the swelling where her child—his child—grew.

He can't take my baby, can he? Dear God, don't let him take her.

Chapter Twenty-Five

One by one, pieces fell into place, and, like boulders, flattened Richard's dearly held belief in his own intelligence. The man who helped England side step the hidden traps of enemies and allies alike at the Congress of Vienna had missed the obvious.

Lily is pregnant. He couldn't take his eyes from the swelling beneath her gown. Very pregnant.

He pulled his eyes to her face. Terror stared back. *She should be worried; she made a fool of me. I ought to be enraged.*

Wonder, worry, and a surge of joy so great it threatened to upend him pushed all other emotions aside. He held his hands behind his back to still their shaking.

"Lily," he began, utterly at sea. Nothing in his experience prepared him for the most delicate negotiations he had ever conducted. He swallowed hard. "We need to talk."

She didn't respond; her anguished look didn't alter.

"Talk is needed," Sahin Pasha agreed. He pulled Lily's hand forward. She stumbled a step or two toward Richard.

"Sahin Pasha, may I have a moment alone with Miss Thornton?"

"One is never alone here," Sahin said sadly, "but I will remove myself from the room. Perhaps Sir Robert may join me." He raised a questioning eyebrow, but Robert Liston had already walked toward the door.

Sahin gave Lily's hand one more tug. "Talk, little one, and listen to this man. Be a sensible girl. You will be safe." He nodded at the eunuch who had followed Lily and now stood silent and disapproving from his place against the wall.

"Good grief, I'm not going to harm her!" Richard exclaimed. Sahin Pasha's guard remained.

"Ten minutes, my lord," Sahin said and departed.

Richard ran his hand across the back of his neck. Ten minutes? Where to start?

"Lily when—that is, I know when, but why didn't you tell me?" He thought rapidly. Five months? Six? More? His brain refused to calculate the time.

"You can't have her!" Lily burst out. She looked frantic.

"What are you talking about?"

"You can't take my baby."

"What do you take me for? Do you think I'm some kind of monster that would separate a mother from her child?"

"Isn't that what your lot does? Hide indiscretion away?" She sounded desperate. "I've done it for you. Leave me here and—"

"My son will not grow up in some heathen harem!"

"My daughter will be perfectly well with me, and these people are more compassionate and civilized than your London society."

"My society? You were comfortable enough in London six months ago." Dear God. She fainted at Georgiana's. She must have known even then.

She wouldn't look at him. He watched her wrap her arms protectively around her belly.

"Did he just move?" He couldn't breathe.

He did; my son moved. I saw it.

"She did," Lily looked up with a sad smile.

He walked close, fascinated, and grateful she didn't pull away. He put out a hand, and the guard pushed away from the wall.

Lily reassured the man with a simple gesture.

"May I touch?

She bit her lip. For a moment he felt certain she would deny him. She nodded instead.

He reached gingerly for the place he saw movement without taking his eyes off Lily's face, watching for signs she would change her mind. His hand came to rest on silk over a hard, smooth curve.

Too absorbed to think even of Lily, he froze in place. A flutter rewarded his attention and then another. Just before he would have pulled his hand back, a movement so strong he could see it vibrated against his fingers.

"A kick!" He looked up at her then to share his joy and saw only wariness. He jerked his hand back.

"Why Lily? Why didn't you come to me as you should?"

"As you ordered me to? I told you at Chadbourn Park I would manage myself whatever the consequences," she reminded him.

"Even if you didn't want marriage, I would have taken care of you."

"Pushed me into some cottage as far from London as you could manage—kept us there far from prying eyes? You will forgive me for choosing not to be your shameful secret. This is better. In a few years, I can return home a widow with child, and no one need gossip about the Marble Marquess."

Richard groped for words. What did the fool woman expect when she wouldn't marry him? "Lily, we would have managed something." He had no clue what.

"All I wanted from you was my father home. Papa could have helped, but all you had for me was delay after delay."

Fair enough. I failed you in that. I let Castlereagh and Foreign Office come first. It can't be helped now. None of it can.

"Why did you lie about it?" he asked. "You told me no further action needed."

"I didn't lie. No action was or is needed from you," she said, her defiant little chin raised.

"You led me to believe there was no baby."

"You needed to get on with your courtship," she said, red color blossoming on her neck. "How could I let you continue your absurd little dance of worry over me when all London knew you were to offer for Lady Sarah, and I knew I had no intention of taking your help."

A pained look slid over her face.

Idiot! "Are you well? Do you need to sit? Should I call for help?"

"Don't be ridiculous. Physically I'm fine," she said, smiling ruefully, "besides, when I get down on those cushions I have the devil's own time getting back up."

They shared a smile at the image she evoked, the first shared pleasure since she entered the room.

I could get lost in those eyes. I could spend my life laughing with this woman.

"Marry me, Lily." Badly done. He realized it immediately. His grace and poise had fled.

She pulled away immediately.

"Aren't you betrothed?"

"No. It never happened. The Duke of Lisle demanded my attendance. I sent him a polite refusal, and I left."

"Left?"

"I came to find you." A faint smile teased her lips. He loved to look at those lips.

"Marry me. You know we should." He touched the place where the baby lay briefly. "We must."

"I told you no. I will not be the ambitious little parvenu who trapped the great Marquess of Glenaire into marriage. I will not be shoved into some country backwater with my baby when you grow embarrassed by my 'less than desirable background.'"

Did I really say that? His own words hung in the air between them.

"Is this better?" he shouted. The guard moved a fraction. "And Mountview is not some backwater," he mumbled.

"So you did plan to send me to the country!"

"I didn't say that. Don't twist my words."

"To answer your question, yes. This is better. Don't let the walls fool you. Here I have respect and care. Here I'm close to the center of power and politics. Here I have voice."

Lily could waltz through the highest circles in Europe, a magnificent diplomatic hostess.

"Our baby deserves a father. He deserves to know me." He caught her frantic glance around at the impassive eunuch; he thought for a moment she looked guilty. She leaned in close.

"I am a widow," she said. He looked startled. She dropped her voice very low. "Everyone here believes I am a widow."

"You lied to the Valide Sultan?" He whispered back. She bit her lip and shook her head. Her eyes pleaded with him to let it go. He looked up at the guard.

"We ought to marry. You know that. You owe it to your child," he said more loudly.

"Your offer is very kind, my lord, but I respectfully decline," she replied through clenched teeth. She signaled to the guard, said "I take my leave now," and turned to go.

The door opened on silent hinges, and a beaming Sahin Pasha entered. "All is well?" he asked.

"Certainly, honored uncle. The marquess is ready to leave."

"We'll talk again, Lily," Richard said to her retreating back. "We are not finished."

"Ask your spy," Richard roared. The two men faced each other in the same room Lily had just left. Robert Liston stood quiet but observant to one side.

"Ahmet is Lily's protector. He is no spy. His presence was to lend what you English call propriety."

"You could have warned me."

Sahin put on a mask of innocence. "About the guard?"

"The baby, as you well know," Richard replied through clenched teeth.

"You did not know? I expected the English services to have better care for their citizens." Sahin's mocking smile lasted a few more moments.

"This has nothing to do with the government."

Sahin relaxed, and a look of what might have been genuine concern took the place of mockery.

I'm never sure what this damned man thinks.

"Miss Thornton's baby is yours then?"

He jerked his head in a nod and flashed a guilty glance at Robert Liston. His majesty's representative in Constantinople looked grim.

"You will have wanted to do the honorable thing?"

"Of course, damn you. I offered for her immediately and again in London and three times just now. She won't have me."

"Foolish chit," Liston declared.

Sahin shook his head. "Who can fathom the minds of women? Lily Thornton should have more sense than to turn down a future duke."

"She doesn't care about that. She claims she wants a life of politics and diplomacy. What does she think I do? I can give her all that."

"Which she knows very well."

"She may have gotten the impression I look down on her background," Richard mumbled.

"Ah. Do you?" Sahin looked over at Liston. To the man's credit, his face had lost its mockery.

"No! Some might."

"Your most elevated mother?"

"And those who fawn on her. Lily's family isn't from the highest circles, but adequate."

"Adequate?" Sahin laughed. "How that must reassure her!"

"She more than makes up for it in intelligence and talent needed in a diplomat's wife."

Sahin nodded. "That she does. Here we value merit. It is possible to rise far in the Sublime Porte on talent alone."

"Then what does the woman want? She has to be made to see reason."

"It is my experience that women who are nesting rarely concern themselves with grand affairs. Reason, I fear, is not what she seeks."

"What else then? She isn't a fool, but she has acted like one ever since—"

"Since my men borrowed your horses and left you at a country inn? We returned them to the earl, by the way."

"Yes, then. What does she want?"

"You will have to reason that out for yourself, my dear marquess. For now she wishes to stay here."

Richard glared at Sahin. *Not if I can help it. I can bring the power of England to bear. I can—*

"Such a fierce look. I suggest you return to your embassy with your reasonable friend Sir Robert and allow our Zambak time to think."

"Zambak?"

"Our word for Lily. One warning, my lord," Sahin said. "Miss Thornton's position here is at the will of my aunt. The Valide Sultan has conceded a deception that would reflect poorly on her if it were to be known."

Richard shrugged.

"Take me seriously, please," Sahin insisted. "Court the widow Thornton—as well you should—but do not demand the return of an unmarried Englishwoman. We will not allow it." His implacable look gave teeth to what was without question a threat.

Richard leaned into his face. "Make no mistake. I'll do whatever it takes to bring Lily home. She belongs with me."

Chapter Twenty-Six

The bathhouse echoed with every move Lily took. The high ceilings and ornate tiled walls normally rang with the happy voices of women starting their day. Lily came late the day after her confrontation with Richard, late and without pleasure. She bathed alone with a single attendant seeing to her needs.

"Does the lady wish rosemary oil?" the little bath attendant asked in an effort to elicit a response from Lily when she rose from the warm water.

Lily shrugged. A sleepless night punctuated with bouts of tears left her wrung out. "Please, yes," she murmured more out of concern for the girl than because she cared.

I deserved his anger, she repeated to herself for the hundredth time.

The attendant began helping her dress. This morning Lily didn't notice the feeling of silk sliding on skin, the sensation she normally loved.

He ought to have raged at me, but he didn't. Cool, calm, and in control. That's the Marble Marquess.

Richards's immovable self-control made her irrationally irritable. Just once I'd like to see him lose control. Just once. Lily hoped she wouldn't be on the receiving end if that ever happened.

She thought of the look on his face when he recognized her pregnancy, the wonder in his eyes when he felt the baby move. *Just because he stays in control doesn't mean he doesn't care.*

The attendant bowed out. Lily, alone in the warm confines of the bathhouse, lingered. Memories of Richard's friends and family ran circuits in her mind as they had all night: Richard teasing with Chadbourn and Catherine, Richard's affection for the Mallets in defiance of his parents, Richard minimizing his mother's sharp unkindness to wallflowers at the ball. Above all, she kept coming back to Richard in the foyer of Aunt Marianne's house, discreetly helping his friend Baron Ross financially.

He cares for them all. He takes care of those he loves; he—

Grief stabbed Lily to the heart. *I've been an idiot. He takes care of those he loves.* She fought the storm of tears that threatened to overcome her and rose to leave.

She reached the anteroom by the outside door when a group of older women entered, the Valide Sultan and her closest attendants. Lily opened her mouth to give a proper greeting, but anguish froze it in her throat.

The Valide Sultan gestured the other women on and put out her arms to Lily. The attendants passed by with curious glances and respectful silence. Lily sank into the older woman's arms and began to sob.

"One has worries for you, Zambak. Your tears in the night did not go unnoticed."

"I'm sorry," Lily sniffed, struggling for control. "I didn't know anyone heard."

"You should know by now most things come to my ears eventually." The woman smiled down at her. "Better?"

Lily nodded.

"Most but not everything. Was that English lord unkind to you, Zambak? I would not have permitted the meeting if I thought you would be harmed."

"No! He had reason to be angry with me, but he was not." Tears threatened again. "He had a shock, seeing me like this and—" Lily swallowed hard, twice.

"I've been an idiot!" she exclaimed.

"Hardly that, Zambak, but perhaps you've behaved foolishly, no?" The older woman gently touched Lily's belly.

"I told him I would not marry him. I rejected him in insulting terms."

"You rejected this wealthy, powerful man's offer of marriage?"

"Three times," Lily mumbled.

"Foolish behavior indeed, almost as foolish as conceiving this child in the first place. It is his child?"

Lily nodded.

"He is honor bound."

"He believes so."

"And you wish protestations of love. You are as silly as those girls you teach, Zambak. He honored you three times and you insulted him. I do not think he will ask again."

Tears leaked from Lily's eyes in spite of her best efforts. "I must talk with him."

Valide Sultan's shrewd eyes hardened. "You wish us to arrange another such meeting? It can be done, but to what purpose?"

Lily clamped her jaw tight. What purpose indeed?

"Men do not like to be commanded," her companion said.

"No." Lily's laugh held little amusement. "He would not want to be commanded."

"What then, Zambak? What is it you wish?"

I could write. I could tell him I changed my mind. I could apologize. I could—

"I think I must go to him," Lily said. "Nothing less than an apology and surrender will do."

The Valide Sultan took Lily's shoulders in her hands.

"If you go, you cannot come back," she said.

Lily didn't respond right away.

"You've led your marquess in a complicated dance. You will not do the same to us." The woman's imperial power, firm and unyielding, radiated from her.

"I understand, Highness. Your great kindness will rest in my heart forever. I will not abuse it," Lily said.

The old woman searched Lily's face as if looking for any weakness. "Sahin has told you of dangers."

"Yes. I'll be safe at the British embassy."

"I can see that you are guarded that far, but Zambak, you must be certain."

"I am."

As certain as I can be.

THE SUN began its descent to the horizon behind the towers of Hagia Sophia when Lily, swathed in veils, stepped onto the boat that would take her across the Golden Horn. The fabled waterway that divided Stamboul, the Muslim quarter and seat of power, from Petra and the foreign quarter of Constantinople, glowed orange in its light.

Ahmet stepped in front of her, inspecting the quay and the crowd beyond. Satisfied, he helped her to shore.

"Thank you," Lily smiled, even though he could not see her face beneath its covering.

"Are you sure of this, Zambak?" he asked without looking at her. His eyes, she noted, scanned the crowd continually. He had approved of her decision to meet Richard but not this trip to the embassy.

"As sure as we can be." She also scanned the quay. At another time, without Volkov's threats, she might have found this place exhilarating. Not this time. She shivered. Sahin warned her. Even if Volkov were not loose, this place is not safe for a woman alone.

Another bodyguard, a man she didn't recognize, followed her to shore. He clambered up stone steps behind her. Both men were tall, towering above the crowds. Both looked strong. Both wore ornate swords in their belts. Lily suspected other less decorative and perhaps more deadly weapons were hidden on their person.

Don't be a ninny, Lily. These men will protect you. If you fear anything, it should be Richard's reaction to your about-face. What if he sends you away? You can't go back.

The crowd alone would have been difficult to manage in her condition. In another time, without child, she might have enjoyed the flow of humanity and cacophony of languages. This time, she pulled her arms around herself protectively, fearing she might be jostled. In the face of her two companions, however, the crowd parted before them.

They made their way past sellers of figs and silver, vendors of fruits and sandalwood. In that other time, without her concerns about Richard's reaction hanging over her, she might have lingered. This time, she had to be careful not to get lost in thought.

Ahmet reached a narrow passage paved in worn cobbles that opened next to a booth of rug sellers. Lily followed him into the shadows between two stone walls. The rear guard had just followed in behind her when it happened.

Lily heard a grunt behind her and turned to see her keeper on the ground, blood spilling over cobblestones from the gaping incision across his neck. When she spun to run for Ahmet, unseen hands pulled at her veils. She twisted loose but found herself trapped between the unseen danger behind and shadowy figures swarming the man in front of her. He fought like a madman but looked about to fall.

Lily clutched her middle and began to pray.

Chapter Twenty-Seven

Liston's secretary shot Richard a cautious glance and made himself scarce.

When they had returned from Richard's disastrous meeting with Lily the previous night, the ambassador had suggested, politely, that they avoid "disturbing" Sahin Pasha or other officials for a few days. He hinted that Richard might calm himself first. "Delicate diplomacy, Glenaire, delicate is called for." Richard had raged; the ambassador had reasoned. This afternoon, Liston merely disappeared.

The first time Richard asked to see Liston, the man's secretary cheerfully refused him. The second time he tugged at his elaborate cravat and fidgeted nervously in his chair. The third time the full wrath of a frustrated marquess came down on the man's thinning hair. His swift departure prevented a fourth.

You know better than to berate a servant. It isn't his fault Liston made himself unavailable all morning. Damn Liston anyway.

Liston wouldn't dare forbid the Marquess of Glenaire, son and heir of the Duke of Sudbury and Castlereagh's own protégé, from appearing at the palace unannounced and alone, but he had come damned close, and now he avoided Richard completely.

The image of Lily pregnant with his child haunted his dreams and bedeviled his day. She's locked in the damned Seraglio and won't talk to me—not that talk has gotten me anywhere so far. His urge to act, frustrated at every turn, refused to die. It roiled in his gut and drove him to pace like a madman.

Richard prowled the embassy, frightening the maids and growling at footmen. Only the boy who cleaned the steps found him amusing.

"Sunny day, Lord English," the boy said. "Good day for walk."

I haven't slept, Lily refuses to see reason, and Liston refuses to petition Sahin Pasha. Why should I care about the day?

He spun on his heels, went back in, and slammed the door. In the reverberating sound of the slamming door, a second thought struck him.

Why not a walk—to the wharf perhaps? What harm would it do to leave a calling card for Sahin Pasha?

Moments later, hat on head and cane in hand, he went back out the door. The cane, with its cleverly concealed sword, normally sat in Liston's private office. He took it without qualms. It serves him right for avoiding me all afternoon.

"Best not get lost," the boy told him when he ran down the steps. "I can show you where you want to go. I know everything."

Richard ignored him. He gripped the cane, glad for its support. *I'm not a total fool.*

"Getting late, Lord English! Best not go far," the boy shouted after him.

After the second wrong turn, he wished he'd taken the boy for a guide. After a third, he thought he had his bearings, but light faded and he dared not retrace his steps through the maze of streets. He peered downhill through a narrow passage to see golden light at the far end. The docks were all downhill. From there he could pay someone to take him back to the embassy. *What a fool's errand!*

He gripped the sword cane tightly and started down the narrow passage. After he passed one heavy wooden door and then another, he reached the halfway point. Below him, a tall turbaned figure turned into the passage, briefly blocking the light. Richard could see a small person covered with veils behind him followed closely by another tall man.

A wealthy woman and her guards, he supposed. Those bruisers won't look kindly on a foreigner blocking her way.

Caught in the narrow passage, he would have to go back or push himself against the wall. Before he could formulate a response, the farthest man fell like a rock, a door opened in front of the trio, and a swarm of dark figures spewed out.

Richard could see the taller guard under attack from at least three men; the woman needed help. He ran toward the attack when hands reached out to grab her. Sprinting downhill, he saw her twist to escape and run toward her first guard. Her veils fell away.

Lily! What on earth?

Richard ran faster; icy fear and blood red rage drove him downhill into Lily's attackers. The remaining bodyguard blocked his way. The man wrestled with three of them, knife slashing, arms straining. Richard's sword found one attacker, but another took his place. They seemed to multiply in the dark.

Brief snatches of Lily appeared behind the melee. He could see flowing ribbons of bright green silk ripple and jerk. He struggled to focus on the attackers. He felled one attacker with an uppercut that would make Jackson proud, but another blocked him.

Concentrate. You're no good to her dead.

Lily's screams tore at him, and he fought like an animal. The guard went down at last, a dagger in his ribs. Over his body Richard saw a hood go over Lily's head, muffling her screams. He pulled his attention back a moment too late. Searing pain exploded in his head, and he fell forward into darkness.

The voice Richard longed to hear all day came to him in the dark. It must be a dream.

A moment later hands attached to the dream began prodding him in places that hurt like the devil. "Richard! Damn it, wake up."

Lily?

"Did you have me kidnapped? Those men could have injured me, you insane man."

Don't be an idiot. How could Lily believe that, even in a nightmare?

Cool hands pushed his hair from his brow. *Not my head; it hurts like hell itself.*

"Please wake up. Don't die on me. Please don't die and leave me alone with these men."

Men—Lily! The shot of memory sent him bolt upright. The pain in his head put him back down with a groan. His eyes flickered open and blinked twice to clear.

Lily's face, deep in shadow, came close, concern marring it. "Not so fast," she said. "I think they hit you very hard."

"They nearly took my head off," he groaned.

"I was afraid you wouldn't waken," she said, her voice sounded wet with tears.

"I have a hard head," he reassured her. Memory flickered. "I thought I heard you a moment ago. Did you really accuse me of having you kidnapped?"

"Maybe." She sounded guilty. "But that wouldn't make sense. You wouldn't harm the baby. I know you wouldn't."

"Is he—" He tried to rise again, but she pushed him back down.

"She's fine. I'm fine, for now at least."

"I would never hurt you either, Lily."

Did she just sniff?

"I thought you had left us."

"I'm here," he said, looking around. He could see little in deepening darkness. "Where ever 'here' is. Is there no light, or are my eyes failing?"

"No windows, and I fear night has fallen."

He could see her in outline, one shadow darker than the rest of the room.

"Do you have any idea where we are?"

She shook her head. "They hooded me. They pulled off the hood and pushed me in the door before I got a good look. We can't have gone far from the quay because two of them carried me here."

"From the feel of my back, I was dragged."

"Possibly. A few moments after they left me here, they opened the door and dropped you on the floor."

Richard felt along his sides. "Stone floor. No wonder I'm cold. Help me to sit."

He cried out in pain when Lily put an arm under his shoulders, but he pushed himself forward. She helped him feel his way to the wall. He sagged against it and pulled her close with one arm, savoring her warmth.

"No furniture?"

"Nothing. An empty room. I'm not even sure it is a room exactly." She put one arm around his waist and lay her head against his shoulder. He could feel the swell of the growing child by his side. He forced himself not to shudder. Don't give in to fear now. It won't help her.

"Tell me what you saw. Tell me what you heard." He fought back waves of pain and focused his mind on what mattered. Lily. Danger. The baby. Our baby.

"I heard nothing until the attack," she said. He heard her gulp. When she spoke again, her voice sounded thick. "I turned on a sound and saw the guard—that poor man—they cut his throat. My fault. I insisted on coming even though Sahin warned me."

"Hush, hush." Time for recrimination later. "What next?"

"I tried to run, but they grabbed at me from behind, and more of them attacked—" She swallowed convulsively. "Oh God! They killed Ahmet. He was my friend."

He could hear rising panic from the memories she voiced.

"Concentrate on details." He tightened his arm around her.

"Attackers wore black, but you must know that. I saw you. You ran down the passage like a madman."

Like a fool right into their hands. If he had stopped to think he might have been able to—what? He didn't know. "It was not my finest hour," he said.

"You were magnificent."

Her praise gave him courage. *I have to get Lily out of here.*

"I don't feel magnificent. What else do you remember? Did you hear their voices?"

"Not well. The hood muffled sound. Some Turkish and something else—Arabic perhaps. I heard an odd word or two of Russian, 'woman' and 'money.'"

"Volkov."

"Perhaps. They didn't talk to me. They just put me here. I called for help. I called for light. I called to demand their names. I heard nothing until they brought you in."

"What did you see when the door opened?"

"Not much. This space is tiny. I think it is a storage closet."

No room. No weapons. No light. Richard let out a groan of frustration. No strength either. He cursed loudly.

The door swung open.

"Such language in front of a lady!" A disembodied voice mocked him in heavily accented English. Light from a lantern in the hands of the man in the doorway blinded Richard.

"The lady and the marquess also. What a delightful, unexpected bonus."

Chapter Twenty-Eight

Volkov stepped into the room and lowered the lantern. Lily saw his face illuminated from below, a leering mask of pure evil. When she began to shake, Richard's arm tightened on her shoulder, and she moved closer.

Other figures huddled in the doorway. She could just make out two or three faces, avid and alive with curiosity.

"What a disgusting little family tableau," Volkov sneered. "You've disappointed me, Lilias."

Disappointed?

"I had so looked forward to renewing our intimate acquaintance." He tilted his head as if considering her. Lily gagged back her rising gorge. "I thought if you pleased me particularly well we might postpone your punishment."

Richard lunged forward. A brutal kick to his shoulder pushed him back against Lily.

"Do control the marquess, Lilias. My 'assistants' aren't particularly careful, and I would much prefer that he die slowly."

"You want me, Konstantin, not Glenaire. Let him go."

"Touching. I presume he is responsible for your interesting condition? He really ought to pay for that. What will your dear Papa think of all this? Perhaps I should act in his stead since he is nowhere to be found." He put a finger to his lips as if considering something.

"I owe him for your papa's disappearance also, don't I? My men tracked him to Copenhagen but lost him. Did you know that?"

Papa, what did you do? Any relief that Volkov had failed to find her father faded under his current threat.

"This marquess of yours also made life difficult in London." He kicked Richard's ribs. "Yes, I owe this one quite a bit."

"The question is what to do with you? I discovered your destination by sheer luck from an encounter on Malta. I paid dearly to be told when you left the Seraglio." He laughed, an ugly miserable laugh. "Not enough perhaps. I had not counted on finding you with another man's bastard. I truly hate taking someone else's leavings."

Lily had no warning when he yanked her arm with his free hand and pulled her up.

"No!" she screamed.

Richard fell sideways. She could see him try to rise from the corner of her eye. Volkov yanked her forward with his left hand. The lantern in his right swung ominously. The thought of her flowing veils catching fire caused her to yank instinctively on Volkov's hand. She batted at the lantern with her free hand and knocked it against Volkov.

"Damned whore, you'll pay for this!" Volkov shouted when fire singed his jacket. He dropped Lily and the lantern, plunging them into darkness. Lily scooted back into the farthest corner she could find.

In the light of a flickering torch hastily brought up to the entrance by one of Volkov's minions, she saw Volkov swing around to her with murder in his eyes and step forward. Behind him, Richard rose to his knees and staggered upright.

A tall man dressed, unlike his fellows, in a short jacket and loose trousers shouted from the door at Volkov who ignored him and kept coming toward Lily. The man snapped his fingers. Someone grabbed Volkov's shoulder and pulled him back. They shouted in a stream of Turkish, Russian, and other languages. Richard seized the opportunity to move in front of Lily.

"That man told Volkov we're too valuable to damage," Lily whispered in his ear. "He spoke Russian, if poorly."

Two of the men in black subdued Volkov, one holding either arm. They joined the argument with Volkov and then began to argue among themselves.

"It isn't quite Arabic or Turkish either. I think I hear Berber, at least when they speak between one another," she told him. She felt him stiffen.

Volkov ordered them to let him go. "It is none of your business who these people are. They belong to me," he shouted. They spat in his face.

"They're saying he failed to pay them!" Lily exclaimed. Astonishment momentarily banished fear.

The tall man at the door crowded into their prison carrying a torch. He flicked a brief glance at Lily and Richard, but he saved his contempt for Volkov.

"He's listing unpaid bills," she said thickly. She clung to Richard's back.

"Bills for?"

"Murder, beatings, across Greece. Hazard pay for coming into Constantinople itself, I think. He says they grow weary and will take the prize for payment." Lily felt a surge of hope. "What prize?"

"Us. We're the prize." Richard cursed quietly.

Her hope faded. "Who are these people?"

"Corsairs, most likely."

Hope died. Lily's heart stuttered. "Corsairs?"

"Barbary Pirates."

A SWIFT blow from the flat of a scimitar quieted Volkov. He hung limp and unconscious between his two captors. Richard spared him no pity. The corsairs tossed the Russian to the floor and began to strip him systematically until he lay naked and unmoving on the cold stone floor.

The tall man with the torch shone his light on Richard and

shoved him sideways to have a better look at Lily. He reached over to lift a lock of her hair where it hung in disarray on her shoulder.

"Don't touch her." Richard shouted. He extended a hand to stop the man and got a slap across the face for his trouble. The blow snapped his head back and threw him into the wall.

The man moved his light closer to Lily; he examined her face and hair with meticulous care. He spoke to her in Russian. She answered in Turkish.

"What did he say?" Richard asked through swollen lips.

"Not Turkish," Lily answered without taking her eyes from their captor. "I assured him I am not."

"English," the man said, his speech heavily accented but perfectly clear. "Both?"

In the dim light, Richard could see her pulse pound in her neck, but she stood tall and did not look away from the man.

"Both of us, yes," Lily told the man. Her courage strengthened Richard's.

Behind their tormentor, the two black-clad guards finished trussing Volkov hand and foot. One hefted his purse and laughed. Gold flashed in the hand of other man, the bigger of the two. The bigger man had thrown back the mask that covered his face in the passageway. Richard could see the deep scar that marked the right side of his face from brow to chin and the smaller scar across his lips that gave him a perpetual sneer.

Scarface stuffed the gold ring in his robes and strode over to where Richard and Lily stood. He shot Richard a contemptuous look, grabbed Lily by the hair, and pulled out a curved dagger.

"Don't touch her," Richard shouted helplessly just before a blow to his midsection from the third man crumpled him to the floor. The two captors argued over Lily in a language he didn't understand while the third relieved him of his jacket and began to finger it as if assessing its value.

He struggled to his knees and looked up into Lily's eyes, eyes wide with terror. When he tried to stumble forward, the man who had removed his jacket, who appeared to be the younger of the three, twisted his arm up above his shoulder.

"Lily," Richard called through a haze of pain, "what are they saying?"

Her answering voice wavered, the sound coming thin and reedy. "The one with scars says a pregnant woman is worth nothing and I will slow them. He wants to—"

A loud scream from Volkov cut her off. He rolled and struggled against his bonds, unleashing a torrent of invective, drawing all eyes to him.

The older man, the one Richard began to pray was the leader, shouted at him in Russian. Volkov shouted back. All three laughed, and the oldest spat some words.

"What are they saying?" Richard demanded, gasping for breath.

"Volkov called them filthy names and demanded that they follow his orders. This man called him 'yazychnik' and ordered him to be silent or—"

"Or what?"

"Or they will slit his throat."

Volkov opened his mouth as if to speak again, but only a gurgling sound came out. Scarface picked up Volkov's torn shirt, sliced it with his dagger in one swoop, and gagged him with it.

"Yazychnik sounds Russian." Richard whispered. "What does it mean?"

"Infidel," she answered on a breath.

As if at her word, Scarface turned on his heel, but before he could approach Lily again, the older man barked an order, and they began to strip Richard as they had Volkov. Scarface pulled his right hand so hard he thought his arm might leave its socket. He began to pull at Richard's signet ring.

Richard pulled back and started to object, but Scarface took his dagger and threatened to cut off the finger with the ring. Richard forced himself to relax. His grandfather's ring with its intaglio coat of arms carved on a perfect sapphire disappeared into Scarface's robes.

The younger man began to bind Richard's hands. Scarface moved toward Lily, baring his teeth and spitting one word in her face. "Kafir."

"Don't touch her, you dog!" Richard roared, lunging forward only to be yanked back. He shouted himself hoarse; they ignored him. He cursed Volkov for the animal he was. He fought to break loose from his bonds until pain shot through his head and darkness overcame him.

Lily. Oh God, Lily.

Chapter Twenty-Nine

Hard wood cut into Richard's back when he came to. He could not feel his hands, bound as they were behind some sort of post. He had no idea where he was or how long he had been there. His keepers had left him tied and gagged in a dim space that smelled of fish and bilge water. They had left his small-clothes, but they were little protection from the cold.

Gratitude for the looseness of his gag didn't outweigh his other discomforts. No pain came close to fear for Lily. What did they do to her?

Frantic attempts to pull at his bindings resulted only in greater shoulder pain and a banged head.

Where the hell am I and how long have I been here? An hour? Four perhaps? Lily, dear God where are you?

Something soft and clawed ran over his lap and scuffled to the left. *I have company in this hell, four footed, and cunning.* He fought back nausea, bent his knees, and slid his feet close to his body. *How long before they gnaw at my toes?*

An inhuman moan emanated from the gloom to the left. No rat that. Richard stared into the shadows, allowing his eyes to adjust. Not so inhuman. Black eyes glared back at him; Volkov slumped against a similar post ten feet away, face bloodied and swollen. His eyes glowed, though. Hatred glowed in those eyes like red coals. While Richard watched, blood dripped down Volkov's face, across his bare chest and onto the rough loin cloth that was his only clothing. Do rats smell blood? I hope he keeps them busy so they don't come for me.

He knew from the bobbing—and the horrific smell—that they had been carried to a ship. He sensed movement; they were under sail. The ship moved slowly which meant they had not yet reached the open sea. By now they may have cleared the city and crossed the Sea of Marmia that lay below Constantinople. He suspected they were passing through the Dardenelles to the Mediterranean. Escape from a ship should be easy in that narrow passage. Hadn't Byron famously swum across?

He shook with bitter laughter. Escape would be easy? If he managed to undo his bonds, find Lily, and get to the deck without being captured, he still had the problem of swimming to shore with a pregnant woman in tow.

How long before Liston or Sahin Pasha figure out what happened?

Rescue seemed almost as unlikely as escape. Even if the Ottomans knew to follow or cared to, the ship, if it was a Barbary corsair, would be fast.

Richard's only satisfaction lay in the sight of the Russian beaten, bloody, and bound. *At least Volkov couldn't do further harm.*

Richard couldn't measure the time that passed before he felt the ship gain speed. Volkov had slumped, asleep or unconscious, and Richard himself had almost nodded off when footsteps on the stairs to the hold put him on alert. The man who entered no longer wore black, but his scarred face made Richard's guts churn.

Dressed in loose brown trouser and wide-sleeved shirt, Scarface wore the long tunic characteristic of North Africa. He had a lethal-looking curved sword in a red sash and his dagger in his hand, the weapon Richard last saw pointed at Lily.

If this animal harmed Lily, he will pay; I will see to it.

He cut Richard's bonds and aimed the knife at his neck. "You come now," he said in passible English.

Richard pulled out the gag; his tongue and throat felt like old leather. Temptation to attack the man surged. One thought kept it in check. *Not until you find Lily.* Richard did as he was told. He crawled up the stairs and limped across the deck. Wind whipped at his bared skin.

They had reached the open Mediterranean and picked up speed. He noted they sailed on a small frigate or perhaps a corvette, probably captured from the Portuguese or the Americans twenty or more years ago. Small but impressive. *At least it isn't a galley.*

His keeper prodded him forward toward the captain's cabin situated aft. The cabin, stripped of decoration and hard used, had the sparest of furnishings.

"Welcome, English," a deeper voice said. The speaker sat at the broad table built into the deck, the captain's desk with its myriad map drawers. Broken handles and gashed wood spoke to this one's long life. Richard recognized him as the leader of their captors. The man clearly captained this ship. Richard lunged toward him; the point of a sword stopped him.

"Where is Lily?" he demanded, his voice a harsh squawk. "Where is my wife?"

"Wife?" the man arched a dark brow. "Your woman dresses for the Sultan's Seraglio and you call her wife?"

Richard opened his mouth to speak again, but this time the words grated in his throat and died there.

The captain gestured, and Richard's keeper handed him a water skin. He swallowed deep and choked. Rum! Both pirates laughed.

"I am Rais Hamidou. You have heard of me?" the captain spoke in impeccable English. Rais. Richard recognized that word. Leader. Chief. Captain.

"Rais Hamidou is dead. Steven Decatur killed him at Cape Gata."

A roar of laughter greeted this pronouncement. Richard realized three or four more pirates had crowded into the cabin to watch this exchange. He inclined his head and raked his memory; the image of his desk with its dozens of reports on Mediterranean shipping didn't help much. Legends clung to the name Hamidou, but they obscured the question of whether the deeds were true or those of any one man.

Perhaps a Hamidou rises from the ashes like a Phoenix when one is killed.

"I am acquainted with the name," Richard said.

He took a slower swallow of rum to soothe his throat and survey the room.

"Where is my wife?" he repeated with as much diplomatic aplomb as he could muster in his current state.

"Secured below."

Relief swept through Richard. *Lily is alive.*

"She is an innocent."

"An innocent?" Hamidou smirked.

"She is my wife," Richard countered; his eyes dared the man to disbelieve. "I demand to see her."

Shrewd eyes considered Richard's defiance. Hamidou flicked a gesture, and one of the men bolted out the door.

"She is not untouched," Hamidou said. "That will impact her value to some in the slave market in Tunis, but her fiery hair and her obvious fertility may prove an asset. The hair will certainly please. We shall see."

The thought poleaxed Richard.

"Volkov owed us much," Hamidou went on. "We will recoup our losses."

These men intended Lily for the slave markets. Knowing felt far worse than guessing. The trade flourished for centuries. The American invasion of Tripoli and Exmouth's bombardment of Algiers had contained the trade but never stamped it out.

Before Richard could respond, the door opened and Hamidou's man returned. He pulled Lily behind him, her hands bound. The man pulled her with a rope like a dog. Frightened green eyes bore into his over a silken gag. Scarface's sword kept Richard in place.

"She should bring much, this one, with or without the baby. The child is yours?" Hamidou asked.

"Yes," Richard rasped. He racked his brain for an argument the man would accept. Only one would work. "Whatever you think she's worth, I can pay you more."

"You?" the man roared with laughter, looking Richard in his ragged smalls and bruises.

"I am Richard Hayden," he rose up and stiffened his aching spine. Hamidou raised an eyebrow. Unimpressed. "The Marquess of Glenaire." More interest. "Heir to the Duke of Sudbury." *I have his attention.* "Whatever you think she is worth, my government will pay more." He prayed that was true. If Castlereagh balked and his father wouldn't, Chadbourn would see it done.

"Interesting, but not certain," Hamidou answered. "I know the traders in Tunis and Algiers. I don't know you."

But you've heard of me. I'd swear to it.

"What do you have to lose by waiting?" He forced his eyes to stay on Hamidou and not Lily.

The man appeared to ponder his words. "Perhaps I will wait with the woman and sell you. You are worth almost as much as the woman, my lord Glenaire, though not, I think, as much as Volkov owes us. The galleys are hungry for strong backs. Your strength is not first rate, but it will improve over time, and it will amuse them to have 'my lord' to pull their oars."

He felt sick. *If I'm lost in the galleys, it will take years to find me. What will happen to Lily and the baby then?*

"If I wait," Hamidou mused, "she will deliver. If her baby lives, I can sell him also."

A wail, wrung from the depths, escaped Lily's gagged mouth.

Hamidou rubbed his chin and ignored Lily's moan of protest. "What shall I do with you?"

The pirate looked amused. *Does he really have to consider it or is he torturing me?* Richard had nothing else to say, nothing else to offer. He had played his last card.

"I will consider your proposal," the man said at last. "In meantime, you will be fed as will your ... Wife, did you say? We must care for our merchandise. Volkov owed us much. You will make up for it and more, one way or another."

~

Rough hands shoved Lily back into the wooden closet that had been her cell for hours. They removed neither bond nor gag.

Raucous laughter accompanied their forced march from the captain's quarters. Hamidou's quarters. Richard had called him Hamidou, the beast who would sell her baby. She gagged as her rising gorge threatened to choke her.

Two of the captors, who stunk of bilge and unwashed bodies, shoved Richard into the closet to lie in a heap at her feet. Her heart leapt. *Do they mean to leave us together?* The men grinned like fools from the doorway.

Richard struggled to his knees. One pushed him back down when he tried to rise. They pantomimed a mockery of obeisance. Lily forced her rattled mind to clear. She called on her smattering of Arabic and knowledge of Turkish, but she couldn't make all out all of their words. She understood "English lord" at least. She could do nothing to help, bound as she was.

The men tired of their game at last when a third man appeared with what looked like a pile of rags. They tossed it at Richard, slammed the door, and shot the bolt to lock it. Behind the door, she heard muffled words that sounded like "robes for a king."

Richard stumbled up and yanked off her gag. He kissed her hard and fast. She pulled her head away and lifted her bound hands to his face.

"Untie me you blasted man, this is no time for dalliance." He began to work at the knots, but leaned in and stole another kiss.

"What the devil did you mean telling that beast I'm your wife?" she sputtered. "Who gave you the right?"

He looked up from working at her fastenings. "I thought it might help keep you safe," he said. He struggled with swollen hands to untie the knots. "They frown on unmarried pregnancy."

"You have no business ordering my life," she said. "I'm not yours to—" *Yours to bully. Yours to control.* She remembered Hamidou and the sword he held to her heart. "Oh God, Richard, the baby!"

"Don't be an idiot. We need every scrap of protection we can find. At least they put us together. It will be true soon enough."

The ropes came free before she could summon an argument. When he pulled her into his arms, she no longer wanted to argue.

He kissed her long, his mouth gently tugging on hers. Her arms went around his neck to pull him closer while she savored the warmth of his naked chest. She slid one hand down his back. When she felt scratches, he winced but did not relax his hold on her. She lowered her hand to the soft cotton of his smalls and held on to his buttocks. When she broke their frantic kiss and moved her mouth across his neck and collarbone, he laid his face against the top of her head and breathed deeply.

"I thought you were dead," he murmured.

She looked up, startled. "I feared for you, too," she whispered through a throat thick with unshed tears.

The shadow of a grin flitted across his face. "Perhaps my lie had one benefit. At least they put us together."

He looked around. Their cell had nothing but rough wooden walls and a foul-smelling bucket, for relieving themselves he presumed. "Not exactly the Brighton Pavilion, but better than the hold."

"Better?" *How could this hole be better?*

"No warmer though," he said. Lily felt him begin to shiver spasmodically.

"Maybe this will help." Lily picked up the pile of rags and shook it out to find it was a tunic of some sort, like the garment a laborer or nomad might wear. It looked as if it had once been blue but had faded to dirty gray. It smelled vaguely of animal, showed patches worn thin with wear, and sported ragged tears across the hem. She held it out to him.

His look of distaste might have amused her under other circumstances.

"Your choice is this or parading in front of those men in your smalls," she said tartly. She looked fully at his state of undress, which she had ignored in her terror in front of Hamidou, and felt her face grow hot. "They treated you horribly."

"They weren't gentle," Richard said, pulling the offensive garment over his head. "But I fared better than Volkov." He winced when it slid down his back.

"Volkov? Is he alive?"

"Barely. They beat him badly. He's tied up in the hold in his own filth without so much as the dignity of his smallclothes."

"I can't feel pity," Lily said, but she looked as if she regretted that. "Let me look at your back."

"Not now, love. I will keep."

Did he really call me love? In her heart she knew it to be a figure of speech, but an unusual one for the Marquess of Glenaire.

"You don't need to fuss over some scratches," he went on. "We are together and will be fed—or so Hamidou promised. Let that be enough for now."

Hamidou! In spite of her best efforts, Lily crumpled. "He threatened to sell my baby!" She grabbed the front of his robe and wailed, "You have to protect her. Pay him whatever he asks. Tell him he can sell me, but protect our baby."

"Don't even think about making such an offer!" he shouted and quickly lowered his voice. "I won't have it."

"You don't order my life," she sobbed. "I will do whatever I have to."

Richard took both her hands in his. "Hush, Love. Hamidou is no fool. He knows exactly who I am. Negotiation may be touchy, but I can persuade him to let you and the baby go. I'm certain of it."

"Negotiation?"

"He'll want to haggle, once he's done terrifying us, but yes. I've been worthless so far on this adventure, but negotiating with hostile parties is one skill I can use to protect you." He held on to her hands; bitterness gave his words a hard edge.

"You are not worthless," Lily said.

"Am I not? My wife and baby are locked in a Barbary cell, a pirate has terrified you so badly you're willing to die for your child, and I did nothing to prevent any of it," he snapped.

"Foolish man," Lily said. She removed her hands from his, slid them up his chest, and looked up at him. "If you hadn't charged down that hill, I would be in this alone, with no 'negotiating' skills and no hope of ransom."

Blue eyes bore into hers, warm with intense emotion. *Why did I ever think them icy?*

He stood a little straighter. "I'll need help," he said.

"Help?"

"For one thing, you must not show fear. You did well when we were taken. Your courage made me proud. Keep it up. Save your tears for when we're alone."

Lily doubted she had done so well, but his pride lay like balm on her flagging spirits.

"For another," he went on, "I know neither Russian nor Turkish much less Arabic. I'm afraid French is the extent of it, and that only moderately. I could have used your facility many times in my work."

The admission astonished her. "What do you want me to do?" she asked.

"I'll need you to pay close attention to everything you hear."

"Berber," she muttered. Her brow wrinkled in thought. "When they speak among themselves I hear a different language. Berber, I suspect. I can't help with that."

"Do your best. Information gives a negotiator an edge." He pulled her into his arms. "We can do this together. We won't let Hamidou order our life."

Lily sank into his warmth. *He said 'our life.' Our*. Hope took root in her soul.

Chapter Thirty

Hopelessness gripped Richard. The moment of accord with Lily hadn't lasted. She spent most of her time sitting against the wall, arms around her belly, lost inside herself. He couldn't rouse her. Their conversation consisted of him urging her to eat when food came.

Day merged with night in the windowless cell. Food came twice a day, but Richard couldn't be certain how many days. When the ship finally paused and lurched at what he hoped was anchor, he tried to count back. They had sailed perhaps twelve days since they had been locked up together.

He had little time to worry about it. Two guards pulled them from their cell without warning. They pushed Richard up against a wall until his head slammed back and trussed his hands. He watched with impotent rage when they yanked Lily to her feet and did the same to her. One guard tied a rope around Lily's bonds and pulled her along behind. Richard's guard did the same, pulling the two of them up to the deck where Hamidou stood.

"Welcome to Tarcin, English. Your new home."

Richard blinked in the relentless sun. The frigate lay at anchor next to a rocky cove. Richard saw no sign of habitation. He wondered if Hamidou planned to maroon them.

They held Lily ten feet from Richard, too far for whispered conversation, when the guard holding her rope asked a question Richard couldn't understand. Hamidou shrugged as if the question mattered little. Richard tried to catch Lily's eye, to see if she understood what had been said, but she stared at the brown and barren island.

Richard followed her gaze. He scanned the tops of a looming cliff and saw signs of vegetation. Where there is vegetation, there is water. Lily would need it—and food and shade. His heart began to pound in his chest at the thought of Lily nearing her time with no one to help. *No one but my worthless self, utterly useless in that situation.*

The guards chatted between themselves, as cheerfully as two men might at ease at their club in St. James's Street. *Our lives mean nothing to these men; human beings are the commodities of their business.* Pure helpless rage began to push out rational thought until a shout intruded on the conversation. Richard looked up to see a boy waving from the top of the cliff. The guards shouted back, grinning from ear to ear and pointing to Richard and Lily.

Not uninhabited then. His eyes had adjusted to the light. He noticed belatedly a handful of small boats tied at the far end of the cove. Fishing village?

Before Richard could process this new information, he heard a scuffle from below and turned to see Scarface emerge from the hatch. He gave a vicious yank on a rope, and Volkov emerged from below decks.

If Lily's gasp concerned Richard, the look on her face horrified him. She gaped at Volkov; sheer terror warred with compassion. Richard tried to step between Lily and the sight of her erstwhile enemy but was held back. *They've forced her to see what they are capable of.*

Volkov limped across the deck, stumbling periodically when Scarface yanked him forward. He still wore the crude loincloth they had dressed him in. His battered face looked worse, swollen and purple in places. One eye was swollen shut, cuts from beatings seeped on both cheeks, and his lips were cracked and dry where they weren't split, as if they didn't give him water? Bruises covered his arms, legs, and chest. Rat bites covered his legs. A crusted red line circled his neck from ear to ear. Remnant of a half-hearted threat to cut his throat?

Volkov's arrival must have satisfied Hamidou. He barked an order, and two crew members descended the gangplank. Richard's keeper tugged his rope and led him down also. He turned to see Lily being led forward. When she reached the gangplank, her captor put a hand under her elbow to steady her before he led her slowly down. Richard peered closely at the man's face, memorizing the face of the one who showed one small gesture of kindness.

Volkov didn't fare as well. Scarface pulled him sharply forward. Richard suspected he might have yanked him around more but didn't want to lose him over the side of the gangplank.

A crew member above gave Hamidou a cocky salute, and the captain himself disembarked with the arrogant stride of any admiral leaving his ship. Richard scanned the deck and rigging but saw only one crew member left behind to stand watch. They must be damned confident about this anchorage, he thought.

By now the boy had disappeared from the cliff top to the left, but Richard could see that a path led up a gentler rise to the right. A group of people gathered there.

The crew milled around at the foot of the gangplank. In the confusion, Richard inched closer to Lily.

"Steady on, Lily. Hamidou's promised us, 'we must care for you,'" he reminded her.

"'Merchandise,'" she countered through clenched teeth. "He said they must care for their merchandise." She looked at Volkov and quickly away, as if she might be sick.

Before Richard could counter her obvious fear, their captors pulled them forward to the sound of cheering above. Hamidou strode through the center of his crew to lead them up the rise. When he reached the top, he made a pronouncement.

"What did he say?" Richard asked. Lily merely shook her head.

They moved briskly. He watched Lily closely for signs of distress. Her breathing became hard, but she looked able to keep up. The crowd on the rise parted when they reached the top. A cluster of mud brick houses, perhaps twenty or more, lay scattered in a hollow space only slightly lower than the spot they stood on. Women, children, and old men crowded in front of the houses; they cheered at Richard and Lily when they came into view.

Their keepers didn't pause to enjoy the view. They slowed their pace and led them down into town. Barking dogs and shouting children followed alongside them. A woman with a tambourine led the line of march. *Like we are some damned holiday parade, a freak show!*

They promenaded a convoluted route around houses and the few trees. *Hamidou is stretching the show as far as he can*, Richard thought. They stopped in front of what appeared to be the largest house. An open space, more empty lot than plaza, enabled many of their followers to crowd around to view the spectacle.

Richard moved sideways so that his arm touched Lily's shoulder. When she leaned closer, the movement touched him deeply. He wanted to comfort but couldn't find words.

Scarface brushed past them dragging Volkov, who collapsed at Hamidou's feet. Hamidou ignored him. Scarface took his place at Hamidou's right, chin high, arrogant scowl in place. An old man came forward, smiling, to accept Hamidou's embrace.

The men exchanged words, their tone obviously intended for the gathered crowd to hear. He looked down at Lily, but she shook her head. She didn't understand them either. Richard heard one word he had heard before, back during their capture, kafir. He had no idea what it meant.

Hamidou barked an order. For the first time, his eyes met Richard's. He repeated his words from the ship. "Welcome to Tarcin, English. These are your hosts."

Their captors pulled them to their right past the large house. As they left the gathering, Richard heard laughter and cheering. He looked back to see Scarface and another man lead Volkov the other direction toward a clump of trees.

They arrived at a hovel a bit larger than their cell on the ship.

The man with kind eyes, the one who helped Lily descend the ship, untied their bindings and gestured for them to enter. A cloth fell shut behind them to cover the door. Afternoon sun filtered through two small windows. Their prison boasted a platform covered with thin blankets and little else. Lily sank down on it and curled into a ball.

Richard clamped back the impotent rage toward the men who did this to her. Emotion would not serve. He had to think.

"Lily, can we talk?"

"About what?" she murmured without moving.

"What you saw, what you heard."

"Volkov. I saw Volkov."

He sank down beside her. The platform kept them from the dirt floor but was only marginally softer. He moved to kneel in the dirt so that he could put his face close to hers, reached up a hand, and caressed her cheek.

"I'm sorry they made you see that."

She did not respond.

"Please talk to me, Lily. I need your help."

She blinked twice and raised her head. "My help?"

"Remember our conversation about information. I need to know what you saw and heard."

She pushed herself up, her face a mask of concentration.

Better, Lily. "Help" must be the magic word.

"I saw a cove with three small boats. Only one looked like it had recent use."

He hadn't noticed that detail. *We really do need to work together.* "What else? Did you understand any words?"

"Not much. They greeted Hamidou's pronouncement at the dock with applause. I'm not sure, but he may have told them he brought them gifts."

Richard bit his lower lip. "They're poor enough here. Any gift would be cause for celebration."

"I think we're the gift," she said wearily.

He couldn't deny that. Gifts to use? Gifts to sell? Gifts for ransom?

"What is kafir? Do you know it? I heard that word on the ship and today in the square."

"Kafir is the same in Turkish and Arabic, perhaps Berber. It means infidel."

"Like yazychnik, what they called Volkov?"

"The same. Unbeliever."

Richard knew the meaning of infidel. He also knew from reports from both English and American captains and diplomats that the Barbary corsairs had no scruples about the treatment of infidels, as if they believed them less than human.

Lily held his gaze for a long time. How much does she know about the treatment of infidels? If she didn't before, the sight of Volkov must have enlightened her.

He tried to pull her into his arms; she stiffened.

"I need to sleep," she said.

She lay down and curled away from him, showing only her back. He suspected she only pretended to sleep.

Richard covered her with one of the blankets, rose, and went to pull the cloth at the door aside. He found an armed guard, one he hadn't seen before. The man glowered at him, and he dropped the door covering.

He sank onto the bed platform, his back to the wall, his head on his knees. *We are well and truly trapped here. When will Hamidou make his move? I'm helpless to do anything but pray. Pray and plan.*

A long and sleepless night later Lily clung to the windowsill of their hovel and breathed deeply. She had been allowed out once the night before and once this morning to relieve herself. She tried to be grateful. After days locked in a windowless closet on a churning deck, fresh air and firm ground almost compensated for discomfort. It was more than they had before.

A group of children laughed while they tossed about a ball made of rag in a narrow dusty street outside the window. Lily could only think about the baby she carried. Hamidou threatened a horrific fate, and others with their ever-present weapons spoke of imminent doom. The fear and despondency that washed over her in waves for days swamped her again.

Will you ever be able to play freely, dear one? She clutched her belly.

Richard's voice called to her from across the room. "At least they kept us together," he said.

"Thanks to your lies, husband," she said. She didn't turn around to look at him.

"I hoped it would help," he persisted.

"So you said," she murmured. *He meant it Lily. Stop being so horrid to him. Tell him the truth; your own behavior deserves condemnation.*

She forced herself to face him. "None of this is your fault," she said. "If I had stayed in the Seraglio, the baby would be safe."

She found him glaring at her.

"If you had stayed in London like you were told, you would be safe," he said through stiff lips. He stood grim-faced, arms folded, leaning against the wall.

Lily bristled, her own regrets forgotten. "Yes, your orders were clear, my lord. If your protection is so effective, where was my father? How did Volkov get past you?"

"It works better when my charges do as they are told," he spat back.

Arrogant, insufferable man. Their brief period of comradery died in the face of misery. Lily clenched her jaw to hold back a retort. Bickering did nothing to alleviate their situation.

He glared back for a moment before dropping his eyes as if he had had the same thought. "Why did you leave the Seraglio where you felt safe? What were you thinking?" he asked.

She sighed. How long ago was that? It seemed like months.

"After you left, I considered what you offered."

Considered? I cried all night. "Whatever qualms I have about the life you offered, I felt compelled to admit you were right."

His grin irritated her, but Lily had to admit he was right. "Our child deserves to know her father," she went on. "You didn't plan to put me away. You offered marriage. Only a fool—" She held up a hand to stop him when he looked like he would interrupt. "Yes, I know I was acting foolishly. Who would turn down your offer of security for her child?"

She looked into watchful blue eyes and continued. "I was on my way to tell you that I had changed my mind, that I would marry you." She looked away at the intensity of his response.

"Now"—she shrugged—"who knows what will happen."

She turned back to the window, swallowing her fears and tears. Richard came up behind her and slid his arms around her middle. He kissed the spot where her neck met her shoulder.

She couldn't resist the warmth that engulfed her. She closed her eyes and leaned into him.

"I claimed you as my wife to Rais Hamidou," he murmured against her skin.

"Lies," she sighed, breathing in the male scent of him. His breath on her skin heated her whole body.

"But you didn't deny it, tantamount to agreement."

She snapped upright, but he held her fast. "What are you saying?" she asked.

"In some parts of the world, a declaration of that sort constitutes marriage," he told her. "We'll want to formalize it when we can, but, Lily, make no mistake. You are my wife. Nothing that comes next will change that."

He turned her in his arms and claimed her with a fierce searing kiss, a kiss of possession. The last of her resistance crumbled. She matched his passion in a response that left no doubt. However much she might regret it later, she belonged to him—heart, body, and soul.

The little burden between them brought them back to reality with a sudden flurry of movement. Richard pulled away only far enough to look down; he kept his arms around her. With a sad smile, he set his forehead against hers.

"I will get us out of this, Lily."

Or die trying. He didn't say the words, but Lily heard them in her heart all the same.

"Hamidou hasn't sent for ransom," Lily told him.

"Not yet. He will. Money matters. In the meantime, we're safe enough here."

Pray God that's true. He can't possibly know for certain. She didn't point that out to him.

"I hope they plan to feed us, though," he said when he released her. He stretched shoulders she knew ached him. "The sun has been up for over an hour."

"They sent grains last night." She shrugged. "It could be worse."

The ragged door to their prison swung open. A young woman stood, as if on command, holding a bowl of barley cakes and dates. The scar-faced guard loomed behind her. At the sight of the man who had held a dagger to her throat in Constantinople, Lily froze.

Hamidou may negotiate reasonably, but does he control Scarface?

Chapter Thirty-One

The girl, who had given Richard only a nervous glance, spoke a few words to Lily. Lily accepted the food and spoke back. *Thanking them? How does she do that?* Lily picks up languages as if she absorbs them through her skin.

Lily crossed the room to offer him food with her head inclined.

"What?"

"Just take it," she whispered with her head bowed. "They expect you to eat first."

He took a little. "How often will they bring it? You come first." He took a bite.

"How should I know? I suspect twice a day. Just eat," Lily said, smiling back at the girl who seemed to examine Lily closely.

Lily withdrew from Richard, and the two women continued to study each other. Lily still wore the silken brocade robes of the Seraglio. Her head covering had disappeared. The girl clucked in what Richard thought was disapproval.

Unlike upper class women in Constantinople, none of the women Richard had seen in this village covered their faces. A striped scarf with broad bands of red, yellow, and black covered this girl's forehead and wound up into a sort of turban around her head. Black hair escaped the scarf down the sides of her face on either side of her chin.

I imagine that arrangement makes hard work easier to accomplish, he thought. *She looks harmless enough, but I wouldn't trust her.* When the girl reached out a hand to touch Lily, he set aside the bowl and took an involuntary step forward. Scarface responded with a step inside, his face thunderous. Richard stepped back.

Is he more worried about the girl's safety or about keeping us in our places?

The two men eyed each other warily while the Berber girl fingered Lily's silken shawls avidly. Her own dress had been woven with rough fiber in bright colors. A loose dress covered her from chin to sandal-clad feet. The same fabric made a sash. A fish-bone design had been tattooed from lip to chin to neck; it disappeared down her dress.

Lily reciprocated the girl's interest. She reached a hand to feel the sash.

"Soft. Softer than I expected," she said. The girl looked puzzled at her English words. Lily tried Turkish. The girl responded in a flurry of speech.

"What does she say?" Richard asked. He once more envied Lily's command of languages.

"I can't make it all out. Her Turkish is primitive, and some of it was in Berber. She disapproves of my uncovered head."

The girl pinned Richard with a look and spoke again.

"She congratulates me on baby I think," Lily said. "She asked if I couldn't find a better man. This one let me fall into the hands of pirates."

"She didn't say that."

Lily raised her eyebrow. "I believe that's what she meant."

A growl from the guard followed more rapid speech in mix of Turkish and Arabic.

"He grows impatient. You are to eat and go with him," Lily translated.

"Good. Perhaps we can make progress."

"The last thing she said is odd."

"How so?"

"She said, 'Don't worry, lady. The Rais is kind and good. You will have help with your baby.'"

Kind and good? Richard looked at the fierce, scarred face at the door. *Beg leave to doubt it.*

~

Like most of the houses on the God-forsaken island, the one in which Hamidou held court had been constructed of mud and brick. Slightly larger than the others, it had a floor of hardened clay that felt cool to Richard's bare feet. A dozen or so men sat on cushioned benches built into the hardened mud walls on three sides, their eyes curious and assessing.

The Rais himself sat at a table like the one in the captain's quarters onboard ship. Unlike the one in the captain's quarters, the table had been oiled and polished. It, like the room, showed every sign of tending. Richard found the terracotta platters adorning the wall to be decorative, if primitive, and the colors of the cushions attractive in the dim confines. Someone cared for this place.

"Ah, the English lord. Come, sit, have tea," Hamidou greeted him in English.

I'll tell you where to put your tea, Richard thought before he swallowed the anger that boiled in his guts. Lily needed him clear-headed. *It never does to lose one's temper too early in a negotiation.*

"My cousins wish to see this powerful man in our midst," Hamidou said. He swept a look at Richard from bare feet, across ragged robe, to filthy hair. His eyes gleamed. He didn't need to understand words to understand the amusement of the dozen or so men sitting on benches built into the walls on all sides.

Richard, still standing, looked around the room slowly with a face he prayed looked calmer than he felt. "Your home looks comfortable," he said.

Hamidou's mouth twitched. "This is the house of my uncle." He nodded to an older man in baggy homespun who grinned back through a gap in his teeth. "My own in Algiers is somewhat more"—he hesitated as if seeking the right word—"spacious."

Two men on the surrounding benches laughed. *Either only two of them know English or only two have been to Hamidou's "spacious" house.* One of them said something Richard couldn't translate that provoked more general laughter. One man clapped the old man he assumed was the uncle on the shoulder. The old man shrugged ruefully.

I need Lily, he thought. *But I don't want her anywhere near these men. If only she could give me her command of languages.*

"Sit, English," Hamidou commanded.

Richard sat and accepted tea, green like none served in any good English household and served in a glass. He raised the glass and sniffed. The aroma of mint wafted up from the drink.

"We will not poison you, English," Hamidou said. "Drink."

He did. He sipped it slowly to give himself time to study the room. He recognized a few of the men from the ship. Others, less formidable in appearance, less festooned with weapons, appeared to be locals. Less festooned, but not unarmed, he noticed while he waited for Hamidou to make the first move. He didn't have long to wait.

"Shall we do business, Marquess? What is it you can offer me that I don't already have?"

Odd question. Aside from money what might he want?

"Money."

Hamidou shrugged. "We ask for ransom, ships come. My people die." He leaned forward. "Hostages die. Slavery is better."

"That will not happen."

"You can guarantee this?"

"Yes." Richard took a sip of tea to cover his uncertainty. "Captains will do as I say. If they see me. If they recognize whom they see. I can guarantee your safety."

"Why should you do that?"

"To get freedom for my family." The word felt strange but right. He had a family. A surge of protective determination hardened his resolve.

"I too have family," Hamidou said. "Many depend on me. Volkov promised much."

"How much?"

The sum staggered. It would purchase one of the grand ducal palaces in London with enough left over to furnish the place.

"I doubt it," Richard said.

"You doubt my word?"

Two men, the ones he thought understood English, moved, one with his hand on his sword. Richard refused to flinch.

Never show weakness in negotiations. This pirate won't respect weakness. "Volkov couldn't get his hands on anything close to that," he said.

"Volkov is a lying pig. He promised what he cannot do." Hamidou glared back. Words, translated and passed on, caused a billow of excitement among the "cousins."

"He is indeed a pig," Richard agreed. "Perhaps you misunderstood him." He watched Hamidou under lowered lashes.

For a long dangerous moment, Hamidou's hostile eyes held his before the corsair's eyes crinkled up in the corners and took on an amused cast.

"The man did garble his Turkish," Hamidou acknowledged. "But our expenses were high," he continued briskly. He mentioned a sum two-thirds as high as before. Richard watched translators pass that on. The men on the benches looked solemn.

"I will give you half that." Richard racked his brain, trying to dredge up every piece of information he had ever read about the slave trade. He had to offer more than he, Lily, and the baby would be worth at auction.

"Three fourths," Hamidou countered.

The pirate likes to haggle. Relief flooded him. He stood on familiar ground now. He had brought Czar Alexander to agreement at the Congress of Vienna. He could manage Rais Hamidou.

Richard's next offer increased only slightly; Hamidou came down by a similar amount. The haggling went on for several long moments, with Richard never moving further than half way to his goal. Hamidou proved equally skilled, a fact that might have amused Richard if the stakes weren't Lily's life and freedom.

"So we are agreed?" Hamidou mentioned an amount close to Richard's goal.

"Yes." *Let's end this farce.*

Hamidou gave him a hard look. "You give me your word there will be no harm to this island, these people, no revenge, no violence?"

"You would believe my word?"

"I don't need to. I hold your wife."

"Do you give me yours that we will come to no harm?"

Hamidou nodded sharply. Richard glanced at Scarface; he held no lever to ensure Hamidou's promise, but he had to accept it.

Richard leaned forward and growled in a voice for Hamidou's ears only. "If any harm comes to my wife or baby, I will move heaven and earth to destroy you."

Hamidou's mouth tightened, but he didn't reply. He gestured for writing materials.

Richard wrote out a formal report to Castlereagh seeking ransom and copied it for his father. The government would try to short him; he requested just enough more to ensure that the correct amount came. He raised his hand and looked at Hamidou.

"My ring."

"Your ring?"

"You took my grandfather's ring. I need it to verify this request, to assure them I am making it myself."

A sharp command sent a young man scrambling. Richard watched him climb a ladder to the upper story. He reached for another piece of paper and began to write.

Will,

I have no time for explanations. Lily and I are in bad straits, being held on an island near Algiers. The Barbary corsair demands the ransom at the foot of this message. Castlereagh and Sudbury have been notified, but may balk. See to it.

Richard raised his pen. "See to it?" *Will isn't some flunky, you damned fool.* Richard felt himself sink into an abyss; hope ebbed. He thought of the heavy-handed ways he treated his friends, all of them: Jamie, desperate for money; Andrew, wounded and dying in France; Will, fixated on his fields and family. He had forced his solutions on them, and they found their own way, often in spite of him. Will ought to ignore me, he thought. How does one beg for help? He never had to do it before. He pushed on.

Lily is almost eight months gone with our child. I trust your discretion in that matter. You must see the desperation of our situation. I know you, Jamie, and Andrew will do whatever is humanly possible. I count on it. I beg you not to fail.

Richard

His friends wouldn't fail him. He squeezed his eyes shut and prayed he wasn't wrong. A noise brought him back to the man across the table. Hamidou showed Richard the signet ring but pulled it back and sealed the messages himself. Richard choked back the urge to snatch it from him.

"Uncle admires this ring," Hamidou told him, "but perhaps if the money comes, and if you do as I say, you may have it back. Perhaps. We will send by fastest ship to Malta."

"Gibraltar. They will get it to London faster," Richard said.

While he scrawled the addresses on each missive, Hamidou turned to his men in hurried conversation. The discussion went on at some length, but the men appeared to reach agreement.

"Gibraltar is more difficult to approach, but we will do it. Speed is good," Hamidou said. He handed the messages to three men who left immediately.

Richard rose to follow them, anxious to get to Lily. Hamidou's hand pulled him back.

"English lord," Hamidou said, "You will come to no harm at my hand."

"What of your men?" Richard looked directly at Scarface when he said it.

"They do as I say."

Richard's shoulders and back sagged with relief until he noticed the hard black look in Hamidou's eyes.

"You will see no harm if the ransom comes." Hamidou held his eyes, and Richard felt his heart pound in his throat.

"My cousins have needs," the pirate said. "If the ransom does not come in sixty days, we will sell you."

Chapter Thirty-Two

Berber women chattered like women anywhere, sharing hot sweet tea and nibbling figs and dates. The latter, Lily surmised were a treat, having come from off-island with Rais Hamidou.

When Richard had been led away, two other women had crowded into the little hut, bringing treats. Their generosity touched Lily. The eyes of all three were avid with curiosity. Lily's grasp of the language had not progressed enough to understand all of the rapid talk, but they appeared to bear her little ill will. At least not immediately.

If the fabric of her gown and shawls interested them, her red hair fascinated. All four touched and smoothed both hair and gown while Lily forced herself to be still.

Generosity doesn't mean they wouldn't sell me to the slavers in a heartbeat. If Richard fails—

She couldn't bring herself to finish that thought. As if disturbed by her mother's emotions, the baby began to kick.

The women smiled at that and burst into chatter again. One word dominated talk that followed. Baby, Lily suspected. With simple words in Berber, a smattering of Turkish and gestures, the women made it clear they wanted to know how far along she was. She held up seven fingers and said "month" in Turkish, then "moon," in case they didn't understand.

The oldest one clucked and shook her head. She said something to the woman who brought food, the youngest of them, who seemed to have the best command of Turkish.

"It will be soon, then," the young woman said.

Tears sprung to Lily's eyes. Soon. Even if Richard's negotiations went well, she doubted rescue would come soon. Regret flooded into her. She regretted the foolish notion to leave the Seraglio. She regretted leaving England. She regretted resisting Richard's proposal in the first place. *I've put you in danger, little one. I am sorry.*

The older woman reached out and took Lily's hand. She spoke in soothing tones.

"She says you must miss your sisters and aunts," the younger woman said, and Lily realized with a pang she had none. She thought of Georgiana Mallet and her friend the Countess of Chadbourn. *I should have gone to them.* More regret.

The young woman didn't notice her deepening sadness. "Not to worry, English lady, we will help. This woman"—she indicated the older woman patting Lily's hand—"my grandmother, has helped with many babies. Many."

A midwife? Lily looked at her more closely.

Before Lily could reply, another woman barged in. Of indeterminate age and fierce expression, she wore a red headdress with a chain of coins looped across it as a sign of wealth. She must have held some position of importance because the others quickly moved aside, deferring to her. She barked some harsh words, only one of which Lily understood—infidel again. Clearly, she did not approve of kindness to a captive.

The old woman glowered at the intruder and then smiled sadly at Lily. Lily found herself smiling back. She took Lily's smile for permission and put both hands on Lily's belly. She began to probe. She had Lily stand and pull her gown taut so she could see how the baby lay. She helped Lily onto her back on the bed platform and probed again. Finally satisfied, the old grandmother sat back on her heels and nodded cheerfully.

The woman in the red headdress snarled at the grandmother.

The grandmother answered in a gentler tone. The only word Lily recognized was the word for baby.

The youngest woman glanced nervously at the angry woman, leaned closer to Lily, and whispered, "Grandmother says all is well, but baby is not ready yet. Soon."

"What did the other one say?" Lily asked. The girl merely shook her head.

The coins on the woman's red headdress jangled when she turned and left as abruptly as she came, apparently satisfied with what she came to find out. The other women visibly relaxed.

Soon. At least it isn't early. She found this strange grandmother's attention as reassuring as the woman in red had been unnerving. She untied one of the silk shawls from around her shoulder and handed it to the older woman.

The grandmother beamed. She nodded repeatedly. Her thanks needed no translation.

Thank God for the kindness of these women. I'm going to need them.

A RIPPLE of excitement among the women, a subtle shift in the emotional pool around her, alerted Lily to Richard's return. She longed to turn and demand a report on his discussion with Rais Hamidou, but her new young friend held her still.

She saw the girl glance briefly toward the door, but the girl's hands held her still while she tugged on the headdress she had arranged on Lily's head. She gave the two curls on either side of Lily's face a swift pat and smiled at her handiwork.

"Your man has returned, Lady," she whispered in Lily's ear. Lily smiled back. "I had better make myself agreeable, no?" The girl translated to the older women who cackled knowingly. They rose with no further delay and fluttered to the door with sly smiles and Lily's silk shawls.

Lily stood to face Richard. His fierce expression made her look away and make a show of smoothing the bright Berber sash she had gotten in exchange for her finery.

"If they stole from you, I—"

"No one stole from me. Communicating with those women helps our cause. The great Marquess of Glenaire does not need to fix my part in it. What happened with Hamidou?"

"You gave them your shawls? Why would you do that?

"Under the circumstances, all that silk felt perfectly useless. It snagged every time I moved. Besides, they admired it."

Richard's brows rose.

The poor man looks confused, and that irritates him, she thought. "I got this practical sash in exchange. See how it holds up my skirts from the dust." She swirled to show him.

"I can see your ankles," he complained.

"You don't like my ankles?" She could see from his face that he liked the sight very much.

"I don't like every man in this village ogling your ankles."

"Silly. I'm too big to attract any man's eyes."

The look he gave her caused heat to run from between her breasts and up her neck to her cheeks. "I beg to differ," he rasped.

Lily put her hands on her face to cool her cheeks. "Besides, I'm locked in here."

"No longer. We're to have the run of the island."

"What on earth has changed? What happened with Rais Hamidou? Did you convince him to let us go?"

"No. I can't work wonders, Lily." His bleak expression struck her in the heart. "I can only negotiate. At least I know how to do that much." He avoided her eyes.

Lily sucked in the breath she didn't know she held. *The man is doing his best to fix things, Lily. He'll hate himself if his best isn't good enough. He'll hate himself if harm comes to you.* The realization roiled her emotions ever further, comfort warring with fear for him. She swallowed hard and forced herself to stand straight, chin high.

"If you could negotiate, then all is well. No one does it better," she said.

Richard looked at her then, gratitude clear in his expression.

"We did negotiate," he said. "There is to be ransom." He outlined Hamidou's terms.

"Sixty days?" She asked breathlessly. "Do you think it will take that long?" She didn't dare ask, "Do you think it will come in time?"

"We have to pray it doesn't take longer," he said as if reading her thoughts.

"The baby won't wait that long," she told him.

Anguish twisted his face. "I can't help it. It may be faster if response comes from Gibraltar directly and word does not have to get to England. If the government responds quickly maybe, but there are no guarantees—" He looked as if he meant to say more.

No guarantees they would respond at all. Lily didn't need to have him spell it out.

Lily put a hand over his mouth. "Listen to me, Richard. You can't fix everything. Our daughter will be born when she is ready, here or on our way to England. We can't possibly make it to London in time."

His arms went around her, and he pulled her close. "I'm sorry I can't do better. I have no idea about childbirth, but I'll do my best to see to you."

That statement and the image it conveyed made her chuckle, laughter bubbling up from deep inside. "Foolish man. I don't believe childbirth is your expertise either. I will manage the thing."

"So you like to say." His worried frown didn't lighten.

"In this case I'm right. I have to be. The women will help. That young woman's grandmother is a midwife. You will remember my efforts to build a bridge to them."

He jerked his head up. "I won't have some village peasant assisting in the birth of my son!"

"What do you propose? You can't transport some Mayfair accoucheur here on time, even if you could convince one to come."

He opened his mouth to argue, and she shut it with a kiss. She snuggled her head against his shoulder. The words he spoke at Chadbourn Park came back to her. "There is nothing I can't manage if I have all the facts." This must be killing him. "No one expects you to do the impossible," she murmured.

"I do," he growled.

She listened while his heart slowed.

"You kissed me," he said moments later.

"I did." Lily smiled against his shirt.

He took her face in his hands, sliding long fingers under her side curls. She waited for his kiss. When he paused, uncertain, she said, "I won't break, Richard, as you discovered on the ship. Kiss me."

He covered her lips with his and kissed her gently until she opened to allow his tongue to explore more deeply. When he tried to pull away, she held him close.

"There's one thing I know you do very well. You did say we're as good as married."

His eyes widened. *I've shocked him.*

"You're inviting me? What about the baby?"

"I learned many useful things in the Seraglio. One is that there is no reason to forego all lovemaking." She looked at her expanded girth. "You just have to be careful."

The poor man looks poleaxed. She watched emotion play across his face: desire, hope, and then caution.

"No reason except a village full of curious people, bright sunshine, and an ever-open door."

He took a step away, but held tight to her hand. "Walk with me, wife. It appears we're to have the freedom of the island as long as we don't attempt to escape."

"Should we? Escape, that is."

"Ask me after I've had a look at the island. I suspect not, or he wouldn't allow the freedom." He led her toward the flimsy cloth that served as a door. "Besides, we need to continue the conversation tonight. After dark. When the village sleeps."

His look, full of passion and promise, made her knees week.

"See, little one," she murmured, "your father is a clever man."

He took her hand and led her outside. No guard stood at the door.

"What else did they say while you negotiated?"

"A lot I didn't understand. The one word I do understand is becoming too familiar—kafir. Scarface uses it as his favorite insult."

Lily looked around the village. *How many of these faces hold kindness? How many hate?*

Chapter Thirty-Three

It took little time to walk a circuit of the island and less time to be certain they could not escape it. They began with the rise above the cove.

Hamidou's frigate still lay at anchorage, but preparations to bear his messages to Gibraltar were underway. The few small boats kept for fishing, transport to the frigate when it anchored further out, or travel to the mainland lay in a shallow cove under guard. Richard's heart sank. Lily clung to his hand.

"Could we overcome the guard?" she whispered.

"Don't be daft!" He sucked in breath. "Alone, I might try it.

"But not with me," she sighed. "I'm a burden."

"Never that. We have a baby to protect, Lily."

She didn't argue; she leaned her head against his arm without letting go of his hand. He needed to comfort her; he almost took her in his arms in full view of the village in broad daylight. What would Her Grace make of that? She would whip me with her outrage if she hadn't already fainted at my appearance. That thought brought a smile to his face. He squeezed Lily's hand and led her on.

Their route took them around the outer perimeter of the houses. The sea, the great churning blue wall to their prison, stretched in every direction they looked. They had circled back past the little square and Hamidou's uncle's house when Richard noticed a path leading up the rocky outcrop behind the village, one that must lead to the top of the cliff.

"Let's explore that rise." He nodded toward it.

He followed the path upward with his eyes when they walked toward the back of the uncle's house. He heard Lily cry, "Dear God!" She grabbed his arm with both hands and turned her head into his shoulder. He looked down at what she saw, and bile burned hot in is chest.

Volkov sat in front of them. Ropes circled his chest and ran under his armpits, holding him upright. His hands were bound in front, the bindings brown with dried blood. His state of undress had not changed; bits of rotten food, mud, and excrement clung to him, thrown, Richard guessed, by children who had been given full rein to torment the man. A crude paper sign with Arabic writing hung around his neck.

Compassion, natural and unbidden, tore at Richard's heart. He brushed it aside, swiftly calculating what it meant to Lily and his own situation. "Can you read the sign?" he asked Lily.

She lifted her head and forced her gaze back to Volkov. "Infidel," she whispered.

"Thus anyone who cheats Rais Hamidou," Richard murmured. *And England damn well better make good on my deal with him.*

"No one deserves to be treated this way."

"Perhaps not," Richard said, "but some poor souls in Newgate for debts don't fare much better." He turned her toward the path, guiding her away from the man.

"Shouldn't we do something? We can't just leave him like that."

"No."

"Richard!"

"No. I won't jeopardize your safety by approaching this man who hired his very captors to kidnap you. It would get back to Hamidou in a heartbeat. He brought it on himself. Let it go."

A rough path zigzagged upward over jagged boulders. Richard held her hand and helped her up. They reached the top after several minutes. Richard forced Volkov from his mind. He hoped Lily did the same.

One bronze-skinned teenager hunkered down by a rock where he could scan the horizon in every direction. Hamidou's lookout. The boy grunted and turned away, ignoring them.

A brisk Mediterranean wind roiled Lily's skirts and put her hair to flight. She held on to her Berber headdress. Around them lay rocky coast. The village occupied one small flat area.

"Look—the mainland." She pointed across the water. They could see the coast of North Africa, bright brown and gray in the sunlight with thin lines of green here and there.

They stood shoulder to shoulder for long moments. Lily confirmed Richard's suspicion that they shared one thought when she murmured. "A person could swim it."

"Do you swim, Lily?" He'd never known a lady who could swim.

"Not in women's skirts," she replied, "And certainly not in this condition." She looked down ruefully.

But she can, he thought, astounded. "I'll have to see how well you swim some other time."

He stared at the shore, lost in thought. *I could swim it, but could I bring help for Lily quickly enough*? Unlikely. Whatever lay in that land didn't include the British Navy. The thought of Volkov sickened him. Thus those who cheat Hamidou.

"You could," she said, as if giving voice to his thoughts.

"I wouldn't leave you."

"I know. I'm sorry to be a burden."

He did take her in his arms at that. *Let watching eyes and London strictures be damned.*

"Never that," he said. He pulled her head against his shoulder while the wind howled around them. "Never that."

They lingered until the sun began to dip; he led her back down. With every step, his heart sank deeper. *No escape. None. I can only rely on my friends.* He squeezed Lily's hand tighter.

"You're hurting me," she complained. "Do you want to break my fingers?"

He loosened his grip with an apology but did not let go. At the bottom of the rise, he turned her toward the far shore, away from the luckless Volkov, and back to the hut where Lily's nameless young friend waited with food and drink. She smiled at their joined hands and bowed out, dropping the door covering as she went. Quiet and privacy descended.

In the fading light, Richard took Lily's face in his hands, long fingers cupping both sides of her chin. He meant to kiss her, but when she smiled wanly, he pulled back. Purple patches lay beneath both eyes, and her mouth looked pinched.

"You look exhausted," he said frowning. She didn't deny it.

He lowered her to the rough bed that also served as their settee and brought her tea. She took a cautious sip.

"Mint!" she said, and tried another sip. "Good."

He pushed food on her, but she took little. He held bread dipped in a sort of meat sauce to her mouth but suspected the nibble she took wouldn't keep a mouse satisfied.

"You should eat."

"I did," she said pulling off her headdress.

"Not enough for even one grown woman, much less for the two of you."

"The women gave me goat's milk this morning."

Is that good for a pregnant woman? He had no idea. He had no idea how to care for her on his own.

"I'm sorry to be a—"

"Don't say 'burden.' Don't ever say it," he growled. "When we get back to England, I'll hire an army of servants to care for both of you."

"And so you will fix everything." Her scowl took him aback. Now what? She looked like she would tear the skin off his back if she weren't exhausted.

He took the dish away. He went down on his heels to loosen her sash and lay her down. She attempted to smile, failed, and let her eyes drift shut.

He began to finish the food, dipping bread into the savory meat sauce and devouring the bits quickly while he watched Lily's breathing become even. His eyes fixated on the gentle rise and fall of the swell where his son lay. *Lily says daughter*. He smiled at the sleeping woman and tucked the thin blanket under her chin. *That's the least of our problems now.*

Light faded away, and in the darkening, he remembered their brief intimacy in the afternoon. Lily's words resounded in his mind. There is no reason to forego lovemaking. Sitting alone in the dark, the logistics of the thing seemed awkward any way he imagined it. Clearly some parts of his anatomy stood eager to try, if only Lily didn't need sleep so badly.

He shed his robe and climbed gently over the sleeping woman to lie against the wall. Lily lay on her side facing the door; Richard snuggled up behind her, his chest against her back. He embraced her swelling belly with one arm, kissed her neck, and tried to convince his overly eager manhood to settle down. To distract himself he began to devise ways to escape their predicament and reject them one by one, until he finally nodded off.

Lily jerked awake deep into the night. He pulled her back against him and kissed the spot where her neck met the slope of her shoulder. "Go back to sleep."

She reached for his arm and pulled it tight around herself. "Don't leave me. Don't ever leave me."

"Bad dream?"

She nodded. "You tried to swim."

Tried. And failed. She didn't need to say it out loud.

"I won't leave you, Lily. You can be sure of that, if nothing else. I won't leave you."

Her warm bottom moved across his groin, causing an immediate swell of desire. He groaned with pleasure; Lily repeated the action. Minx!

"Please," she said, rolling over, seeking his kiss. He obliged her. One of his arms circled her head, and his other hand roamed over her growing middle. Astonishment greeted the unexpected discovery that a breeding woman responds quickly to a man's touch, if he is gentle and knows exactly which places need a caress.

Such a touch to her nipples elicited a moan, the invasion of a finger, moisture. She threaded fingers into his hair and held his mouth on hers. "Please," she repeated, attempting to pull him closer.

"Easy, Lily. We must have a care. Let me." He rolled her back to her side and nestled behind her, pleasuring her with his hands until she squirmed restlessly. When she leaned her head back onto his shoulder and whimpered softly, a smile spread across his face. Her pleasure delighted him—delighted and inflamed.

He slid into her moist heat from behind. His last coherent thought was *You're a treasure Lily, never a burden. Never that.*

The grubby toddler in Lily's lap pointed to her eyes. Most of the children obsessed on her hair until Grandmother finally told them to quit touching it. The boy in her lap was the first to notice her green eyes. She smiled at him. The smile he returned made her heart flutter.

"Green," she said pointing to her eyes. She looked around but found little on the rocky island in the same color. She spied a wide stripe on her young friend's sash and pointed. "Green."

The toddler followed her gesture. His little eyes squinted. He looked back at her face. One tiny hand came up to the side of her eye. "Green," he repeated.

Whispers of the word went around the little circle of women around Lily. She looked at their eyes, curious and eager. *Of course! These women are as anxious to learn as I am. They are no different than the intelligent women in the Seraglio or in London. The more they know, the richer their lives become.* The teacher in Lily emerged from its sleep.

"Let's begin, then," she said in English to baffled expressions. "I am Lily." She put a hand over her heart. "Lily. Zambak."

When she pointed to the girl, the young woman didn't disappoint. She put her hand on her heart and said, "Izza." She pointed to Lily and said, "Zambak." She giggled then and added, "Lily."

Introductions passed amid much laughter. Only one refused, the woman with the most heavily decorated headpiece who invaded Lily's peace the first day. She rose in a huff and retreated to her own home.

"She is Wasila, wife of headman," Izza explained. Lily decided to ignore the rebuff and forge ahead. She learned as much as she taught when they moved on to exchange simple words: house, sash, tea, tree, boat, man. Man or guard? Hard to tell.

The sun had risen high above before the women began to drift away reluctantly. Lily looked up and saw Richard watching her from the door of their hut.

"How long have you been there?" she asked.

"Long enough. You're teaching them English." His expression looked grim.

Lily's mouth tightened. "Do you find harm in that?" she demanded.

"No." Still his expression didn't soften. "English and did I hear Berber?"

"Some Turkish, a word or two of French. We're exchanging." Richard stared down at his feet deep in thought.

"They learn quickly. Most people do when given an opportunity," Lily said into his silence. *What bothers the man now?*

"Could I?" he asked. Her eyes flew open wide. "Could you teach me Berber—or Turkish at least?" he said at last.

"I don't know."

His scowl in response would have frightened children.

"I mean I can try," she rushed on. "You realize I don't know much Berber, don't you? I've just been picking it up."

"You started 'picking it up' the moment Hamidou's men burst into that filthy cell in Constantinople. You absorb it like a sponge. How do you do it?"

"I don't know. It has always been so. I watch and listen. I observe how people act upon their words and their expressions. I listen to tone and inflection. People, in the end, aren't all that different from one another."

He doesn't look like he believes me.

"Are you saying you can't teach me?" he snapped.

Heaven help me, the Marble Marquess found something he can't do easily, and he hates it. Is he resentful or just afraid to fail?

She pulled on his arm and put her hand over it as if they were about to enter a ballroom; she led him toward the rocky rise, this time approaching from the other direction, avoiding Volkov.

"That isn't what I mean, Richard," she told him. "I can teach you what little I know, but when you meet with Hamidou, I suspect you will hear words I don't."

His scowl softened. "If you stood at my side, the problem would disappear, but I won't have you around those men if I can help it."

Lily felt her mouth curve up. He would take my help if he could.

"You have to look past the surface, Richard. You care for your country. Hamidou cares for his people. Are you so very different? Watch how he talks to his men. Watch their expressions. Make educated guesses."

"If I bring words back, you can help me ferret out the meaning."

"That might work." They began to climb. "What words concern you now, in English I mean. What should I watch for?"

He flicked a glance at the boy hunkered at the top of the hill. "Lookout," he said. The corner of his mouth twitched, and Lily grinned broadly.

"What else?"

"Slave. Dealer."

Lily's heart sank. Yes, it might be good to watch for that.

"More."

"Rescue, navy, ship—" Soon they had a list of a dozen words that worried Richard most. Lily began to consider ways she might introduce ideas with the women that would elicit the vocabulary she needed.

"Now, let me teach you the words I do know. They will help us ask for food if nothing else."

He grinned finally. "That may prove useful. But let's carry our lesson back to our hut."

He stepped down the rocky path in front of her, holding one hand to steady her steps. He dropped his voice so it couldn't be heard above the wind by anyone but Lily.

"One thing, though. Don't teach any of the boys."

She glanced up at the watcher on the hill and nodded.

Partway down, he hesitated again. He turned to her but did not meet her eyes. "Lily," he began, "You—" He stopped and looked up. "That is, thank you. I can't do this without you." He turned on his heel, stepping quickly, and leaving Lily to trip and right herself.

What did that admission cost him? She wondered. His retreating back looked stiff as a wooden plank. A bubble of joy rose inside her, carrying one thought: he needs me. It hummed through her as she strode down the hill after him until at last she stumbled down into the village. The cluster of mud-brown hovels sobered her quickly. *First things first, Lily. You have to get off this island—and not into the markets in Tunis.*

Chapter Thirty-Four

Days slip quickly when you want them to last. Seven more passed with little progress, and Lily's time moved inexorably closer. No rescue appeared on the horizon. No word came from Gibraltar. No prayers saw answer.

Lily tried to walk serenely through each day. Every morning she sat with the women, grinding grain and exchanging languages as if they were family friends and not strangers who would sell her and her baby into bondage as easily as they would converse with her. Every night she clung to Richard and accepted the comfort he tried to pour into her with his gentle touch.

Every day she smiled. Every day she felt shadows shroud her soul. Every day her hand slipped more often to protect her growing belly. Every afternoon she climbed the cliffs to hope for rescue.

Weeks into their imprisonment Richard climbed with her as he often did. The steps had become more difficult, and he put an arm to her waist to help her.

"You shouldn't do this," he said.

"Exercise is good for me," she replied, breathing heavily.

"That may have been true last week. No longer."

"Will you forbid it?" she asked, raising one eyebrow.

"I wouldn't dare," he said wryly. "I only advise."

Lily tried to ignore the worry lines she watched grow deeper on his face daily. She put one foot in front of the other. A few steps later she wondered if he might be right. The climb grew more difficult.

At the top, he sat her on a mossy rock to catch her breath. Hamidou's lookout gave an embarrassed nod and looked away as the boys always did. This one looked particularly young; Lily guessed him to be nine or ten.

Richard stepped up onto the rock above her. Lily craned her neck to look and saw that he scanned the wide Mediterranean, looking northward as he always did toward Gibraltar. She relaxed back down and turned her own eyes toward the coast.

Blue fog clung to the coast late this day. Lily watched while it began to thin and scatter. While she watched, a flicker of movement caught her attention. At first she thought she imagined it; she didn't. She rose to her feet in excitement.

"Richard! There—what's happening?" she called, pointing toward the moving object.

The lookout leapt to his feet and followed her pointed finger. He ran to the edge and shouted down to men in the village and then pelted down the hill.

"It certainly excited our little friend." Richard had climbed down and stood next to her. "It's a ship, but what kind?"

"It looks like four masts."

"Whose do you think it is?" she asked.

He shook his head. "Too far to tell." Hamidou's frigate had returned several days before and sat at anchor in the cove.

"It is coming from the south. Could it be English?"

"Possible, but I wouldn't count on it. It is sailing directly at us, though."

They stood and watched the ship draw nearer.

"Dutch," Richard said, "From the looks. I don't see the flag."

The ship neared the island and moved away from the shoals on the East, turning toward the cove on the north side.

"Not the Union flag, not one of ours," Lily sighed. "What do you think is happening?"

"At a guess, it looks like the pennant of the Bey of Tunis."

Tunis. The slave market. Lily gripped Richard's hand fiercely. "It has only been twenty-seven days!" Hamidou cannot be trusted.

Richard put an arm around her waist and pulled her to his side. He leaned to kiss the top of her head. "Don't leap to assumptions, Lily. It may be a friendly visit."

When they made their slow and plodding way down the path, hindered by Lily's girth and Richard's determination to protect, they found the village alive with excitement. Friendly visit indeed.

She could see the visitors, obviously Berbers, appear over the rise and march toward the square. Richard steered her in that direction when she would have fled to their hut.

"Better to know soonest," he said.

Hamidou and his uncle stood in front of the house in welcome. Scarface stood at Hamidou's right. The sight made Lily's heart race. Scarface's mouth twisted into a mockery of a smile.

Just as the men from Tunis entered the square, a ripple of talk erupted at Scarface's right shoulder and drew her attention. Before she could wonder about the cause, two men dragged Volkov into the square and dropped him in front of Hamidou. He looked painfully thin but no worse than they had seen him before.

The Tunisian leader greeted Hamidou and immediately began to inspect the man on the ground. His scowl deepened moment by moment. He looked up at Hamidou and let lose a torrent of words in Berber, too much and too fast for Lily to understand.

"He says this one is worthless." Izza had slipped in next to Lily. "He offers little coin," she said disdainfully. "He asks why Rais takes no care of the—" Izza bit her lip as if trying to recall a word.

"Merchandise?" Lily suggested.

A bright smile lit Izza's face. "Yes, Lady." Her lips formed the new word silently as if she wanted to store it for future use.

"Rais says this one cheated him. Says lowest dog of infidel."

The Tunisian prodded Volkov with his foot. The Russian jerked away. He's alive at least.

Richard's arm came around Lily's shoulder when the Tunisian turned abruptly and eyed them with a thoroughness that made her knees buckle. She righted herself. "You must not show fear," Richard said. She breathed in and lifted her chin. He had called her courageous; she did not want to fail him.

The Tunisian agent spoke to Hamidou without taking his eyes off Lily.

"He wishes to know how much for you, Zambak," Izza said. "He offers much." Izza's eyes glowed as if a high slave price could be an honor.

"Rais said no, did he not?" Lily asked her.

"He say 'not now.' Says he gave his word there will be more days." She held up ten fingers and waved them three times.

Thirty days? "Thirty-three," Lily corrected.

Scarface spat some words at Hamidou, who stopped him. Scarface turned in disgust and went into the house.

Izza shook her head. "Disrespect to argue with Rais in front of strangers," she said.

More talk, which Lily took to be haggling, went on less dramatically. When they finished, Izza frowned. "Price very low. Not enough to buy grain for winter."

The Tunisian gave an order, and his men began to drag Volkov to the cove. He turned and spoke again to Hamidou before turning on his heels to follow his men.

"He say, 'I'll be back,'" Izza said. She wrinkled her brown eyes and tried to remember the word, "In Thirty days!" she concluded proudly. "He will pay much," Izza continued, a wide smile spreading across her face.

"Thirty-three," Lily murmured, dreading what might happen. "Pray God we're gone by then."

"King's knight to his bishop's third."

Richard stared at Hamidou's move and attempted to focus. It was damned difficult to remember strategy while attending to the words of eight men conversing around him. So far only one word stood out:

English. English what? Fleet? Navy? *More likely poor hapless English lord. Me. Lily could puzzle it out more quickly.*

He fingered a rough-hewn piece. The squarely cut chessmen looked crude but recognizable. "Queen's knight to her bishop's third," he said, mirroring his opponent. Not terribly inspired.

Eight perfunctory moves by Richard later Hamidou slid a knight into place. "Checkmate," he said.

Richard sat back in his seat. *I don't remember the last time I had lost a game before coming to this God-forsaken island. I'm losing my mind.*

"Not well played," Hamidou said, shaking his head. "You may hope your bigger game plays out better."

"Bigger game?" Richard feared he knew the answer.

"Thirty-three more days, English." Hamidou took a sip of tea. "As I told my Tunisian friend."

"I understand he offered you a lot of money."

Hamidou shrugged. "We'll see what your government offers in the end," he said.

The offer must not have matched. Praise God for that.

Scarface looked up from a game five feet away and snarled something. Richard had no idea what.

"Our Tunisian friends do business. They do not threaten our people," Hamidou continued as if Scarface hadn't spoken. "If your game includes harm to this village—" He left the threat implied.

"I gave my word."

"I gave mine. We'll see whose carries weight. The game isn't over, my English friend."

Chapter Thirty-Five

Izza batted Lily's hand from the grinding pestle.

"Grandmother tells you not work today," the girl said.

Lily pulled the blanket she carried around her shoulders. The wind grew colder as the days grew cloudier. The women wore heavier overgarments now.

The old grandmother followed Lily's gesture with a concern that reinforced Lily's growing unease.

Discomfort increased daily; the baby felt lower, and the pressure that caused made her legs ache. It kept her up the night before. Only Richard's patient back rubbing made it bearable. He no longer attempted intercourse, but he never stopped holding her, caressing her, whispering sweet nonsense in her ear. She hoped he slept better than she did. Surely this baby will make her appearance soon!

Wasila, she of the over-decorated headdress, Lily's nemesis, barked a complaint at Izza that brought Lily out of her thoughts. The old grandmother spoke sharply to the woman.

"She say you must work, not be lazy," Izza said. She followed it with a discreet giggle. "She never work herself. Grandmother tell her to leave you alone."

Grain in the basket ran out. One of the younger women rose to fetch more. Lily rose with her and took one handle of the wide basket. She needed to stretch her legs and was grateful for the excuse. Izza scurried behind. Lily recognized the woman carrying the other side of the basket as a young mother with three small children.

They reached the grain storage and slid off the lid. The younger woman moaned when she looked in. Lily peered over her shoulder. Supply looked low. It sank quickly with so many to feed.

Izza and the other leaned in and scooped out a bucketful, the other woman's face wrinkled with concern. It occurred to Lily for the first time that some might resent two extra mouths to feed.

"I tell her not to worry, Zambak. Soon we have much coin to buy grain," Izza said cheerfully. She pulled out another bucketful.

"Yes, my government will send ransom," Lily agreed. She hoped it was so. She helped dump the grain into their basket.

"I don't know this ransom, Zambak, but the Tunisians promised much coin," Izza chirped. Lily's hands froze in their work.

Izza did not seem to notice. She picked up one handle of the basket. The other young woman took the other and they walked back toward the women's circle.

Lily leaned against the brick storage bin, one hand around her middle, and swallowed convulsively. She had thought Izza a friend, Izza who cheered at the thought of selling Lily, Richard, and the baby.

Do not show fear. Move about as if all is well. Believe it.

She followed the other two women. The young mother appeared to be complaining about the grain supply when Lily joined them. She gestured at the basket and pointed back to the bin in animated description.

Wasila took up the conversation, pointing at Lily and carrying on in rapid Berber. Izza's answer seemed to mollify her.

"What did she say?" Lily asked Izza.

"She say we will starve if Hamidou goes soft. I tell her not to worry. Much money will come. It has been offered." Izza went about the business of grinding grain.

One other woman held up an object and looked at Lily inquiringly.

"Hammer," Lily told her. Teaching continued. One could go through the motion, Lily found, even when one's heart died a little.

~

Lily, proud and defiant, challenged Richard. Lily, wan and listless, crushed him. Hamidou's messengers had returned from Gibraltar weeks before, empty handed. As near as Lily could tell him, the governor said he would do his best, but he needed time. What little time they had disappeared daily.

Lily acted as if she ignored it all. She withdrew inside herself, spent long hours in bed, and refused to eat.

"You must eat," he urged in spite of three previous refusals. He knelt next to their bed, holding a bowl of the ever-present porridge. Lily sat with her legs over the side and shook her head.

"No more. Please. I can't."

He held the spoon a moment longer.

"It makes me gag."

He dropped the spoon to the bowl.

"You eat it. One of us should be strong," she said with a weak smile.

He sat back on his heels and did as she asked. The food had gotten bland and monotonous as though their keepers had grown tired of feeding them.

Lily winced and grabbed her belly; he put the bowl down hard in his hurry to reach out to her.

She relaxed as suddenly as she had tensed and leaned her head onto his. "Nothing," she said.

"False like the last?" he asked.

She nodded. "The old grandmother said false pains are normal. I must be patient."

"Isn't it too soon?" he asked. He slipped an arm behind her and lay her down on her side. He pulled off the Berber headdress and ran a hand down her hair to caress her cheek.

"For the baby? Not much, I think. It is time, or near enough. She won't wait for rescue."

"Lily, I wish—"

"Hush. You do what you can. What woman could ask for more?"

"If we were in London—" he began again.

"If we were in London, women would close ranks, a midwife would order me about, and you would hide at your club safe in the knowledge that you were not needed," she smiled. "I rather like having you close by."

Her words warmed him but did little to calm his fears. Women died in childbirth even with expert help.

"Then I will stay here, wife." He pulled a blanket up around her shoulders and rested his hand there.

"I don't mean you must be in my pocket all day," she said on a yawn. "Go, prowl the village. I will be well for a short while." She yawned again. "Let me sleep. I need to save my strength."

He pulled his hand away and rose. He stood and watched her for a long moment before turning to the door.

He paced the short length of the village lost in thought; he reviewed His Majesty's fleet in his head. What is the fastest vessel? How fast can it get here from London? He considered how long it would take the Foreign Office to gather the ransom. There would be discussion and debate. Castlereagh had declared that England must not pay ransom. Will he make an exception? He might if he found it in England's interest. His Grace would take steps to rescue his heir, but he might not hurry, and he was not likely to raise dust over Lily.

Any way Richard calculated it, he hated the answer. Help might reach them in the full sixty days, but even that seemed unlikely. Now? Much too soon. The baby will not wait for rescue.

Without a conscious decision, his steps turned to the path up the cliff. How far from here does the coast lay? Perhaps I can spy a landmark to help me calculate it. His persistent logical mind reminded him that shoals and currents could not be so easily calculated. He had rejected escape once before, and he ought to do so again.

Too late, echoed in his mind as he climbed the path. Too late to try. Too late to leave Lily alone.

He knew with sudden insight that even in London no women

would pry him from her side, at least until the event itself. However unfashionable, however déclassé, even in London he would see Lily through the birth of his son. Nor would he leave her now even for a well-intended effort to seek help.

He stopped his climb, numb with the realization that events moved relentlessly forward and he could do nothing to stop, delay, or prevent what would come. The ragged blue robe whipped around him while he stood suspended halfway up, unable to go forward, unwilling to climb back down. He knew only one thing with clarity. *Lily matters more to me than anything else ever did, more than duty, more than the damned House of Sudbury, more than England. I would die for her.*

Before he could turn, a shout drew his intention upward on time to see the boy on duty pelt down the hill and brush past him shouting alarm.

Chapter Thirty-Six

If Lily could have slept, it would have been brief. Izza barged in soon after Richard left, dislodging a cloud of dust, disrupting Lily's sleep, and devastating her peace of mind.

"You not come today, Zambak," she said. "Grandmother sent me to check on you." She fluttered around Lily in concern. "Grandmother worries. Is it time?"

Lily pushed herself up on one arm and attempted a smile. "I am well. Tell Grandmother thank you," she said.

Izza dropped to the floor and sat cross-legged, prepared for a long chat. Any hope Lily had for solitude died.

"Do you wish a boy or a girl child, Zambak? Me when I have children will have only boys." The girl began to chatter about her nonexistent children, listing the names she planned to give her sons and the exploits they would have.

"They will bring much honor and much coin to their mother," she assured Lily. Lily shuddered, thinking how Izza's sons would obtain coin for their mother.

The baby chose that time to push hard against Lily's diaphragm. She must have her feet up under my ribs. Strong legs. Will she be a horsewoman? Lily smiled at that thought and then winced when the baby kicked again, harder against her ribs.

"Starting now, Zambak? Shall I get Grandmother?" The girl looked disappointed when Lily told her no. Lily realized she had all the curiosity of any young unmarried girl and hoped to learn things from Lily's experience.

"Do you think it will hurt very bad? My friend Mara said very, very bad. A woman must be strong, no?" When she launched into a tale of her aunt's cousin who died and her baby with her, Lily began to search her mind for a way to get rid of the girl.

"I think I would like to speak to Grandmother," she said.

"I can bring," Izza replied. She jumped to her feet.

"No, I can go." Lily tried to rise but fell back onto the bed. Izza held out a hand and helped her up. The girl had a kind heart. *She's the enemy, Lily. Accept her kindness and return it if you can, but don't forget she's not your friend.*

Lily staggered to the door of the hut. Izza skidded to a stop just outside, alerted by shouting in the village. If the previous event had been cause for excitement and celebration, this one engendered panic.

"Men say ship comes, Zambak. Not one of ours!"

Villagers ran in every direction. Women gathered small children close and hustled them into their houses. Men rushed toward the uncle's house. Some people ran up the hill to the lookout point. More of them gathered above the cove.

Richard had disappeared. Lily glanced toward the cliff, knowing he probably went there. She couldn't attempt the climb, not with so many others jostling on the path. Izza beckoned her toward the cove, and Lily hesitated only briefly before she made her ungainly way to the crowd above it. Curiosity won out. Richard said it was too early for the rescue, but what if he were wrong?

She stood with the others and squinted into the sun until a spot came into focus below the horizon. The ship sailed in from the north. She could make out very little. Could it be Ottoman? Dutch? The Dutch, she thought, have diplomatic relations with the Barbary States.

A group of men ran from the uncle's house, passed through the crowd, and hustled down the hill. Two she recognized as men from Hamidou's crew stayed above.

Around her, people pointed and shouted. Fear marred some

faces, and anger others. Wasila caught sight of Lily and wheeled around, pointing at her and shouting. She barged toward Lily as if to knock her down. Before Lily could step back, one of the pirates stationed his body between Lily and the enraged woman. Wasila continued to rant and point to the ship. The man ranted back.

Why is this man helping me? She remembered him as the kind-faced one who had helped her aboard ship but could see no reason for him to come to her defense.

Lily looked frantically for Izza who could translate Berber into Turkish. The girl had disappeared. Below she could see that the frigate had been brought in close to shore due to high tide. Hamidou's men were hoisting anchor and preparing to escape the cove. Some people cheered them on, but the crowd thinned as others melted away to seek their houses. To hide? Store their possessions? Gather weapons?

I shouldn't be here in this crowd. She turned her head frantically from side to side. She couldn't find Izza any more than she could find Richard.

Should I go back to the hut? Should I hide? Where is Richard? I need Richard.

She began to inch away and turned for one more look at the approaching ship. As she looked, it turned and its flag unfurled in the sun. The Union flag. An English ship!

"Hamidou says you come," a harsh voice said in heavily accented English. "You come now." She looked up into the harsh face of the guard she had thought kindly.

The English ship pulled up and turned fully broadside to the frigate in the cove, trapping it. It lay some yards out, but Lily could see its cannon aimed directly at the cove, at the frigate and its crew, and at the village.

A rough hand clamped tightly on her arm.

"You come now," the man said.

~

"You promised safety!" The harsh light in Hamidou's eyes frightened Richard more than the knife in Scarface's hand that lay cold against his neck. A second Corsair held his arm at a painful angle behind his back.

"So I did," Richard said, as calmly as he could muster. "They have to see me, alive and well, first. If they don't, I promise nothing."

Hamidou signaled Scarface, a mere twitch of eyebrow, and the man backed off an inch.

"They will. They will see that your life is in my hands," Hamidou replied. He looked behind Richard. "Where is the woman?"

"Not in her hut," a voice replied. "Meddur went to the cove to look for her."

Richard didn't need a translator to identify the spew of words from Hamidou as curses. "We have no time for foolishness," Hamidou barked. "Bring the English." He swept out of the house in a billow of red robe and menace.

Richard, half pushed and half dragged, stumbled over the doorway. They rounded the house and had almost reached the path to the cliff before the man Meddur caught up, panting and shouting. He pulled Lily along beside him; her ungainly gait the obvious cause of his delay.

Richard's captor loosened his grip, and Richard took advantage to pull Lily into his arms. The click of a trigger pulled back echoed over the commotion around them. He turned his back to it, shielding Lily. *When did they bring out firearms? They must have stored them in the uncle's house.*

"No time for this," Hamidou growled. "Climb now." He waved his sword and led the way upward.

Richard held his arm around Lily's waist and helped her climb. "I am sorry, more sorry than I can tell you," he murmured against her ear.

Lily, white lipped and drawn, merely shook her head. They reached the top, and a cluster of seven men, the core of Hamidou's crew, surrounded them. Hamidou barked orders. Strong arms pulled them apart and faced them toward open sea. The pain in Richard's twisted arm paled beside the sight of Lily, great with child, in the clutches of a ruffian twice her size.

All seven held the newly uncovered firearms that Richard had not seen before. One corsair, and then another, pointed their Portuguese snaplock muskets at Richard.

Scarface snatched off Lily's headdress and lifted an ancient but deadly looking flintlock pistol to her head. Her red hair tumbled to her shoulders and swirled in the wind. Their captors pushed them forward to the edge of cliff.

Richard forced his attention to the spectacle below. A fully rigged ship of the line had pinned the pirates' frigate in the cove. It lay broadside, the island within range of its 32-pound guns. Marines lined the deck—armed, red coated, and ready for action. The Union flag snapped in the wind.

Can they see us? He looked down at the rags he had been given with which to cover himself. *No one looks less like a marquess than I do. If they see us, will they recognize us?* Lily's hair, flying in the wind brushed his cheek; his own was almost as long. Richard smiled grimly. *Surely no Berber has hair that color—or the color of mine for that matter. The captain must make out that much in his spyglass.*

Hamidou, who had hopped up onto the highest rock to Richard's right must have the same thought when he forced them forward. He stood with his feet planted wide apart, one hand on his hip, and waved his sword in circles above his head.

Time froze. The ship of war neither attacked nor backed down. The men holding them stood firm. Richard could smell the fetid breath of the man pinning his arm and hear the rasp of it in and out.

After an eternity, or perhaps a few seconds, he saw movement on the ship's quarterdeck. A ship's officer in blue appeared among the red-coated marines, and two men in civilian clothes followed him. The officer raised a long pole and unfurled a massive banner, a white flag of truce to propose a parlay. Neither he nor the civilians made any further move.

"They wish to talk?" Hamidou asked.

"It appears that way," Richard said. "You best reply in kind."

Hamidou looked as if he meant to refuse, but he called to a boy who had followed them up the hill. The boy ran and returned quick time, carrying a sheet. Two pirates pushed Lily aside so that she moved closer to Richard. He grabbed her hand and hung on. The two pirates unfolded the sheet between them and held both ends.

Lily turned so that her left shoulder lay against Richard's right. Scarface, distracted, dropped his gun. All eyes watched the ship of the line.

The civilians onboard waved their arms as if agitated, and sailors moved to lower a small boat. The officer in blue came over the side and began to climb down to the bobbing boat. They were coming to talk.

Chapter Thirty-Seven

Lily felt the tension in every cell of Richard's body. They both strained to watch two men make their precarious way down a rope ladder to the yawl heaving in the waves beneath them where four sailors manned oars. Neither man looked accustomed to the task.

The first man descended awkwardly but arrived safely. The second moved painfully slowly and fell at the last, falling with good fortune into the landing craft.

"Andrew," Richard breathed, "you damned fool."

"Andrew Mallet?" Lily demanded, startled.

"I suspect so. The man who just fell favored one leg, as my brother-in-law does. He'll feel that for a long time."

Lily squinted toward the landing craft that pushed away from the ship and began its journey to the island. She couldn't make out faces. They were soldiers, all of them, Richard's friends. But they are also family men, who should be safe at home with their wives and children.

"How can that be? It has only been fifty-two days since you sent that message."

"I'm damned if I know," he growled. She felt his breath coming rapidly in his chest.

"This has to be good, doesn't it? They will have brought the ransom, and Hamidou will let us go," she said. She shot a surreptitious glance at Scarface.

Richard didn't answer. She looked up then and recognized the look he had when his brain worked over time analyzing all possible outcomes, most of them bad.

"Don't," she said. She raised a hand to his cheek.

"Don't what?" he asked, grasping her hand.

"Review all the possible ways this could blow up, all the reasons why it could go wrong."

His eyes held hers. "Just remember, Lily. Whatever happens here, I love you and I did my best."

He loves me!

It echoed in her heart, but she had no time to savor it.

"Enough!" Hamidou barked. "You have been seen. They look like they mean to talk."

Lily looked out at the yawl that moved rapidly toward the island.

"We go down now and see how we can avoid English traps," Hamidou said.

Strong arms hauled her away and kept her upright down the rugged hill. Others forced Richard down in front of her, in spite of his effort to turn toward her. They frog-marched him swiftly through the cluster of houses toward the cove.

Lily followed as best she could, grateful that her captor accepted the limits of her condition. By the time she reached the rise above the cove, her breath heaved and she felt faint. Her captor dropped her arm, but when she teetered, he put a hand under her elbow to steady her.

Such a mix of violence and gentleness! Will we ever understand these people?

Hamidou, Scarface, and the others holding Richard gathered above the cove. The uncle and a few other villagers stood around. Most villagers hid in their homes or on the rocky far side of the island.

From her place slightly behind the men, she could see that the yawl had reached more than halfway to the island and closed rapidly. The civilians sat shoulder to shoulder in the center. One most certainly was Andrew Mallet. She could now see that the other was the Earl of Chadbourn. Relief warred with fear, and her vision began to dim, but she forced herself not to faint. Richard's friends had come for him.

~

"No gold until we talk to His Lordship." For a man who would rather be a farmer, Will Landrum, the earl, managed aristocratic hauteur well enough.

Hamidou's men searched the boat and the terrified English sailors. They found nothing. Richard watched his friend take control of the situation after Hamidou demanded gold "Or your English lord will die on this beach." *Keep it up, Will. These animals don't respect weakness.*

"Harm any of us, and the HMS Boreas will reduce this island to gravel," Will retorted. He and Hamidou took each other's measure for a fraught moment.

"Understand me," Will went on. "Your blood money is aboard ship. When we have the marquess and his lady safe, you will have it."

"They stay until we have the gold," Hamidou spat back. "And know this. Your lord promised safety to the people of this island. If he does not deliver that, I cannot promise the safety of his wife." Hamidou looked slowly up to the top of the rise, slow enough for Will to follow, and fixed on Lily who stood pale and shaking in the clutches of a Berber pirate.

Will's eyes widened at the word "wife," but he looked where Hamidou pointed. He paled slightly at the sight of her and looked at Richard in surprise. "Nothing happens until my colleague and I speak with His Lordship. Privately."

Hamidou waved a hand, and Lily's captor led her downhill. "Very well," he said. Another gesture and Scarface raised his pistol to place it against Lily's head, hatred in his eyes "You may talk," Hamidou concluded.

Richard's captors dropped his arms. His first instinct consisted of a murderous need to push Scarface into the sand. Only one thought held him back. If I jump him, the gun may go off. The man's knowing smirk almost broke his resolve, but he forced his feet forward toward two of the men he respected most in the world.

"You're a pair of fools," he murmured. "But I've never been more glad to see anyone than the two of you." He took them both into a two-armed embrace. The three stood facing one another in a tight circle, heads in.

"Where is our friend the major?" he asked.

"Jamie disappeared before you left London. He never turned up."

No time, Richard thought. No time to worry about Jamie Heyworth now.

"Ransom?" he asked. He pitched his voice low.

Andrew's eyes flickered behind his gold-rimmed glasses. "Of course." Richard started to ask them how they did it so fast, but he had no time for explanations. "Most of it," Andrew went on in a whisper. "They'll have to count fast or look carefully to find the lack."

"On the Boreas," Will added. "Did you really promise them safety?"

Richard nodded. "Most of these people are just going about their miserable lives. Hamidou and his crew—"

"Hamidou is dead!" Andrew snapped.

"This man begs to differ. He commands in that name, have no doubt of that. Leave the islanders alone. Let him and his crew leave this place. What happens on the high sea in a fair fight is up to His Majesty's Navy."

"Good luck convincing the captain of that ship." Will indicated the Boreas with a shrug of his shoulder.

"Tell him the Marquess of Glenaire commands it," Richard said. *Damn but it feels good to command something!*

"That should work," Will said with a grin.

"What next, Richard? How do you want us to play this?" Andrew asked.

"You two go back to fetch the gold. Demand to take Lily with you. He won't let us both go without payment, but he might send her."

A slight smile played on his brother-in-law's mouth. "Your wife, Richard? And from appearances, in an interesting condition."

"As good as, Andrew, and don't say differently. She's about to birth that baby any day now. I need to get her out of here."

Will looked over Richard's shoulder. "Our host looks impatient. Let's get this over with." The three men turned back to Hamidou. "Nice suit, by the way," Will put in, looking at Richard's tattered robe. "And remarkable hairstyle," he added peering at the pale blond hair, now shoulder length, blowing in the wind.

"Get us out of here and you may tease me the rest of your days."

"I plan to." Will's grin passed quickly. He approached Hamidou.

"I am satisfied," he said, "That the marquess and marchioness are safe. We will go back and make arrangements for the gold. The marchioness will go with us."

Hamidou shook his head. "These captives are valuable assets. No gold, no release."

"If I may suggest," Andrew put in, "I will stay here in the lady's place."

Richard put a hand on his arm. "Georgiana won't thank me."

Andrew smiled up at him. "I have no desire to make any more trips up and down that ladder than I have to." If he meant to say more, a loud wail from Lily prevented it.

Richard shook off an arm and ran toward her. Her face twisted in pain, and she bent over. A wet stain ran down her skirts. She fell forward toward him, and he sank to his knees holding her. She sobbed, "I can't go anywhere. The baby isn't going to wait." She moaned again as another pain washed through her.

"I'm sorry. I'm so sorry," he whispered in her ear.

Chapter Thirty-Eight

"Your ship is ready, Rais. Prepare your men to evacuate..."

Another loud wail from the back room of the uncle's house distracted Richard. Only Andrew's hand firm on his arm kept him in place.

Concentrate, Richard. This negotiation is life or death.

"You believe that captain will let us go? What of the village?" Hamidou demanded.

"My orders are to leave the village alone and to allow your ship out of the cove. The captain will follow those orders. Once you are under sail, I can't promise."

Hamidou nodded. "When the gold comes, we will see," he said.

"The earl will return with your gold, Rais," Andrew put in. "You may count on it. My presence here is surety."

Richard heard Hamidou reply, but Lily's cries distracted him. *Can those women be trusted? What if they harm Lily? What if they harm my son?*

"Your wife will be well, English. The grandmother has assisted hundreds into this world," Hamidou told him.

Am I that transparent?

Every fiber of his being pulled him toward the back room of the uncle's house, the room to which Hamidou led them when Richard carried Lily up the hill. She had labored for an hour already. *How long do these things take?*

"Are we agreed then?" Andrew asked. "When the gold comes, the Boreas will pull out to allow your crew to leave. You will have one hour to do so. They will remain off shore until you are gone and they see that we are safe. Then they will come in to evacuate the marquess and his family. That will allow you time to make your escape. Agreed?"

Hamidou gave a sharp nod. "If the earl returns with the agreed upon gold, we will do it."

When the Rais left to inform his men to prepare, Richard sagged in relief.

"Almost there," Andrew said, sinking back onto a divan.

"We're in danger until they are gone. Don't let the lack of a guard fool you," Richard told him. "And those women... I need to stay with Lily." He turned toward the back room.

"A moment, first, while we're alone."

Richard turned back, puzzled. Concern covered his brother-in-law's expression.

"They won't welcome you, you know. The women, I mean."

"They won't have a choice. What do you need to tell me?"

"Castlereagh gave orders to your agents around the Mediterranean. His Majesty's government will not pay ransom for captives."

"He said as much some months ago: let a few suffer to kill the practice. It looks different when you're facing slavery. How did you convince him otherwise? And how, come to that, did you do it so quickly?"

Andrew smiled a crooked smile, his scarred visage tilting upward. "We'd have been here sooner, but we had to piece the gold together. Will and I were in Gibraltar when your request came."

"Why on earth?"

"Looking for you, of course. You went haring off on your own with little thought and no preparation. We thought you needed help. When we discovered you'd left Gibraltar alone on a fishing boat, we became convinced you lost your mind."

Richard sat down, distracted by the tale. "I was a damned fool, and look where it got me. I could have reached Lily eventually without all this."

"Yes, Lily. I take it she agreed to your romantic proposal at last?" Andrew smirked.

"No romance, little choice."

"I doubt that sat well with her," Andrew said. "I can imagine Georgiana given no choice."

"It's why she ran," Richard admitted. "I didn't handle it well."

You bungled it, you looby.

"This marriage of yours is legal?"

"It would be in some parts of the world."

"Not ours?"

Richard shrugged. "An Anglican priest willing to back date marriage lines would be convenient," he admitted.

"Particularly if it's a son."

"I hadn't thought of that, but yes. I would not want my firstborn excluded from the succession."

"And Lily has decided to go along with it?"

Richard bit his lip. Had she? She intended to in Constantinople. She said she didn't think she could be a duchess, which is nonsense. "I'm not sure, but yes. I think so. I will ask her again as soon as I can."

Dear God! Lily! He rose to go to her but paused. One part of the story teased his brain.

"How did you gather the money so fast?"

"Will convinced the governor in Gibraltar that the foreign secretary would make an exception for his protégé. He knew you, of course, and cobbled together about a third of the cost from his reserves and sent the messages on to London."

"And the rest?"

"We became convinced there wasn't enough time to wait. Will took a bank draft to Lisbon. That's what took so long. His Majesty's government will owe the earl a pretty penny."

"I'll cover it—or rather His Grace will. I'll see to it."

"It wasn't enough. You agreed to a staggering sum."

"It was a bit over half what he asked. I had to guess how much would be more than the Lily's slave price and mine. Where did you get the rest?"

"That's the interesting part. A ship arrived from Constantinople. We got the final third from them. Sahin Pasha's people had been scouring the Mediterranean for you. They were authorized to contribute. I saw the notice. Their ship is close by, just out of sight, by the way. Something about making sure all debts are paid. He seems to think he owes you something."

"Damn well does, the old reprobate."

Richard jumped when a loud scream broke into their conversation. He bolted for the bedroom door.

"God go with you, Richard," Andrew said softly. He wondered where Hamidou kept strong drink. He knew from experience it would be a long wait. He leaned back and began to recite The Aeneid in his head in Latin.

Lily clung to Richard's hand for dear life. Neither the grandmother's scowl nor Izza's outright disapproval moved her to let go.

"He will stay," she said over and over. The feel of him holding her hand got her through one wave of pain and then another. She had no idea how much time passed since he came to her. An hour? Two?

"Lily, can you trust these women?" he whispered.

"I have to," she replied. "Oh God. Here it comes again." She gripped him tightly and breathed as the old woman had shown her.

Richard took a damp towel, wiped her face, and smoothed her hair back. The sight of the mighty marquess, his tattered robe askew, his face marred with worry, tending to her needs tore at Lily's heart.

I wish I could banish your fear, she thought, *but we both know better. Women died in childbirth every day even when not surrounded by Barbary pirates.*

A particularly violent pain tore through her. The grandmother pushed back the sheet that covered her and raised her knees to check her progress.

"Grandmother say you have good fortune, Lady. This birthing going fast," Izza chirped.

"How much longer?" Richard asked.

The girl shrugged. "Hour. Maybe two. Maybe more."

"That is not fast," Richard ground out through clenched teeth.

Lily moved beyond speech. The contractions came, hard and long, much faster now. When she began to thrash about, Richard attempted to put his arms around her, but she struck out at him.

"Best leave alone, English. Grandmother says end part is too—" The girl waved a hand in the air and bit her lip, searching for a word. "Busy," she concluded.

Lily thought perhaps she had become delirious. She could hear Richard's voice whispering that he loved her over and over. Once she thought he said, "I'll never do this to you again."

Waves came one right after the other.

A commotion at the door caught Lily's attention, reminding her of her reality. *Are the pirates gone? Are they back?*

"What of the English ship?" she managed to rasp during a lull.

"Andrew says Will has returned with the ransom. He wants me to come. I won't leave you."

"Hamidou insists that you finalize the handoff, Richard!" Andrew's voice sounded far away and muffled as if his head was turned away.

"No!" Richard said, holding her hand through yet another one.

"Go," she whispered.

"I won't leave you."

"You have to get us out of here. Finish it. Go!" It took all Lily's remaining strength to send him away. She held herself together while he searched her face. "Go," she repeated in a whisper. "Make us safe."

Chapter Thirty-Nine

The Boreas's yawl and its cargo reached the cove the same time Richard did. He bolted down the hill.

"Let's get this over with."

Hamidou nodded, staring at the yawl. His crew helped pull the boat weighted down with the Earl of Chadbourn, a five-man crew, and a chest.

Will leapt out of the boat with a bundle wrapped in paper under his arm. He handed it to Andrew and faced Hamidou.

"Payment, Rais, as you demanded," he said. The boat crew carried the chest to the sand. Will opened it.

"Is it all there?" the pirate barked.

Richard's heart sank. If Hamidou decided to count it they would be there all afternoon. If he found it short, the entire deal might fail. He'd keep the money and sell them all.

"I think the tide does not favor delay," Richard said. "If you want to get out of here, go." He pointed across the water. The Boreas had not pulled in her guns, but she turned away from the shore and had begun to move away.

Hamidou looked up at the villagers gathered on the hill. Richard didn't understand his short speech, but he suspected the man told them he would return with their share of the gold. Hamidou pointed at Richard. *Making me responsible for their safety.*

Hamidou stuffed some coins in a cloth bag and handed them to the uncle. He closed the lid of the trunk and gestured for two of his crew to carry it onto the frigate. For safekeeping.

He doesn't trust us not to renege if he leaves it here. Doesn't trust us any more than I trust him.

Hamidou looked at Richard then and reached into his robe. He pulled out Richard's signet ring. "Yours, English."

"Keep it," Richard said rapidly before he had time to regret the impulse. "Send it to me in London when you see that the village is safe and I have kept my word. Keep yours."

The two men locked eyes for a long moment. Hamidou looked away first. He pocketed the ring.

"We will not meet again, English."

"I hope not," Richard replied. "I will have to kill you next time."

Hamidou grinned, saluted, and trotted up the gangplank.

"Is he really Rais Hamidou?" Will asked.

"Probably not," Richard said, "But to these people, it makes no difference. He's their savior."

The three men stood shoulder to shoulder watching the frigate pull away. Andrew handed the bundle he held toward Richard.

Richard looked at it curiously. "What's this?" he asked.

"Open it," Will said.

Richard turned to leave. "Later," he said over his shoulder. "I need to go to Lily."

"You might want it," Will and Andrew both insisted. Richard turned back, took it from them, and tore a corner of the paper. His fingers touched black serge. He looked up at the smiles of his friends.

A large boulder lay at the bottom of the path leading to the village. Richard put down the bundle and opened it all the way. A silk shirt, trousers, and a jacket tumbled out. A rumpled neckcloth lay under the jacket.

"No boots. Sorry. We can worry about stockings on ship. Go greet Lily like an Englishman," Will urged.

"No time." He shoved the bundle back into Andrew's arms. "I'll bathe in the surf and use these later." He began to run. *I've worn this filthy rag for two months. Another few hours won't kill me.*

Richard ran until he skidded to a stop inside the uncle's house.

The silence he found alarmed him; he darted forward. *Is she well? Has someone taken her? Has she—* He couldn't allow the thought that she might die. He shoved open the door and hung on the frame, panting. His heart turned over.

~

The old grandmother insisted Lily put the baby to her breast as soon as she cleaned the little one.

"Grandmother say healthy for mother. Helps empty," Izza had no words for afterbirth. She waved a hand as if that explained everything. Izza's face sagged as if in disappointment. "So sorry, Lady. The baby only a girl. I go now." Just like that she left.

Lily didn't care. She watched her baby suckle and wondered how any woman could choose not to nurse her own child. She continued while grandmother cleaned up all signs of the birth and grumbled about the unreliable Izza.

The old woman approached the bed with a warm soapy towel. "Bathe now," she said, but the sound of running feet interrupted further conversation.

The door flew open and Richard stood, breathing heavily. He must have run all the way from the cove, Lily thought, watching his chest heave. She removed the sleeping baby from her breast and pulled up her shift. She lifted the little bundle higher.

"Come meet your daughter," she called. Her voice sounded hoarse from crying out. Richard stumbled to the bed, transfixed with wonder, and dropped to his knees beside her.

"Are you well?" he asked, searching her face.

"As you see. Tired but otherwise fine. So is the baby," she tipped the swaddled bundle in her arms toward him.

"Daughter." He echoed what she said, staring at the white fluff on the little head. "You were right." Tears began to run down his face. He dropped his head to the bed.

Crying? Her heart sank. She put out a hand to touch his hair.

"Are you disappointed?"

His head bobbed up. "Heavens, no. Relieved beyond words. She's beautiful," he said, wiping his face. "I just—" He let the apology die and put out a tentative hand to touch the wrap surrounding their baby. "Are they all so small?"

Lily chuckled over that bit of nonsense. "I believe so. You wanted a son, though. I'm not sorry."

"We have a healthy daughter in spite of everything. Right now she is all that I could want," he said without taking his eyes from the little one.

"It is better that she is a girl, Richard, better if your son is born after we legalize this marriage you claim we have."

"Probably. We would have found a way—Will and Andrew are working on it, in fact—but yes, this one is a great blessing." He meant it. He couldn't take his eyes from her.

"Do you want to hold her?"

Panic lit his face, quickly suppressed by longing. "May I?" He rose and sat on the edge of the bed.

"You certainly may," Lily said. She handed the bundle over to her father, lay back, and watched Richard fall in love with his daughter.

"Her eyes are green," he said. "Like yours."

"They may change. Sometimes—"

"No. I forbid it. Our daughter will look like her mother."

He smiled down at Lily.

The grandmother came then and reached for the baby. Richard looked as if he would refuse.

"Are we not free to go?" Lily asked, old familiar fear driving through the fog of contentment that had enveloped her.

"Yes! I should have said. Hamidou and his men have gone. The landing craft and its crew wait for us in the cove."

Lily struggled up onto her elbows. "Then we must go as quickly as we can."

The grandmother pushed Lily down with alarm.

"Lady sleep now," she insisted. She made shooing gestures with her hands.

"Do we have time for me to nap?" Lily asked over a yawn. Her eyes began to drift shut.

"A little," he said. If he said more, Lily didn't hear.

She awoke moments later, or perhaps much longer. She couldn't tell. The grandmother had disappeared. Richard sat on a stool next to her with a basket at his feet. His ragged blue robe had disappeared. He wore clothing that may not have been the height of fashion, but which was decidedly English. His hair looked damp.

"The baby?" she said, pushing up on her elbows in panic.

He pointed to the basket. It had two handles for carrying. Inside, the baby slept peacefully. "You both needed rest after your hard work."

Lily felt like she could sleep for weeks. "But we must leave."

"The boat is ready, but Lily, we need to talk first."

Of course. Real life has returned. Her heart sank.

"Please don't take her from me, Richard. That's all I ask."

Chapter Forty

"What are you talking about?" Richard demanded. *Lily looks pale and drawn*, he thought, *but otherwise normal.*

Tears pooled in her eyes. He hated tears.

Does childbirth make women lunatics? Why can't women be simply managed without all this emotion?

Richard sighed. He had learned a thing or two in the past several weeks. He sat on the bed and pulled her into his arms. She began to sob in earnest.

"Hush, Love, hush. I just wanted to talk to you about 'legalizing this marriage you claim we have,' as you said."

"We can't. I can't," Lily wailed.

"Why on earth not?" he demanded, wondering again if her mind had slipped.

"No priest. Baby already here. Your family will want a society wedding, your mother will be outraged, and the scandal will—" Lily had a full head of steam now.

"My mother has no say in it. No society wedding, you foolish woman. There is a Church of England on Gibraltar. We can probably convince the priest to backdate the lines."

"You mean lie?" She sniffed.

"Not exactly. I told you we're as good as married. He'll merely formalize it."

"You can't want to marry me," she said wiping her face.

Stubborn woman, now what maggot eats your brain? "I went

halfway around the world, confronted eunuchs in the Seraglio, and fell in with Barbary pirates pursuing you. How can you say I don't want you?"

"I'm a mess. My hair is matted. I must stink."

For a moment he considered saying, "All true, but..." but thought better of it. Drawing on his diplomatic expertise and newly acquired knowledge of wives, he said, "You have never looked more beautiful to me than you do now having given birth to our daughter." That should do the trick.

"Oh, Richard, I can't." This time she looked serious, and he began to fear she truly meant to reject him.

"What do you mean 'can't,' madam?" He had begun to lose patience, not to mention his wits.

"I can never be a duchess," she mumbled. "I'll disgrace you and you'll send me away."

Richard drew in a deep breath.

"Duchesses come in many forms, Lily. Don't mistake my mother for the example of the type." He put a finger to her lips when she started to reply. "Listen to me." He turned her so she had to look directly into his eyes.

"You will make a brilliant diplomat. You will manage a salon and dinner table that foreign dignitaries, ambassadors, and visitors will clamor to attend. Besides—"

Her eyes widened.

"—I don't want a duchess. I want a wife. That's what I came to Constantinople to tell you." The look in her eyes gave him heart. "You will manage the future of England over wine. We will do it together."

"We will?" she asked in a small voice.

"Well, that last part only if Castlereagh doesn't dismiss me from his service after this. Even if he does, our home will be a haven for foreign relations. Think how you will regale guests over dinner with tales of the Barbary Coast."

Her mouth twitched, twisted, and exploded into a smile.

That's my Lily.

"Do you think I can?"

"I know you can. No other woman on the planet could be the woman I want. No other, the one I love."

He watched her eyes soften and glow. She sighed contentedly and leaned against his shoulder.

"So, Lily, will you marry me?"

No immediate reply. *What does the blasted woman want?*

"I love you, Lily. I always will."

She looked up at him then, eyes shining. "Of course I'll marry you, silly man." He leaned in to kiss her.

"Now that that's settled, can we leave? Much more time and we'll lose the tide," a voice exclaimed. Will and Andrew grinned at them from the door; Lily blushed furiously.

Lily reveled in the warmth of the blankets Richard wrapped around her. She reveled even more in the confusion on his face. She almost giggled at the sight of the Marble Marquess finding family impossible to manage. He looked down at the baby and back at her.

"Oh, for heaven's sake, Richard," Will said. "I can carry the baby. "I've had practice. I know you don't trust anyone else to carry Lily."

She wrapped her arms around his neck and felt herself lifted into the security of his embrace. They set off for the cove—Will, Andrew, Richard, and Lily with the little one in her basket.

"Georgiana," Lily suggested thoughtfully, against Richard's shoulder. "Shall we name her after your sister?"

"No," he said emphatically.

Lily glared at him. "What then, my lord?" she demanded.

He didn't slow his pace and didn't answer.

When they reached the rise above the cove, she suggested, "Mary, my mother's name." He shook his head. *The wretch. Is all life going to be a conflict?*

"Hush," he said.

Richard followed his friends down the hill, and Lily clung to the security of his arms, her face muffled against his shoulder so she couldn't argue.

Four sailors and their officer stared at them anxiously. "Best get moving, my lords," the officer said.

Richard lowered Lily and let her slide until her feet touched the sand. Before he could help her into the yawl, she raised her chin and suggested, "Hortense." As she started to laugh, Richard's kiss silenced any opposition.

"We will call her Zambak," he said. He lifted Lily into the boat and handed her their daughter.

Epilogue

Gibraltar, three weeks later, November 1819

Lily stared down at the date in the registry, clear and easily read in the chaplain's elegant hand: June 15, 1819, her wedding date. Or so Richard had declared. It was, of course, five months from the actual date, but who would gainsay the Marquess of Glenaire? Certainly not the bride herself. No one would ever call their daughter a bastard.

Richard urged her to a chair while the army chaplain calmly covered the date with one hand and invited the witnesses, two local clerks in the army headquarters, over to sign. Obscure witnesses, they were unlikely to speak about it to anyone in London.

Lily glanced back at Andrew and Will sitting patiently in the rear of the garrison chapel. They would carry back to London the vaguely worded fiction that Lily and Richard met in Gibraltar in June, implying they married before embarking on their great "adventure." Richard insisted it was almost true—a common law marriage at least—if only to spare his friends the burden of lying.

The two friends would leave in the morning, but Richard and Lily would stay for a few months to give Zambak time to flourish—and to make her age less likely to be questioned. As always, he had arranged life neatly to his own satisfaction. No one would dare question him.

A brief flame of resentment, quickly snuffed, flared through her. *He is, of course, quite correct, as always—damn it.* Still, Lily couldn't fault her new husband for his determination to protect their daughter, and, she admitted, Lily herself.

She glanced down at the dress Richard had conjured for the

wedding, beautiful for all it was locally woven in bright colors with Spanish, or perhaps Portuguese, motifs. He even located a nosegay of flowers somewhere on this barren rock, a thoughtful touch she never expected. She'd come to appreciate his drive to protect, even if it was heavy handed.

On that thought, she let out a yelp when her husband lifted her up into his arms without a by-your-leave. "I can walk! I'm not ill," she protested.

With a nod at the smug (and probably richer) chaplain, he carried her out the door, their friends following. "I'm sorry," he murmured in her ear. He didn't even choke on the words he so rarely said.

"For carrying me?"

"Don't be ridiculous."

"Whatever for, then?"

"I know it wasn't the wedding of a woman's dreams," he said.

Will hurried past to chase a pair of monkeys off the donkey cart that had carried her out of town to the garrison.

"I didn't even give you the King's Chapel at the governor's house," Richard went on, lifting her into the cart, wrapping the soft red cloak he'd bought around her, and pulling her into his arms. Andrew hauled himself into the driver's seat with his formidable upper body strength. Will climbed up after him.

"You've done well by our daughter. I'm content," Lily said, her eyes only for Richard.

He paused, and the relief in his glance startled her. He dropped his head for a brief kiss as they clattered down the hill toward The Convent, as the governor of Gibraltar's residence was called.

"I'll make sure you are celebrated with a grand ball once we return to London," he said. "We'll place an announcement in the papers: 'The Marquess of Glenaire has returned, having married Miss Lilias Thornton while abroad during the previous year.'"

"Do we have to?" she moaned.

"The ball or the announcement? It is true enough."

"The ballroom will be full of inquisitive eyes and cutting conversation." she shuddered.

"Nonsense. We'll give them the Hayden family glare. It will stop them in their tracks." He swallowed. "Even my parents won't dare."

"We'll invite them?"

"Of course. Short of illness, they have no way to refuse, even when we invite Georgiana and Andrew."

Will turned from his seat in front of them and cut in. "You're a brave man, Glenaire."

Richard gave him a haughty glare down his aristocratic nose.

"That doesn't work with me, remember?" Will chuckled. "I suppose there is no arrangement for a wedding breakfast, either." They hadn't even told the governor the purpose of their errand. The less, Richard dictated, that the governor knew, the better.

"It doesn't matter. I'm anxious to get to my daughter. It will be time to feed her shortly," Lily said. Her determination to feed her baby herself was the one war she had won with Richard. He announced he had found a wet nurse, and Lily put her foot down. She judged that he'd come to appreciate it because he certainly enjoyed sitting with her when she did.

"I did suggest to the kitchen staff that the marchioness would be making her first appearance at dinner and they might want to be sure the occasion was marked with their best. I expect they will present a celebratory feast tonight," Richard said, his smug grin telling her that he would guarantee it.

Andrew's crooked smile was rueful. "I think you'll find my brother-in-law has his own way to care for those he loves, Lily, even if he stumbles. He had little training when he was young."

Richard growled, but Lily smiled back and snuggled against Richard's shoulder. She didn't object when he carried her up to the nursery.

~

Deep in the night, Richard took his daughter, sated from feeding, from her sleepy mother's arms. He raised the coverlet and tucked it around Lily as her eyelids fluttered closed. His wife. *Wife.* The word lodged itself, solid and steady, in his heart. His brave and brilliant, strong and stubborn wife. For all the fear and uncertainty they had lived through, he wouldn't change anything. He had found his perfect partner.

When the mite in his arms squeaked, objecting to his hold, he settled her more gently. This one would be just like her mother.

Moments later a groggy nursery maid handed the baby bundled in a soft shawl with clean gown and nappies back to him. Changing her was a bridge too far for the marquess, but he would rock her back to sleep before returning her to her cot. His father would sneer, and his mother would shake her head in horror. He thanked the Lord, Lily, and his sister Georgie for showing him the difference.

The next morning, he gave in when Lily insisted on walking to the docks to see their friends off home. He owed them more than he could ever repay. Money was the least of it. That they both respected and cared for Lily was another thing on their side of the ledger.

"Enjoy your time here, Lily. See if you can locate a baby cart so you can take the little one along while you enjoy the sea and explore The Rock," Will suggested, indicating the great cliffs above them with a gesture of his head. "The views are spectacular."

"We would look like a gypsy caravan," Richard grumbled with a shake of his head.

Will kissed Lily's cheek. "Do it anyway," he whispered.

Andrew laughed, hugged Lily, and stunned them all by hugging Richard before he could object. "I can't wait to entertain Georgiana with the stories I have to tell."

"God help me," Richard shuddered. "You could make better use of your time, by seeing what you can find out about Jamie." The fourth of their band of friends, Jamie Heyworth, had been missing for weeks before Richard left England.

Andrew winked at Lily. "I am sure you already have your

minions on that task, but we'll see." He followed Will up the gangplank.

Richard and Lily stood shoulder to shoulder and watched until the ship moved to the mouth of the harbor. The packet would have them to England as swiftly as it was possible to get there.

"Will was right," he said suddenly.

She looked up expectantly.

"We have time to explore the entire peninsula, you and I. No pressure, no prying eyes." He turned to study her expression, uncertainty gripping him.

"I thought you were going to write reports on shipping, defensive preparations, and so on," she murmured.

"I'll scribble something to pacify the foreign minister, but England can manage without me for a while. There's little here to get between us or distress us. Let's use this interlude of peace as a sort of honeymoon."

Her beautiful eyes held his, unwavering, and his tension eased. "Yes. Together. As a family."

His entire being seemed to melt. For once the marble marquess was beyond words. He did the only thing he could. He kissed his wife, reveling in her response, oblivious to staring eyes.

Author's Note

I hope you enjoyed Richard and Lily's story as much as I enjoyed telling it. The setting and background for this story fascinated me. I've included some historical notes at the bottom in case you are interested in learning more.

For more on the lives and loves of Will and Andrew, be sure to read: *Family Honor, Book One,* and *A Lady's Honor, Book Two.* Watch for Zambak's own story in Book Seven, *The Empire's Honor.* For now, however, *Tattered Honor,* the missing Jamie Heyworth's story, comes next:

Coming Next

The afternoon Lily and Richard boarded the Boreas, in a low-class neighborhood in Rome, on a street notable only for crumbling window sills, fierce residents, and rotting garbage, Jamie Heyworth, lately Baron Ross, haggled with a rag dealer over the value of his dress uniform. He got more than the man offered, enough to eat for another week—or enough to keep him in wine. It would have to do.

Here is Tattered Honor, Chapter One.

Rome, 1820

"Major Bently? Are you in there?"

Bently? Jamie Heyworth covered his ears. *Some damned fool wants my Uncle Charles.*

Pounding, urgent and loud, echoed through his room.

He ignored the noise. *Perhaps it will stop.*

It didn't.

"Major Bently!"

There it was again. *Uncle Charles can answer.*

His Uncle Charles lay dead the past eight years. Jamie peeked out from under his ragged pillow and stared at the cracks in the ceiling.

Another loud knock made his cot bounce and vibrate. It sent pain like nails into his already aching head.

"Major Bently, kindly open. You promised."

Promised? He never made promises. He rolled to sit on the edge of his cot with a loud groan, a colorful curse, and a gasp so sharp it filled his lungs with pungent Roman air and jiggled his languid brain cells. Memory flooded back.

That morning he had no money, nothing left to sell, and no reason to get up—except more knocking. Louder.

"Stop the damned pounding," he mumbled.

"Major, I heard your vulgarity. I know you are in there."

Jamie's senses began to clear, and he realized some woman pounded on his door. *The vexatious chit from last night*, he thought. The woman had invaded the tavern he frequented like the black crow of death and would not leave.

The little blackbird had good credit, he remembered. He eyed the three empty wine bottles on his table. He distinctly remembered only having money for one. He had spent his last coin on that bottle. *She must have funded the other two*. There had been food, too, he remembered, and a very fine cheese. Jamie Heyworth never forgot a good meal.

"Major, please! It is past nine in the morning, and we will be late," the woman's voice called.

Late for what? He struggled to recall.

After he plied her with tea and calmed her down, she had fed him some tale about dying brothers, evil nuns, a menacing count, and nieces held prisoner in a tower. *Maybe not a tower*, he thought. He felt sure he remembered the rest correctly.

"Major Bently!"

Ah! Bently. Using his mother's maiden name amused him when he gave it to her. Major Lord James Phineas Heyworth, Fourth Baron —and so on—sounded ludicrous attached to his pathetic self even if he didn't have good reason to avoid being found. He preferred not to use it. Bently sounded safer. He hoped it was.

Did I promise anything?

"You promised you would meet me by the fountain in the piazza at 8:30 this morning," said the voice behind the door.

Her answer stunned him. He could think of no reason why he

would promise some chance-met blackbird anything, much less an early morning rendezvous.

"Are you well?" the voice persisted.

No, damn it, I feel like the very devil.

"Yes. I am well. We were to meet at 8:30 in the evening, were we not?" he responded.

No sane person runs about at 8:30 in the morning. He began to wonder if the woman really was mad, one of those hysterical females who reads too many novels.

"Don't be ridiculous. The nuns wouldn't let us in the hospital in the evening," she said.

Nuns again! And more infernal banging. He doubted the door, though thick as a post, could stand against his ravening crow.

"Major, you promised! You said—"

Jamie threw the door open. The woman stumbled against him. Soft curves pressed against his entire length and jarred his sluggish body awake.

I'm not dead yet! The thought improved his mood considerably. He produced his cheekiest grin and made no effort to remove her soft body from his person.

"What did I promise, exactly?" he asked, staring down into a delicately sculpted face, inches from his. He liked the feel of her. *She's hiding her best parts under all that English wool. Doesn't the foolish woman know she is in Rome?*

The chit pushed herself away, slipped under his guard, entered the room, and frowned in distaste. *No schoolroom miss, this one.*

In daylight, she looked more like a wren than a raven. Dressed in sensible brown, she radiated bright, searching eyes and flowing energy. *Too damned much energy for so early in the morning.* Her eyes darted over the bottles, scattered clothing, and the dirty dishes on his broken chair.

"You said that you..."

She stopped abruptly and gaped.

He glanced down.

"Luckily, I fell asleep in my shirt," he said, lips twitching. "I'm sure I can locate my trousers and smallclothes, if you'll give me a moment."

For an instant, blue sparks flared in her eyes, which were rimmed by thick honey-gold lashes. Just as fast, she turned her back.

"Quickly, please." She spoke toward the window. He wondered what color she would turn if she knew how well she showed off her derrière when she pulled her frock tightly to one side with white-knuckled fury.

"What exactly did I promise that has brought you running, fleet of foot, to my quarters this morning?" he asked.

He moved with deliberate slowness around the room, picking up clothing discarded the night before and searching his brain for promises discarded just as easily.

"You agreed to speak with the nuns, to interpret for me," the woman said.

That was it. The wren needs an interpreter, needs one so badly that she let some excitable waiter drag her into a seedy tavern she had no business entering to meet an English "gentleman." More fool she.

"I should not be surprised you don't remember. You were much the worse for drink last night," she complained.

She has me there.

"You're acquainted with the effects of drink?" he asked. *Intriguing.*

"More than I wish. My husband—oh, do hurry up!" She stomped her foot and, much to his regret, let go of her skirts.

Husband? Pity, he thought. *Inevitable though.*

"Are you ready?" she demanded.

"You might wait until I'm finished with my trousers. Your husband will—"

"Do nothing!" She sounded furious.

"I beg your pardon?" He buttoned the fall of his trousers.

"My husband will do nothing. He died three years ago."

"Ah, then there is no one to be concerned about your presence in a man's room in a foreign city in which you speak not a word of the native language. What's the hurry?"

"The hurry, Major," she almost spat out his rank, "is that I am only permitted to visit Isabella during very strictly set hours."

"Isabella?"

"My niece!"

Of course. The niece.

"Do pay attention. Sister Amelia Maria will be at the hospital, but I am told the others will allow me a visit, only the briefest visit, in their common room," she went on.

Ah. No tower. The niece is imprisoned in a—Good Lord!

"You are taking me to a convent?" he gasped.

"Of course."

"I must have been 'much the worse for drink' indeed, if I agreed to that."

"You did agree. You gave me your word," she insisted.

My word. When had anyone last requested my word or respected it when given? The novel idea rolled around in his head. He had given his word.

"You may turn around, unless—" He caught a glimpse of wide-eyed curiosity quickly squelched when she turned to face him."—the sight of a man buttoning his waistcoat and jacket offends you."

"Certainly not. I have seen an unbuttoned waistcoat once or twice," she snapped.

"I see. The husband."

Jamie turned to the basin near his bed and shaved with the economy of movement habitual in a man long used to the privations of camp and campaign.

"This would be easier if I knew your name," he said from the side of his mouth. She didn't faint at the sight of a man shaving either.

"I must have—but no, I didn't, did I? I am Eleanora Haley—Mrs. Charles Haley."

Jamie wiped his face and ran a hand carelessly through his hair to smooth it. He had no brush; its silver handle fed him for almost a week.

"Well, then, Mrs. Charles Haley—" He choked on the words when he turned around.

"It's what we agreed to," she said, holding out a leather purse.

She believes she has employed me?

Jamie stifled a surge of hope. His fingers trembled and brushed hers when he took the bag. He pulled out a silver coin. The imprint of the papal coat of arms gleamed up at him—a Papal scudo, Rome's primary currency.

"It's what we agreed. Don't think you can push for more."

More? One scudo alone was worth more than four guineas. He hefted the bag and reconsidered his assessment of the previous night. The woman was definitely mad, no "maybe" about it. At least now he understood why he promised to meet her.

"You paid me this to escort you to a convent?" he asked.

"Certainly not," she said. "For a month of your time. To serve as my interpreter."

Not so mad then. He knew he should refuse.

A gentleman would refuse the money, he thought.

Luckily, Jamie was no longer a gentleman. His fingers tightened on the soft leather. The money would keep him alive for a month, long enough to do whatever it was the woman hired him to do.

He smiled broadly. "Let's go see these nuns of yours."

Historical Notes

The Eastern Question

The diplomatic issues surrounding the gradual disintegration of the Ottoman Empire are generally referred to as "The Eastern Question." Our marquess's statement that the weak Empire didn't concern Britain but expansionist Russia did is correct. The Eastern Question centered primarily on the Balkan states and the fate of that region in a power vacuum. While Britain tended to support the Ottomans later in the century, they took the side of the Greeks in the revolution that was just beginning to rumble in this novel, and that primarily to contain Russia. It broke out in the open in 1821. Support for the Ottoman Empire against Russia ultimately led to the Crimean War. Instability in the Balkans in time drew in all the major powers and eventually tipped Europe into war in 1914.

For a more in depth explanation see: http://staff.lib.msu.edu/sowards/balkan/lect10.htm.

The Barbary Pirates

Barbary piracy raged for over two hundred years before this story takes place. The lucrative slave trade prompted corsairs to prey on Mediterranean shipping, and even to attack coastal areas of Ireland and Great Britain.

After the American Revolution, ships of the US no longer enjoyed the protection of the British navy, and they suffered at the hands of the pirates. The new US had no interest in paying tribute as Britain had. It attacked Tripoli successfully in the First Barbary War from 1801-05, but the situation deteriorated again during the War of 1812, abetted in part by Britain, which was anxious to weaken the American Navy. In 1815, the American fleet under Stephen Decatur defeated the corsairs and forced a treaty with the Dey of Algiers. Bombardment of Algiers by Lord Exmouth in 1816 completed the defeat. While those events did not completely end piracy, they did put a stop to Algeria's dominance in the Mediterranean. However, the slave trade continued to be a thorn in Britain's side in 1819 when our story takes place. The trade didn't end entirely until the French conquered Algeria in 1830.

Rais Hamidou was an actual pirate, admiral of the Algerian fleet, considered the best and most skilled. He is something of a hero in Algeria to this day and is known for his gallantry and chivalry. As our marquess said, he died at the Battle of Cape Gata in 1815, killed by Decatur's ships. Of course, he threw himself overboard and his body was never found. Our Hamidou could feasibly be the man himself, a miraculous survivor, or, more likely, someone using his name in the manner of the Dread Pirate Roberts.

For a more in-depth explanation, see:

https://history.state.gov/milestones/1801-1829/barbary-wars

https://vivalalgerie.wordpress.com/2012/07/16/rais-hamidou/

http://www.bbc.co.uk/history/british/empire_seapower/white_slaves_01.shtml

The Seraglio

There was little room in the story to expand on the workings of the Ottoman court. However, every effort was made to accurately reflect life in the Seraglio in these ways: The valide sultan was a powerful figure under most sultans. Her administration was vast and complex. The Seraglio was a place of learning and culture, even among the women of the harem. By the nineteenth century, the power of the valide sultan had waned somewhat from earlier centuries, but she continued to be an influential figure.

A few words about language: "Seraglio" is the term for the

sultan's personal living quarters within the palace complex. "Harem" is the word for the women themselves.

For a more in depth explanations see:

http://www.nadinevalidesultan.org/ottomanharem.html

http://www.theottomans.org/english/family/harem.asp

Frankenstein; or, The Modern Prometheus

Lily's conversation with Catherine about Frankenstein takes place in February 1819. The small London publishing house of Lackington, Hughes, Harding, Mavor, & Jones actually published the work March 11, 1818. Mary Shelly published it anonymously, with a preface by her husband Percy Bysshe Shelley, and with a dedication to her father, the radical philosopher William Godwin. It got largely, but not entirely, unfavorable reviews.

About the Author

Award winning author, Caroline Warfield, grew up in a peripatetic army family, and the need to travel never left her. After a varied career (largely around libraries and technology) she retired to the urban wilds of eastern Pennsylvania to be closer to family and to write. She remains a traveler and adventurer, enamored of owls, books, history, and beautiful gardens (but not the act of gardening).

Caroline calls her books family-centered romance, and this one is no exception. Family makes her characters what they are, for better or worse. She takes them as they are, scarred and wounded, and sets them on their path to their own happily ever after, because *love is worth the risk.*

Soli Deo Gloria

<u>Find Caroline on the Web:</u>

Website http://www.carolinewarfield.com/

Amazon Author http://www.amazon.com/Caroline-Warfield/e/B00N9PZZZS/

Facebook https://www.facebook.com/groups/WarfieldFellowTravelers

Newsletter: http://www.carolinewarfield.com/newsletter/

BookBub https://www.bookbub.com/authors/caroline-warfield

You Tube: https://www.youtube.com/channel/UCycyfKdNnZlueqo8MlgWyWQ

Instagram: https://www.instagram.com/carowarfield/

TikTok:https://www.tiktok.com/@owlwise7

www.ingramcontent.com/pod-product-compliance
Lightning Source LLC
LaVergne TN
LVHW091032080826
845145LV00002B/460